THE
FIRST
THIRTY
DAYS

From the Ashes of Despair, a Melody of Hope Rises

SCOTT T. YOUNG

PALMETTO
P U B L I S H I N G
Charleston, SC
www.PalmettoPublishing.com

Paperback ISBN: 979-8-8229-4441-1
eBook ISBN: 979-8-8229-4442-8

This book is dedicated to my daughters Alysen and Ella,
the inspiration behind this story.

Your love is my guiding light, my rock, my reasons.
I hope this story helps you fully understand the depths of my
love and lets you see yourself through my eyes.

PROLOGUE

September 23rd

Dear Diary,

I find myself pondering the existence of true love. Does it exist, or is it simply a product of our imagination? It's easy for me to immerse myself in the world of romance through movies, songs, and my writing. Still, sometimes, I question if it's just a fleeting fantasy devoid of reality.

Although I have experienced love in various forms, I long for that deep, soul-stirring connection with a partner. I yearn to be cherished, adored, and swept off my feet by genuine and enduring love. The desire to be romanced and appreciated consumes my thoughts, urging me to believe such love awaits me.

Despite the uncertainties that creep into my mind, I refuse to abandon hope. Destiny will bring me face-to-face with the one who will awaken my dormant soul. Our paths will intersect at the perfect moment, and our hearts will recognize each other's presence.

Each day, my heart grows more potent, fueled by the flickering flame of hope. I remain steadfast in pursuing love, refusing to let doubt cloud my vision. The universe conspires to lead me to the love story I've always yearned for.

With unwavering determination, I keep my heart open and my spirit resilient. I trust that love will find its way to me when the time is right, or I will find my way to it. Until then, I embrace the journey, hoping true love will grace my world.

CHAPTER

ONE

Garrett Anderson was awakened by a trickle of sweat sliding down his forehead. His heart pounded hard against his chest, and he blinked open his eyes, relieved to find himself in his rented room, escaping the vivid dream that had tormented him. Every night, ghosts of his past reappeared. They haunted him relentlessly, leaving him with a constant reminder of the mistakes he had made.

Sitting up slowly, he winced at the sharp ache in his lower back, a reminder of the day before. His gaze shifted to the matching bed beside him, where his daughters Alexa and Jasmine slept. Getting to spend this time with another was something they all loved, however, Jasmine, nearly sixteen, was getting to an age where she wanted her own space, while Alexa, a newly minted thirteen-year-old, still liked him close. Sunlight filtered through the shades, casting a soft glow on their serene faces. It was a sight that filled Garrett with profound love.

As he looked back on the past year, he realized how far he had come on his journey of forgiveness. Though his absence had caused wounds that turned into scars, they slowly faded. It had been a difficult road for him and his two beloved daughters, but the effort to rebuild the relationships that mattered most had been worth it.

The oversized clock atop the nightstand caught his attention, displaying 8:05a.m. He contemplated lying back down, craving more sleep, but quickly dismissed the idea. Restlessness urged him to rise and embrace the day. With tender admiration, he gazed at the two precious beings that held his heart in their small hands.

Garrett couldn't believe how much Jasmine and Alexa had grown. Jasmine's long, curly dark hair framed her face like a halo, while Alexa's light brown locks were neatly tied in a bun. Both girls inherited fair skin from their mother, but their vibrant, fluorescent green eyes were a trait they shared with Garrett. Throughout his life, he had received countless compliments about his exotic-looking eyes, a feature he saw mirrored in his daughters.

After savoring the sight of his slumbering beauties, Garrett slipped on his shoes. He went downstairs to the lobby of the Simsbury 1818 Estate. Nestled in Simsbury, Connecticut, this grand mansion, built in 1818 and converted into a bed and breakfast in 1995, had an air of mystery surrounding it. Locals whispered stories of hauntings, and the establishment's website boasted testimonials from visitors who claimed to have encountered paranormal activity. Each room housed a pamphlet recounting the estate's tragic history of betrayal, death, and unexplained occurrences, giving Garrett a new perspective on his surroundings.

He descended the creaky wooden staircase and traversed the narrow hallway leading to the main lobby. A Persian beige rug lay atop the rustic hardwood floors. He smiled at a few guests sitting and enjoying their breakfast on antique-looking wooden chairs and tables. The enticing aroma of freshly brewed coffee and hot food filled the air, eliciting a rumble in his stomach. As he approached the coffee station, he spotted Gretchen, the short, plump super, coming to him with an ear-to-ear grin. She wore a black sweater with black pants and shoes.

"Good morning, Mr. Anderson! How did you sleep?"

"I slept fine, Gretchen. How was your night?"

"It was uneventful, thank God!" Gretchen chuckled, her eyes lingering on Garrett with a flirtatious gleam. "Has anyone ever told you how beautiful your eyes are?"

Garrett laughed softly, finding her compliment endearing. "Never!"

"Well, they are gorgeous," Gretchen remarked, her northeastern accent adding charm to her words. "How was your day at Six Flags with the girls?"

Garrett's mind drifted back to the day spent at Six Flags of New England. Goosebumps pricked his arms, and his heart swelled with affection. He had traveled to Connecticut to visit his daughters, who lived with their mother in Avon, a quaint town near Simsbury. Like many other small towns in

Connecticut, Avon boasted a picturesque setting of lush green trees and elegant homes inhabited prominently by affluent residents. Being close to New York City and Boston, Avon served as a weekend retreat for some well-to-do city dwellers.

"Six Flags was a blast," Garrett replied, his voice filled with fondness, as he reached for a coffee mug and began shuffling through the choices of creamers.

"The Irish Cream is my favorite," Gretchen said in a playful voice as she batted her long eyelashes and continued smiling.

Garrett was enamored by her charm. He leaned against the reception desk, his eyes meeting hers. "That seems like a good choice, but the French vanilla speaks directly to my taste buds."

Gretchen let out a melodious laugh, its sound echoing through the lobby and catching the attention of other guests nearby. "I had no idea coffee creamer could speak," she exclaimed, a mischievous glint in her eyes. "What speaks to your heart, Mr. Anderson?"

Garrett's cheeks flushed with a shy smile forming on his face. He cleared his throat, trying to compose himself. "Right now, a full body massage would do wonders. My body is sore from being thrown around on all those rides. Jasmine, Alexa, and their friends insisted on riding every attraction at Six-Flags. It was an adventurous and tiring day, Gretchen."

Usually, Garrett's visits revolved around spending time solely with his daughters. But on this particular visit, he had allowed each of them to invite a friend to Six Flags. It was an unforgettable day that opened his eyes to a new side of his daughters. Observing them with their friend's revealed facets of their personalities that were only exposed in the presence of their peers. It was an insightful learning experience for Garrett, making him feel closer to his daughters—something he cherished more than anything.

"It sounds like you had quite an adventure with the girls. Friends truly are like family to teenagers. I'm glad you got to witness that bond firsthand."

Garrett nodded, appreciating Gretchen's insight. "Yes, it was extraordinary. I've realized that including their friends in our activities brings us closer and allows me to connect with my daughters differently. Do you have a newspaper around here?"

Gretchen leaned closer, her voice lowering. "We do, right over there on the counter, Mr. Anderson. I'm so happy you could enjoy those precious moments with your girls yesterday. Can I interest you in anything else? Maybe a massage? My room is just around the corner."

Garrett felt a blush creeping up his cheeks. He cleared his throat, trying to hide his growing embarrassment. "Wow that is a tremendous offer, Gretchen. But for now, the paper will do just fine."

Garrett approached the covered front porch outside the main entrance with the newspaper in hand. A sense of tranquility washed over him as he found a comfortable wooden chair and table facing the expansive park-like lawn that stretched before him. The charming house, perched atop a small hill, offered picturesque views from every vantage point.

It was the beginning of fall, Garrett's favorite time. The air felt cool and brisk against his skin, sending pleasant chills down his spine. The scent of the surrounding trees and the dying leaves filled his nostrils, carrying a sense of nostalgia and the promise of change. He enjoyed watching the leaves slowly transitioning into vibrant hues, their colors dancing in his vision. The tall trees, their branches dense with leaves, created a sheltering canopy that enclosed the world within their embrace.

Garrett settled into his chair and took a sip of his coffee, relishing its hot and comforting embrace as it traveled down his throat. The flavors mingled with the crisp autumn air, creating a sensory symphony invigorating his senses. With the local newspaper open before him, his eyes were drawn to the bold print marked September 23rd, 2016. It was a significant day that he had prepared for but seeing it in print sent a surge of emotions coursing through him.

Closing his eyes, Garrett leaned back in his chair, allowing the memories of that day six years ago to flood his mind.

As Garrett left his office, he saw the text from Julie. "I'm sorry about our fight earlier today. Please reconsider going to Bob and Linda's tonight. I know we will both have a wonderful time."

Garrett slid into his luxury sedan and started the engine. The leather seats felt frigid against his skin.

It is that time of year in Boise, Idaho. Soon, I'll be scraping ice off my windows.

Before he put the car into gear, he reluctantly replied to Julie's text, "I'm on my way home. We can discuss the party when I arrive." As Garrett sat in rush hour traffic on I-84, he thought of his argument with Julie earlier that day. Julie had called begging Garrett to go to a dinner party at their friends Bob and Linda's house.

"I don't understand you, Julie. You say I have to quit drinking, but you continue dragging me to drinking parties. I barely know the other couples attending. I'm not in the mood to sit and listen to drunken conversations."

"I'm not asking you to listen, Garrett; I'm asking you to stay sober and participate in the conversations. You've always been a social person. Why are you acting like this is so hard for you?" Julie's voice was sharp and harsh to his ears.

"You don't understand how different I feel when I'm sober at these events. I feel awkward, like I don't know how to relax or be myself. Maybe it would be different if I wasn't the only one not drinking."

"You always have an excuse to drink. You have a serious drinking problem. If you could drink like normal people, I would be fine with it, but you can't." Julie's voice rose. "I am sick and tired of you passing out at ten o'clock and embarrassing me. You do not know how to pace yourself!"

With these words, Garrett felt his chest tighten and defensive energy running through his veins. "Just because I drink more than you do does not mean I drink more often. If you don't want me to drink tonight, that is fine, but I do not want to attend this party. Let's go and do something else, just you and me."

Julie sighed and softened her tone. "Linda has been begging me to come over all week. You know she will be upset with me if I'm not there."

"So, you are more worried about how Linda feels than how I feel?" Garrett felt a stinging sensation in his heart. His voice surprised him as it cracked.

"Oh my gosh, Garrett, you are so selfish! Everything is not about you!"

Garrett's emotions raced, and he knew he would regret continuing this conversation. "I have a conference call, Julie. I have to go. Good-bye."

Now, as he pulled into the driveway and heard the third-car bay opening, he noticed Julie's SUV was not parked inside. Relief washed over him, slowing down his labored breathing and racing thoughts. Garrett was changing in his closet when he heard the familiar sound of the garage door creaking on its tracks. As he changed from his business attire to his jeans and black T-shirt, his heart pounded against his ribs. The uneasy feeling escaped him as he was reminded of what mattered most in his world.

"Daddy, where are you?" Jasmine and Alexa screamed almost in unison.

"I'm upstairs, sweethearts." Like a herd of cattle, he heard them stampede up the carpeted stairs, laughing and screaming that the last one up would be a rotten egg.

"Hi, Dad!" Jasmine said as she stood before him in her favorite light blue summer dress. Alexa was right behind her, looking at the ground as if it was too painful to look elsewhere.

"Hi, girls! How was school today?"

"It was great, Dad! We had a half-day today and watched a movie. I wish every day were just like today." Jasmine's eyes were wide open, and her innocent smile melted Garrett's unease.

Alexa wore black tights and a white sweater with a giant elephant on the front. Garrett turned his attention to the defeated expression his youngest child displayed.

"How was your day, honey?"

"It was fine, Daddy," she replied with a heartbreaking frown, still not looking up from the spot in the carpet she was transfixed upon.

"Did you lose the race?" Garrett asked with empathy, knowing this was the reason for his daughter's unhappiness.

"She cheated, Dad! She got a head start. No fair!"

"Well, guess what, Alexa?"

"What?"

Garrett scooped them up in his arms, twirling them in a circular motion. "You both win!" He spun around in circles until he could feel their bodies convulse with laughter.

But the sound of his daughter's giggles was interrupted by the stairs creaking as Julie ascended them. "Girls, I need both of you to help Mom put away the groceries."

"Okay, Mom," they said as they stampeded back down the stairs.

Julie entered the closet to deposit her purse and scarf. Garrett sat on the bed and waited for the discussion to begin where it had left off. He felt emotionally spent and wanted nothing more than to return to the blissful moment with his daughters.

Julie came out of the closet, looking at Garrett with soft eyes and a grin that made Garrett's heart feel funny. "I have a surprise for you." She sat down next to Garrett, putting her hands on his legs.

"What kind of surprise?" Garrett asked, feeling the warmth of her skin radiating through his jeans.

"Well, I thought about what you said regarding the party. You don't want to go because everyone will be drinking. It would be best if you didn't drink since you've recently been getting overly drunk. So, I decided to buy your favorite red wine. You only get too wasted on liquor, so I figured this would be a great way to meet in the middle."

The hopeful feeling she had initially given him vanished. He had hoped she would accept his offer of a date night. All their free time was spent with other couples, and recently, Julie was choosing an older, more affluent crowd that Garrett did not enjoy. He struggled to relate to middle-aged doctors, lawyers, and professors.

Garrett and Julie were both in their early thirties and had undergraduate degrees from Boise State University. Julie was a homemaker, and Garrett was a sales director for a local wireless phone company. Although Garrett made great money, he always felt left out, even insecure around these other men. As a result of his insecurities, he began to drink heavier than usual—even more than Julie realized. Garrett had bottles of vodka hidden all over the house and in his office.

Garrett found comfort in the temporary escape that alcohol offered. It became his refuge from the demands of his job, the uncomfortable social situations, and the weight of being the sole provider for his family. Justifying his excessive drinking became second nature to him, allowing him to indulge in the oblivion he believed he deserved. He knew it upset Julie, but the allure of letting loose and numbing his pent-up emotions was too enticing to resist.

Garrett understood that Julie had found a compromise that allowed him to drink without arguments. A sense of defeat consumed him as he looked into her eyes, but he mustered the courage to make a request. "That sounds like a fair trade. Can you promise me something, though?"

Julie's eyebrows raised, intrigued by his words. She opened her eyes wider, waiting for him to continue.

"Can you promise me that we can leave when I'm ready? I love Bob and Linda, but some couples are hard to tolerate for long periods."

Julie's expression softened, understanding the underlying need behind his request. "Yes, honey, I promise."

Bob was a new oncologist in the neighborhood, while Linda stayed home to care for their two children. After Garrett's promotion to Sales Director, Garrett and Julie moved to the neighborhood a few years ago. They had grown up in Boise and had no desire to leave. They believed it was the perfect place to raise their family, with its low crime rate and abundance of outdoor activities they enjoyed together.

The winter months brought them joy through snow skiing at local resorts. Summers were filled with camping, fishing, and thrilling white-water rafting adventures. Golfing had become one of Garrett's favorite pastimes, and he had improved his skills over the past few seasons. Additionally, Garrett's family owned a cabin in a small town called Cascade, about an hour north of the city. It was a beloved destination for their daughters.

As the evening wore on, Garrett's patience waned. He became increasingly irritated by two guys he had recently been introduced to, John and Brett, who were lawyers. Though uncertain how they knew Bob and Linda, their drunken behavior tested Garrett's tolerance. Sensing his growing frustration, Garrett approached Julie, asking her for a private conversation.

They stepped onto the back patio, surrounded by the harmonious chirping of crickets. The air felt unpleasant in Garrett's lungs as he addressed the issue. "I know it's still early, Jules, but John and Brett are obnoxious. Everyone is getting hammered. Would you mind if we said goodbye?"

Julie's demeanor changed in an instant as she processed his words. She crossed her arms tightly against her chest, a sign of resistance. "Seriously, Garrett? It's eleven, and we've only been here for a few hours. Is asking you to play nice for a little longer too much? Please?"

Knowing he couldn't win this debate, Garrett realized he would be the "bad guy" if he left alone or insisted on Julie leaving with him. However, an idea sparked in his mind, leaving him unexpectedly pleased.

"Fine, Jules. We can stay a little while longer," he acquiesced, trying to keep a straight face.

Julie seemed surprised by his lack of resistance, her hands falling to her hips. Her narrowed eyes locked with his, seeking reassurance. "Thank you, baby. You're going to stick to the wine, though, right?"

Garrett's chest constricted as he broke eye contact, diverting his gaze to the cloudless sky adorned with twinkling stars. Thoughts of other guests, including Julie, indulging in expensive cognac, whiskey, and vodka swirled in his mind. He despised feeling different from others, especially after he had asked Julie to quit drinking to support his path to sobriety. Her dismissive response, "I don't have a problem with alcohol, Garrett, you do," had hurt him more than he let her believe.

Looking down from the night sky, Garrett locked eyes with Julie again. Justifying his intentions, fueled by resentment, he maintained a straight face and adopted a reassuring tone. "Yes, Jules. I'll stick with wine."

Garrett kept his word, but he downed the glasses of wine as if they were a refreshing drink on a scorching summer day. By midnight, he felt good and relaxed as the crowd around him spiraled into intoxication and oblivion.

Standing in the kitchen beside Bob, Garrett laughed at a story his friend had shared. Suddenly, John stumbled into him, clumsily spilling his whiskey and coke all over Garrett's clothes. The strong scent of alcohol permeated the air as it soaked into his cotton garments. His eyes burning with rage, Garrett placed his wine glass on the granite countertop and stood straight, moving closer to John.

"Seriously, man!" he exclaimed, his voice filled with pent-up anger, ready to confront the drunken fool before him.

"I'm sorry, I tripped over the cat." John's eyes were half opened, and he wobbled back and forth, struggling to keep his balance. His goofy-looking grin only fueled Garrett's anger over the situation.

"They don't have a cat, you freaking idiot," Garrett retorted, his heart pounding. He could feel the adverse effects of alcohol on his mood and reactions, amplifying his anger and making him more prone to confrontations, especially with disrespectful men.

"Or what?" John puffed out his chest, his grin disappearing and his lips tightening. He stood taller, inching closer to Garrett, as the tension thickened in the alcohol-laced air, silencing the drunken guests in the kitchen.

Before Garrett could respond, a sudden impact jolted his lower right chin. Given his fifteen years of martial arts training, the punch wasn't unfamiliar to him. He instinctively turned his head to identify the attacker. It was Brett, standing beside him, preparing for another strike. Acting on pure instinct, Garrett sidestepped to the left, evading Brett's assault. Seizing the opportunity, Garrett grabbed Brett's shirt collar and began landing punches on his face.

Suddenly, someone tackled Garrett from behind, interrupting the escalating violence. Looking up, he saw a terrified face above him—Susan, Brett's wife. Tears streamed down her trembling cheeks as she pleaded, "Please, stop hurting my husband."

"Okay," Garrett managed to utter, his mind jolted back to reality. The fear in Susan's eyes shook him, snapping him out of the animalistic rage that had taken over. He rose from the floor, observing the stunned silence of the onlookers, including Julie. They stood frozen, resembling mannequins in a department store, their lips pressed tightly together and their eyebrows forming a V-shaped frown.

Feeling angry and embarrassed, Garrett left through the front door, heading home. He sat on the front steps, practicing controlled breathing as his body relaxed. It felt like an eternity before Julie approached the house. She stopped before him, hanging her head low, tears streaming down her face.

His heart sank as he watched his wife break down over his behavior. "I'm sorry, Julie, but Brett cheap-shotted me for no reason," Garrett defended himself, seeking understanding and justification for his actions.

"I don't care what he did, Garrett, just stop! You ruined my night and my life. I doubt anyone will ever invite us over again because you chose to act like a drunken idiot," Julie exclaimed, wiping away her tears and locking eyes with him, her gaze filled with disappointment and frustration.

"I wasn't acting like a drunken idiot. Brett and John were. You've got to be kidding me right now!" Garrett retorted, tears welling up.

Julie wiped the remaining tears and pointed a finger at him. "You drank liquor tonight, didn't you? You reek of liquor! I can't believe you couldn't keep your promise. How dare you lie to me!"

"I didn't drink liquor ..."

"Stop lying!" she screamed. "I'm sick of your lies. I'm tired of you embarrassing me in front of our friends."

"I'm tired of these friends, Julie. Why do we always have to be around other people? Why can't we hang out with each other and our family?"

"Because I care about these people. They are important to me, and you ruined that for me. I hate you!" Julie's words struck deep, intensifying Garrett's pain.

Without saying another word, Garrett walked towards the garage. He punched in the code, and the door rolled up. All he wanted was to escape her, disgusted by her reaction. He didn't want to break down in front of her. He needed to be alone, and he knew exactly where to go.

"Where are you going?" Julie's voice echoed as she tightened her jacket around her body. Garrett remained silent, opening the car door as the beeping started. He ignited the engine, put the gear in reverse, and glanced at Julie through the rear-view mirror. Ignoring her frantic gestures, he turned the corner, feeling a sense of relief as he left his wife behind.

The sound from Garrett's phone startled him, and he glanced at the caller ID to see that it was Matt, his best friend since middle school. Seeing Matt's name on the screen provided a much-needed distraction from his tumultuous thoughts. He tapped the green circle and brought the phone to his ear.

"Hey, Matt," Garrett greeted, trying to sound composed despite his turmoil.

"Garrett, where are you, my man?" Matt's enthusiastic voice brought some relief to Garrett. He felt his shoulders loosen, realizing how tense he had been since the incident.

"I'm heading toward your place on the way to Barrels. Let me guess, Julie called you," Garrett replied, not surprised that Julie had reached out to Matt. She knew he could help reason with Garrett during difficult times.

"Yes, she did. I heard it wasn't the greatest dinner party tonight. How about you stop by and pick me up? Would you mind a little company?"

Matt and Garrett had been best friends since seventh grade. Matt had been through two failed marriages, attributing them to his inability to have children. But Garrett knew that Matt needed help with long-term commitment in general. He was free-spirited and passionate about outdoor activities like traveling, mountain biking, and snow-skiing. Julie loved Matt but wasn't comfortable with Garrett spending too much time with him, believing he needed more maturity. Garrett knew her discomfort stemmed more from the beautiful women Matt surrounded himself with rather than his maturity.

A smile formed on Garrett's face. "Not at all, brother. See you in ten minutes."

Garrett pulled up in front of Matt's single-level home and reached for his phone to send a text, but Matt opened the car door before he could. Sliding into the passenger seat, Matt offered a warm smile that faded as he waved his hand before his nose.

"You smell, my friend. You better let me drive."

Garrett quickly put the car in reverse, not allowing Matt to escape. "I'm fine. Jerk-off John spilled his drink on me. I've sobered up. I'll let you drive back home, though."

Matt stared at Garrett for a moment before fastening his seatbelt. The locking mechanism clicked, and his attention shifted to the road ahead, scanning the dark streets for any obstacles.

As Garrett approached a stoplight, he saw the lights of their destination a few blocks away.

"I heard you laid that guy out pretty good," Matt shifted his focus from the empty streets to Garrett.

Garrett could feel Matt's gaze but kept his attention on the lights in the distance. "Yeah, I guess I did. I'd had enough by that point. Julie and I were fighting. I tried to leave before things escalated, but she begged me to stay. She doesn't understand me, Matt." His face flushed, his throat tightened, and his chest trembled.

"I know she doesn't, Garrett. But don't worry about that right now. Everything will be fine."

The traffic light turned green, and Garrett pressed down on the gas pedal. Still struggling to hold back tears, a powerful surge of energy suddenly ripped through the right side of the vehicle. The sound of metal bending and pulling filled Garrett's ears as his body crashed against the panels and glass of his car door. Fear and panic were all that consumed his mind as darkness slowly took over his vision.

Garrett awakened from the darkness that had engulfed him, drawn back to consciousness by an unfamiliar beeping sound nearby. Pain coursed through his entire body, and his head throbbed on the left side while his limbs ached. He struggled to open his eyes against the glaring brightness of the lights above. Thoughts raced through his mind, but forming coherent ideas seemed impossible.

He blinked repeatedly, trying to moisten his dry eyelids before opening them again. With effort, he succeeded, but his vision remained blurry, and the room spun. Gradually, the lights above him became focused, revealing that he lay on a bed in what looked like a hospital room. Closing his eyes, he tried to recollect how he ended up here, but panic set in as he realized his right arm was restrained.

He looked down at his right wrist and saw it was handcuffed to the bed railing. Fear engulfed him, and he felt like the air had been sucked out of the room. Hoping desperately that he would wake up from this nightmare, Garrett's lungs struggled for breath.

The door creaked open, and Julie entered, looking worn out and exhausted. Her eyes were swollen and red, and she still wore the clothes from the previous night. Garrett focused on her, relieved she was in this dreadful dream. As he watched her approach, memories flooded back—Bob and Linda's party, the altercation with Brett, the pained expression on Susan's face, the argument with Julie, and driving with Matt. Matt ... Wait, what happened after I picked up Matt? Garrett's mind raced, panic and fear gripping him once more.

Julie took a seat in a brown leather recliner beside Garrett.

"What happened, Julie? Why am I here? Where is Matt? Oh my gosh, what have I done, Jules?" Tears streamed down Garrett's face as he sobbed uncontrollably, realizing something terrible had occurred.

Julie cried alongside him, holding his left hand against her cheek. "You were in a car accident, baby. The police aren't sure what happened yet. The surveillance video shows a pickup truck running a red light at the intersection of First Street and Main. It collided with your car at fifty miles per hour."

"Where is Matt, Julie?" Garrett struggled to speak above a whisper.

"Oh, baby, I'm so sorry. Matt didn't make it."

Confused, Garrett looked at Julie as if her words didn't register in his mind. He couldn't process the reality of what she had told him. Matt didn't make it? It couldn't be true. Not Matt. He was strong and healthy. He couldn't be gone. Lost in his thoughts, Garrett was jolted back to reality by Julie's anguished cries. As he watched his wife sob uncontrollably, the realization that Matt was truly gone shattered his heart into a million pieces. The pain was so intense that it threatened to invade his consciousness. Darkness crept in, luring him away. He wanted to embrace Julie, but the handcuffs reminded him of his confinement when he tried.

"Julie, why am I handcuffed to the bed?" Garrett's voice trembled as he gently lifted Julie's head, forcing her to meet his gaze.

Her bloodshot eyes quivered, and her lips trembled. "Your blood alcohol level was twice the legal limit. They're charging you with manslaughter. Your bond has been set at one million dollars." Julie looked away, the weight of reality settling upon her as well.

"They're saying I killed my best friend! Did I kill Matt? Please tell me this isn't true! It can't be true, Jules! Not Matt!"

The machines beside Garrett blared their alarms, and two nurses hurried into the room. Garrett screamed for Matt, wanting the tubes out of his arm, desperate to escape the bed. One of the nurses swiftly administered Ativan, a powerful sedative, into Garrett's IV. He felt the medication instantly, a warm and tingling sensation growing in his chest and stomach. Julie, the nurses, and the room itself blurred before his eyes. His body relaxed, and the world faded into darkness all around him.

When Garrett regained consciousness, Julie was nowhere to be seen. Instead, his eyes met with a distinguished-looking man in a finely tailored business suit, seated in the spot where Julie had been moments before. He introduced himself as Justin Rose, an attorney. Justin explained that Julie had contacted his firm and enlisted his services to guide Garrett through the upcoming days.

Garrett longed to escape the harsh reality that had befallen him. The physical pain was unbearable, and he begged for the existence of waking up in bed, convinced that this nightmare was merely a figment of his imagination. Meeting Justin's gaze, he carefully examined his face, searching for any hint or clue in his light brown eyes.

"How bad is it?"

Justin briefly lowered his gaze before meeting Garrett's eyes once more. He took a moment to collect his thoughts, preparing to deliver the sobering truth. "It's not looking good, Garrett. Based on the police reports, it's clear that the older gentleman who collided with your car suffered a stroke, making the accident his fault. However, due to your intoxication at the time, they're holding you responsible for the death of your friend. They argue that you could have reacted defensively without being under the influence. According to the law, you are deemed at fault when an accident occurs while driving over the legal limit. At this stage, Garrett, my focus is not on proving your innocence before a jury. My task is to negotiate the shortest possible prison sentence for you."

CHAPTER

TWO

"Hey, Dad," a voice called out, bringing Garrett back to the present. It was Jasmine, sitting across the table from him.

"Good morning, sweetheart! How did you sleep?" Garrett replied, his gaze shifting from the distant memories to his daughter's face.

"I slept great! The beds here are super comfy," Jasmine said, a trace of accent in her voice—a reminder of their years in Avon. After the accident, they moved to Avon to live with Julie's father. At the time, Garrett had little say in the matter, as Julie, being a homemaker, had no career or prospects. Reluctantly, he accepted her decision despite his initial disagreement.

"I agree. The beds are great. I like this place. What do you think?" Garrett took a sip of his now-cold coffee, noticing the pleasant aroma of bacon lingering in the air.

"Out of all the places we've stayed in over the past year, this one is my favorite," Jasmine replied as Alexa joined them on the porch.

"I love it too, Dad. Especially because it's supposedly haunted!" Alexa chimed in, giving Garrett a warm hug before settling into the chair between him and Jasmine.

"You believe those ghost stories you've been reading?" Garrett raised an eyebrow, a grin forming on his face.

"Gretchen told us all about the strange things that happen around here," Alexa's green eyes sparkled with excitement.

Jasmine added, "Guests complain about knocking sounds from the vacant room beside us. It's become kind of a legend to the locals."

Jasmine and Alexa exchanged knowing glances, playfully exclaiming, "Oooooohhhh," in unison. Garrett felt a powerful warmth as he observed his daughters' youthful exuberance. He cherished these moments with them, knowing he had missed out on so much during his time incarcerated. It wasn't about making up for lost time but about treasuring every precious moment they had together.

"Are you two ready for some breakfast?" Garrett glanced through the window, spotting other guests enjoying their freshly cooked meals. The smell of cooked meat made his stomach growl.

"Yes! The food looks delicious. I'm starving," Jasmine said, rubbing her belly.

Alexa nodded, and the trio left the porch to satisfy their appetites.

After breakfast, Garrett visited the gym at a nearby sister facility. The property boasted a small gym and a large pool, which Jasmine and Alexa were particularly excited about.

Leaving his daughters at the poolside, Garrett descended to the gym. To his delight, it was empty, affording him the solitude he often sought during his workouts. He surveyed the equipment before settling on a heavy dumbbell routine, focusing on isolating his biceps. A full-length mirror adorned the back wall, reflecting his well-built, six-foot-tall frame with jet-black hair cascading past his ears.

As he stretched his tight, sore muscles, he noticed the fading tan from the summer months and the small wrinkles forming at the corners of his eyes. Determined, he picked up a pair of fifty-pound weights and began his routine. Engrossed in the rhythm of his workout, Garrett's mind wandered back to his past, replaying the memories he carried with him.

Following the tragic accident, Garrett faced the harsh reality of his actions. He was charged and convicted of Misdemeanor DUI and Felony Vehicular Manslaughter, leading to a sentence of five years at the Idaho State Correctional Center. It could have been much worse, with a potential twenty-year sentence, if not for the heartfelt testimonies of Matt's parents. Their unwavering support played a pivotal role in securing a lesser punishment.

After enduring six long months of separation, the day finally arrived when Julie, accompanied by their daughters, visited Garrett at the correctional center. His heart skipped a beat as he saw them in the visiting room. Overwhelmed with emotions, he rushed toward his girls. He embraced them tightly, savoring the feeling he had longed for during their time apart. Their little hands and arms wrapped around him, filling him with completeness and euphoria.

"Daddy!" they exclaimed, showering him with hugs and kisses on the cheek.

"I've missed you two so much," Garrett whispered, holding them close, not wanting to let go. He marveled at how much they had grown, but guilt gnawed at him, reminding him of the precious moments he had missed.

With tears welling up in his eyes, he released his daughters and turned his attention to Julie. Their eyes locked, and a bittersweet smile played on his lips as he embraced her, kissing her neck. Surrounded by the buzzing energy of the visiting room, Garrett felt overwhelming gratitude for having his family by his side.

Taking their seats at the table, Garrett sat between his daughters, facing Julie. The visiting room was filled with families, inmates, and visitors engaged in conversations, with cards, board games, and vending machines scattered throughout.

Jasmine, observant as always, looked from Garrett to the other prisoners in matching outfits. "Nice outfit, Daddy. Does everyone have to wear the same thing?" she asked, her nose scrunching with curiosity.

Garrett glanced down at his light blue button-up shirt, belt, and jeans. Above his left pocket, a patch with his last name and IDOC number was written in black marker. He felt a pang in his chest, realizing how quickly his daughter caught on to the uniformity of the attire.

"Yes, sweetie. We do have to wear similar clothing," Garrett explained, his voice filled with embarrassment.

Curiosity still lingering, Jasmine raised an eyebrow and asked, "Why?"

Before Garrett could respond, Julie interjected, diverting their attention to the games and candy available in the vending machines. As they discussed their choices, Garrett's cravings surfaced, his stomach growling loudly in anticipation of the sweet indulgence. But amidst the momentary distraction, heaviness settled within him. Julie gave the girls some cash and directed them to the nearby machines.

Feeling Julie's touch on his hand, Garrett was reminded of the unfamiliarity of physical contact after his confinement. "Thank you for coming today, Jules. I've missed you three so much," he expressed sincerely, his voice trembling with unspoken emotions.

Julie's eyes glistened with unshed tears as she replied, "You're welcome. We've missed you too." Her gaze dropped, breaking the eye contact that held so much unspoken connection. "I need to discuss something significant with you," Julie finally said, her eyes seeking his, conveying the weight of her words. Garrett's heart sank as he braced himself for what was to come. "My dad has offered to move us into his home in Connecticut."

Connecticut? The word echoed in Garrett's mind, causing a stream of adrenaline to surge through his veins. "You can't move away from me, Jules. Why would you even consider this?"

Julie looked at him, disbelief etched on her face. "Because, Garrett, our savings account is dwindling, we're three months behind on the mortgage, and our vehicles are on the verge of being repossessed. I can't find a decent paying job anywhere, and my lack of work experience since Alexa was born is making it even harder."

Hearing her words, guilt began building, a potent reminder of the consequences of his actions. He longed for a momentary escape, a numbing of the emotions careening through him. The urge for alcohol to drown his sorrows resurfaced, tempting him with false reassurance.

"I'm so sorry, Julie. I'm so sorry you're in this position," Garrett said, gripping her hand tightly. A solitary tear rolled down her cheek, mirroring his pain.

"I know there must be other options, our parents, your mom, friends ... something that doesn't involve taking you and the most important people in my life away from me," Garrett pleaded, his heart aching at the thought of losing them to a distant land.

Julie wiped her tear-soaked eyes and met Garrett's gaze again, her voice filled with sorrow and determination. "I've explored every option, and this seems to be the most feasible one. My dad has offered financial assistance, and it would provide stability for the girls. A good home, excellent schools, food on the table, reliable transportation, and clothing to wear would alleviate so much of the stress I'm currently dealing with. I could also find a job that I truly enjoy without feeling the pressure to accept any opportunity that comes my way. It wouldn't be a permanent move; we can re-evaluate the situation as your release date gets closer."

Garrett sat there, watching his daughters eagerly insert

coins into the vending machines, feeling completely helpless. Deep down, he knew he couldn't provide what Julie and the girls needed in their current circumstances.

Julie's father, a wealthy business executive residing in Manhattan during the workweek, had a spacious weekend home—an impressive six thousand-square-foot residence. Garrett treasured the moments spent with Jon and Liz, Julie's dad and stepmom, and relished their trips to the bustling city. He also enjoyed the family vacations in Connecticut, where they would spend time together in Avon, enjoying the company and the scenic backyard with its inviting pool.

Although the thought of Julie and the girls moving away weighed heavily on his heart, Garrett understood the practicality of the decision. "I hate the idea of you leaving, but you're right. It might be the best option for all of you."

Julie kissed him once more, their lips meeting in a passionate embrace. However, amidst the intensity, Garrett couldn't shake the feeling that something was missing. As he looked into Julie's eyes—once vibrant and filled with love—he noticed the deep well of sadness and exhaustion. Garrett realized he was losing his family, which was utterly devastating.

The girls returned to the table, their arms laden with snacks, drinks, and games. Garrett refused to let their impending separation overshadow their time together. For the next hour, the four reveled in each other's company, engrossed in a lively game of Uno while indulging in soda, candy, doughnuts, and chips.

Garrett's heart felt broken when it came time for them to part ways. It was the most agonizing farewell he had ever experienced. Tears flowed freely as the correctional officer escorted him away, each step taking him further from the ones he loved most. His heartache intensified with each passing moment, aching with the awareness that his family was slipping through his fingers, and he was powerless to stop it.

A month had passed since Julie and the girls had visited, and Garrett sat on his bottom bunk, engrossed in a book. The guards approached, delivering the daily mail, and one of them handed him a large manila envelope. His heart sank as he noticed it was from Julie. They had just moved, and he saw the new address printed beneath her name. With a sinking feeling in his stomach, he could sense the contents' weight.

Opening the envelope, his worst fears were confirmed. Inside were divorce papers and a heartfelt letter from Julie. A sour taste filled his mouth as he read her words.

Dear Garrett,

I am very sorry you had to find out this way. I would have come to see you in person, but I don't think I would have gone through with it. I know that your life has been completely turned upside down and that this will only make it harder for you. I don't want to make life more difficult for you, baby.

I have listened when you told me how horrible the food is, how dirty your living quarters are, and how nervous the never-ending violence makes you feel. My heart aches for you and the nightmare you must face daily.

You have failed to understand that my life has also been a nightmare. I have lost my partner in life, my provider, my best friend. Every day, I wake up wishing I could somehow turn back time so that you could still be with us, that I could have somehow stopped you from getting into your car and driving away that night. That is not possible.

While packing the house, I found half a dozen vodka bottles hidden throughout the garage and your bedroom closet. I knew your drinking problem was terrible but discovering this made me feel betrayed. Betrayal of trust that alcohol had become so vital to you that hiding it seemed like a good option.

Alcohol has caused most of our marital problems and has taken you away from our daughters and me. I hope someday you can understand that you are an alcoholic. You will never learn to live a life of sobriety without admitting this first.

I wish I had the patience to wait for you, Garrett, and the trust that life will be different for us when you get out. I don't, however. I know you must think I am weak for giving up. We are all vulnerable, just in different ways.

Please take care of yourself in there. Learn from this experience and become a better man after having gone through it. Know that the girls and I are safe and will be throughout your incarceration. I will never do anything to keep them from your life. They love you dearly and will always be a part of you, no matter where you are.

I do love you, Garrett. I always have, and I always will. Goodbye, baby,

Julie

Garrett placed the divorce papers on his locker, surprised by his lack of emotion. A numbness had taken hold of him, shielding him from the expected shattering of his heart. But as the numbness dissipated, anger seethed within him. He was angry at Julie, the judge who sentenced him, and the older man who caused the accident. He despised his current situation, and, above all, he was furious with himself for his past mistakes.

Without the numbing agent, Garrett struggled to process his emotions, feeling like he was losing his mind. Anger became his refuge, shielding him from the unbearable pain, bitterness, fear, and resentment that consumed his thoughts. Anger guided his every action and behavior, fueling him, and permeating his existence from the moment he woke until he closed his eyes at night.

It all began with one sarcastic comment from one of his cellmates. He couldn't hold his rage in any longer, his chest ready to explode. He grabbed the man by his throat and slammed him against the concrete wall. He could see and feel the fear oozing from his eyes as he squeezed harder and tighter. As the blood completely drained from his face, he finally loosened his grip, watching his body fall to the ground with a loud thud. The man struggled to catch his breath. Garrett was instantly hooked on the feelings this altercation inspired within his turmoiled soul.

After eighteen months of confinement, he had been embroiled in twenty-one brutal fights, earning a reputation as one of the most feared men among the prisoners. Various prison gangs tried to recruit him, and inmates sought his friendship for protection. Still, he remained a solitary figure. Companionship held no appeal for him. When not fighting, he found consolation in reading, working out, and watching movies on his tiny television. He clung to a strict routine, desperately trying to maintain control.

Cellmates came and went in a cycle lasting only a few months at best. When Garrett grew tired of their poor hygiene, disrespect, or lack of cleanliness, he demanded they leave. Some would refuse, and he would unleash the violent beast that possessed his body. Using only legs and elbows, he ensured no evidence of his actions remained when the guards conducted their knuckle checks. This was the way he lived, his reality, and the only way he knew how to hold onto the little sanity he had left.

CHAPTER

THREE

Nearly two years after his arrest, Garrett sat at the steel table in the unit's day room, savoring his post-workout meal. Following a strict workout routine and adhering to a high-protein diet, he had gained thirty pounds of lean muscle and was in the best physical shape of his life. Unlike most inmates, he was fortunate enough to receive monthly financial support from his parents, allowing him to purchase items from the commissary.

As the unit door rattled open, Garrett noticed a new inmate entering. He deduced that this man would be his cellmate since his bunk was the only vacant one. The stranger appeared slightly older, around forty-five, with a clean-cut hairstyle and a freshly shaved face. He made an excellent first impression, and Garrett felt a glimmer of hope that this newcomer might stay longer than his previous cellmates. Little did Garrett know, this man would forever alter the course of his life.

Approaching his new roommate, Garrett extended his hand and introduced himself, "Hi, I'm Garrett."

"Nice to meet you, Garrett. I'm Jerry," replied Jerry, reciprocating the handshake with a firm grip.

Curiosity getting the better of him, Garrett inquired, "So, what are you in for?" He posed the routine question to each new cellmate, pledging he wouldn't tolerate certain felons sharing his living space.

"I was arrested for a felony DUI," Jerry answered. He retrieved some documents from a folder on the table. He handed them to Garrett, who scrutinized them to verify his cellmate's claims. An awkward silence ensued as Garrett examined Jerry's court papers.

Jerry cleared his throat, breaking the silence, "And what about you? What did they get you on?"

Garrett's voice turned cold as he responded, "Manslaughter." He returned the paperwork to Jerry and sat on one of the metal chairs. Noticing the neatness of Jerry's bed and the organized placement of his items, he asked, "Have you ever done time before?"

"Nope, this is my first time."

"All right, let me fill you in on the rules of this tier," Garrett said, authority in his voice. "Everyone is expected to be up by nine-thirty, maintain good hygiene, and work out at least five times a week. Clean up after yourself inside and outside the cell. We take turns cleaning the cell every other day. Don't accrue debts you can't repay. Lastly, and perhaps most importantly, show respect. Will any of this be an issue for you?"

Jerry responded promptly, without hesitation, "Not at all."

Satisfied with the answer, Garrett gathered his shower items and exited the cell. The following month progressed without any significant incidents or conflicts between them. Jerry demonstrated adherence to all the rules, maintained cleanliness and order, and respected Garrett's personal space. This harmonious coexistence left Garrett feeling content and optimistic that this arrangement could endure.

One evening, after the prison was on lockdown, Garrett was taken aback by Jerry's voice breaking the silence. "Hey, do you mind if I ask why everyone seems afraid of you?" Jerry inquired, his genuine curiosity evident in his tone.

Setting aside the book he read, Garrett paused momentarily, contemplating his response. Eventually, he decided to give Jerry a chance, sensing the sincerity in his question.

"I've been in my fair share of fights over the past few years," Garrett confessed, his voice carrying a hint of remorse. "I haven't lost any of them. I guess it's earned me some respect, you know?"

Curiosity brimming, Jerry asked, "Were you a skilled fighter before all this, back on the streets?"

Garrett hesitated momentarily, unsure whether he wanted to delve deeper into his past. However, recognizing Jerry's genuine interest, he exhaled deeply and opened up. "I trained in mixed martial arts for over fifteen years before my conviction," Garrett revealed. "My best friend and I used to spar together at least once a week. So, fighting has always been a part of me." Getting up from his bunk, Garrett brought himself to eye level with Jerry and asked, "Has anyone been bothering you?"

"No," Jerry said firmly. "I was just curious. I wanted to get to know you, that's all."

Garrett took a seat, his expression curious. "What do you want to know?"

Over the next four hours, Garrett and Jerry delved into their past lives. Garrett shared stories about his role as a Director of Sales in the cell phone industry, proudly displaying cherished photos of his daughters. He discussed his interests and hobbies, highlighting the value he placed on them. Jerry, in turn, opened up about his wife and only daughter, passionately describing his career as a Professor of Music at a local university. He spoke of his deep love for teaching others to play the piano and shared his ongoing battle with alcoholism. This topic made Garrett's discomfort evident, prompting Jerry to change the subject swiftly.

"So, what happened with you and Julie?"

Garrett skillfully evaded discussing the reasons behind his divorce, offering a simple response. "It just didn't work out," he said, leaving Jerry waiting for further explanation. Sensing that it might be best to let it go, Jerry decided to drop the matter.

Over the following months, Jerry settled into a routine with the help of Garrett. They diligently worked out five days a week, engaging in bodyweight exercises within the confines of their cell while adhering to a strict diet. Jerry discovered that the prison offered "Daily Recovery," an 8-step recovery program. Determined to make amends, he set a goal to wholeheartedly work through the steps and complete the program before his release.

Jerry set a realistic target of finishing one step per month, recognizing the attainability of this goal while acknowledging the substantial time and dedication it would require. Each morning, Jerry woke up and embarked on his step-work. Occasionally, Garrett would wake to find him in tears, while other times, his infectious smile would warm Garrett's soul. As Jerry delved deeper into his step-work, Garrett noticed a significant change in his attitude. He appeared happier, more at peace with himself. Additionally, Jerry incorporated Bible reading and prayer into his daily routine.

One day, as the sun began to rise, Garrett awoke to find Jerry engrossed in prayer at the small round table. Tears streamed down Jerry's cheeks, illuminated by the gentle pink-ish-orange glow on his face. The scene was so breathtakingly beautiful that God seemed present in their cell. Deeply moved, tears welled up in Garrett's eyes. Jerry's unwavering trust in God profoundly touched him.

After Jerry finished praying, his gaze turned towards Garrett. "What's going on, Garrett?"

Wiping away his tears, Garrett composed himself. "I can tell God loves you. Do you think He loves me too?"

"Of course He does," Jerry assured him. "He knows we are imperfect and prone to making mistakes. He only wants us to acknowledge our faults and work on correcting them. This is where the eight steps of my program are beginning to change my life."

Witnessing the genuine transformation in Jerry, Garrett knew these words held truth. Overflowing with emotions, he brought his hands to his face and sobbed uncontrollably. All the feelings he had suppressed and buried deep inside now resurfaced, refusing to be ignored. Jerry moved closer, positioning himself next to Garrett on his bunk, and gently wrapped his arm around Garrett's shoulders.

"I killed my friend, Matt," Garrett finally confessed, his voice laden with guilt. "He is dead because of me, Jerry. How can God ever forgive that? I was drinking, and he died because of me. He was an incredible person, loved by everyone. He would still be alive if I hadn't been drinking that night."

With each word, Garrett's realization of the destructive role alcohol had played in his life grew more substantial. The memories of Julie pleading with him to quit drinking flooded his mind. Still, he had always dismissed her concerns as nagging, failing to understand his desperate need for the substance. Now, in this moment of clarity, he recognized himself as an alcoholic.

As the weight of his actions sank in, Jerry spoke in a soft, compassionate voice. "God will always forgive us. That is the easy part of His plan. The hardest lesson we must learn is to forgive ourselves. You have made severe mistakes but must find the strength to forgive yourself, Garrett. If you continue punishing yourself, you will never feel God's love and forgiveness."

Jerry's words resonated deeply with Garrett. He finally decided to let go. Suddenly, he felt the presence of God shining upon his face. The turmoil that had plagued his soul for years subsided, replaced by a profound sense of warmth and serenity. A gentle tickling sensation embraced his chest. For the first time in many years, Garrett felt intimately connected with God. Waves of euphoria pulsed throughout his body, a tangible reminder of God's love and affection.

Awestruck by this spiritual experience, Garrett dropped to his knees and prayed—something he hadn't done since childhood. He prayed for himself, seeking the path to sobriety. He prayed for his daughters, family, friends, Matt, and Julie. Holding nothing back, he poured out his heart. When he finished, a boundless certainty settled within him, revealing the course of action he needed.

Garrett looked at Jerry, a smile gradually spreading across his lips. "Will you teach me about Daily Recovery? Please show me how to work the steps. I don't want alcohol to continue ruining my life once I'm out of this place."

Jerry returned his gaze, nodding his head in affirmation before embracing him.

"One more thing," Garrett added, his voice filled with newfound hope. "Can you teach me to play the piano too?"

CHAPTER

FOUR

Garrett finished his workout, racking his weights and examining his glistening figure in the mirror. He had shed some weight he gained while in prison but possessed a strong, muscular physique at two hundred and five pounds. Evaluating his body, he took note of areas that could benefit from further improvement. Overall, he was satisfied with his appearance and had been in maintenance mode for six months. He returned to the pool area after chugging his protein shake and wiping away the sweat.

Jasmine and Alexa lounged on two chairs by the pool, engrossed in their phones, capturing moments to share with their friends.

"Did either of you dare to get in?" Garrett teased, looking at them with a playful smile.

Alexa proudly responded, her damp hair evidence of her aquatic adventure. "I did! I got in the cold water and survived."

Jasmine crossed her arms over her chest, pretending to shiver. "It was too chilly for me. I couldn't do it."

"Sorry, it turned out colder than expected Jaz. Are you both ready to leave now?"

Both girls rose from their chairs simultaneously and said, "Yes, we're ready."

Back at the 1818 Estate, Garrett and his daughters enjoyed a delectable lunch while Gretchen continued to regale them with tales of supposed hauntings. Though Garrett didn't harbor much belief in ghosts, he delighted in seeing his daughters captivated by the stories Gretchen spun.

"Did you know Ms. Clarisse is buried on the hill overlooking this house?" Gretchen revealed, her face contorting into a ghostly expression. "Legend has it that she chose that resting place to watch over those who dwell here forever."

The girls erupted in laughter, thoroughly entertained by Gretchen's theatrics. Garrett joined in, relishing the joy radiating from his daughters.

Watching Jasmine and Alexa from across the table, laughter, and chatter filling the air, Garrett marveled at how much they had grown during his absence. On his first visit after his release, it felt like he was reconnecting with strangers. While locked away, he had done his best to maintain their relationship through weekly letters and phone calls. Their letters, filled with photos and updates, served as windows into their lives, keeping him connected despite the physical distance.

Seeing them now, laughing and conversing with Gretchen, was delightful for Garrett. It was proof of the healing power of time. This new chapter in their lives, forged through hardship and resilience, held an unbreakable bond that surpassed ordinary father-daughter relationships. They respected, adored, and savored their time together as if every moment was a precious gift—a testament to the enduring power of love and family.

After their lunch, the trio retreated to their room to freshen up. Garrett had promised to take them shopping for new dresses, ensuring they would look their best for the special evening dinner. Their destination was Emilio's, a renowned steakhouse in the heart of West Hartford. With its reputation for exquisite steaks, refined atmosphere, and exceptional customer experience, the restaurant had earned glowing reviews, necessitating reservations made months in advance. Garrett had chosen this esteemed establishment to commemorate his first anniversary of freedom. This occasion held genuine significance in his quest for redemption.

Garrett remained actively involved with Daily Recovery, diligently working through the steps with Jerry as his mentor. Each day, he felt himself growing more invigorated and resilient. Attending at least four weekly meetings, even chairing one, Garrett had reached a point where he was ready to give back and mentor others walking a similar path. His connection with Jerry remained steadfast, their daily communication serving as a constant reminder of the support they provided for each other. Jerry, having been released a year before Garrett, understood their challenges and remained a pillar of strength in their shared sobriety journey.

There were times when the program's demands felt overwhelming, causing Garrett to reflect on the lonely days he spent confined within the prison walls. The memories of isolation, the inability to step beyond the fenced borders, and the hopelessness and regret for not being active in his daughters' lives would resurface, threatening to engulf him in a sea of despair. The prison had been more than just a physical incarceration; it had affected his emotional and mental well-being. Garrett recognized that his commitment to Daily Recovery was not solely about maintaining sobriety; it was about preserving his sanity and finding peace amidst the tumultuous currents of his past.

As Garrett sat in the dressing room of a department store at the local mall, a sense of gratitude swelled within him. He marveled at his precious time with his daughters and the financial stability he had been fortunate to achieve. Uncertainty weighed heavily upon his shoulders when he was first convicted as a felon. He knew that his previous career was forever lost, and the prospect of finding a new path that welcomed someone with his criminal record seemed daunting. The tales of employment struggles shared by fellow inmates did little to assuage his fears.

It wasn't until Garrett's release and his temporary stay with his parents that he stumbled upon an unexpected opportunity. Julie had diligently forwarded all his mail to their address. A familiar logo caught his eye as he sorted through the piles of junk mail. It was a statement from an online stock trading account he had opened years ago, originally intended to manage some stock options he had received.

While working under his former boss, who dabbled in penny stocks, Garrett had received a few tips on potential investments. Seizing the moment, he transferred one thousand dollars into his online account. He began buying and selling stocks like a seasoned trader on Wall Street. He'd kept this account a secret from Julie, having opened it just days before the accident that altered the course of their lives.

Garrett distinctly remembered investing in several pharmaceutical companies, and as he carefully examined the statement, a rush of disbelief washed over him. His initial thousand-dollar investment had skyrocketed to an astounding eighteen thousand seven hundred and thirty-six dollars. Of the three companies he had chosen, one had successfully developed a groundbreaking drug that passed all clinical trials and was now prescribed by physicians for patients with specific heart conditions. Overnight, the stock price had surged from mere cents per share to several dollars.

Emboldened by this remarkable turn of events, Garrett decided to explore the realm of day trading further. He immersed himself in researching companies and meticulously analyzing financial data, discovering a natural aptitude for this line of work. Within three months, he had transformed his initial investment of approximately eighteen thousand dollars into an impressive forty thousand dollars. Setting a budget for himself, accounting for travel expenses and other necessary expenditures, Garrett set a goal of generating five thousand dollars in monthly revenue. Remarkably, he had yet to miss his target. With each successful trade, he felt renewed purpose and determination.

Garrett would have already relocated to Connecticut if the circumstances had been different. However, the rules of Probation and Parole presented a unique challenge for felons like him. They prohibited transferring to a state without a friend or family member to provide accommodation. Unfortunately, Garrett's options were limited to his daughters, Julie, and her new husband, which made the situation complex.

With four more years of parole ahead of him, Garrett pondered the future. He knew that his girls would likely be attending college by the time his parole ended. It was a daunting thought, but he held onto his faith in God, trusting that a solution would present itself when the time was right. Garrett believed that divine guidance would lead him to the path he needed to follow.

After spending nearly two hours shopping, Jasmine and Alexa finally found their perfect dresses. Jasmine first emerged from the dressing room, wearing a stunning black sleeveless dress that fell just above her knees. Garrett noticed her flushed cheeks and the familiar smile that reminded him of his little girl.

"Wow, Jasmine, you look stunning!"

Jasmine twirled around, allowing the dress's fabric to float gracefully. "What do you think of the back?" she asked, revealing a low-cut design that exposed a concerning amount of skin. Garrett had to remind himself that his daughter was now a young adult, no longer the little girl he once knew. Suppressing his paternal instincts, he responded, "I give it a perfect ten! Classy and elegant."

Jasmine beamed with joy, grateful for her father's approval. "Yay! Thanks, Dad. I love it. All right, Alexa, your turn."

Meanwhile, Alexa anxiously waited behind a dressing room

door, ready to unveil her chosen dress. With a shy giggle, she emerged wearing a white, short-sleeved dress that landed below her knees. The loose-fitting garment reminded Garrett of the summer dresses she adored as a child. Still, this one had a touch of sophistication. Black silk trim adorned the sleeves and neck, and a black bow with a diamond center sat below Alexa's chin. Alexa had already caught up to her sister's height at thirteen, standing proudly at five feet tall. Garrett marveled at how quickly his youngest daughter had grown, silently yearning to freeze time and keep them his little girls forever.

Unable to contain his admiration, Garrett exclaimed, "All I can say is perfect. Perfect!"

Alexa's laughter filled the room as she twirled in front of the mirror, taking in her reflection. "Do you like the bow?" she asked, glancing at her father, contemplating whether it was too childish for her newfound maturity. This was a constant struggle for Alexa as she navigated the transition from girlhood to womanhood. Everything in her life seemed to change—her interest in boys instead of horses, her preference for video chats with friends over cartoons, and the rigorous hour-long rituals of getting ready. It was a bittersweet challenge for Garrett to witness Alexa's growth. To him, she would always be his baby girl.

"I think the bow is beautiful, just like you."

Content with her father's approval, she turned to Jasmine, seeking her sister's opinion. Jasmine and Alexa had always shared a close bond despite occasional ups and downs in their sibling relationship. Being younger, Alexa looked up to Jasmine for guidance, especially during transitional moments.

Having experienced those same milestones first, Jasmine gladly offered her wisdom and support.

"I love it! You look beautiful! The bow goes perfectly with the black heels you'll be wearing tonight," Jasmine chimed in, appreciating the coordination of Alexa's outfit.

Alexa looked in the mirror once more, seeking final confirmation. "Oh yeah, I forgot about the little bows on my shoes. I agree; they'll go together perfectly."

Garrett couldn't contain his joy as he looked at his daughters. "I will be the luckiest man in the restaurant tonight, walking in with you two beautiful ladies."

That night would be monumental. A night they would surely never forget.

CHAPTER

FIVE

Emilio's, located on the top floor of a downtown commercial building, exuded an air of elegance. Adhering to the formal dress code mentioned on their website, Garrett had chosen to wear a three-piece gray suit. Underneath, he wore a white button-up oxford shirt and a solid black tie, completing the ensemble with shiny black shoes. When he emerged from the bathroom, his daughters expressed their admiration, their "oohs" and "aahs" filling him with pride.

As the elevator doors opened, Garrett stepped into Emilio's and was immediately drawn into the atmosphere. The first thing that caught his attention was the breathtaking views surrounding the restaurant. Floor-to-ceiling windows enclosed the space, offering a panoramic vista of the cityscape. In the center of the room stood a shiny black grand piano. A white-haired man played a soft tune, his melodic voice perfectly complimenting the background. The tantalizing scent of seasoned meat wafted through the air, reminding Garrett of his hunger.

A young woman greeted them at the hostess station and led them to their table. Garrett noticed the glances they received from other guests as they made their way through the restaurant. They were seated in the northwest corner, providing magnificent city views. The dark sky beyond the glass panes twinkled with approval as if praising their presence. The table resembled a cozy booth, with two small brown love seats facing each other, separated by a table.

Garrett's attention shifted to the bar near the piano, where couples enjoyed fancy cocktails while savoring the breathtaking scenery. Seeing people drinking alcohol still held a sense of novelty for him. During his time in prison, access to alcohol was limited. While homemade concoctions like hooch, an alcoholic drink made by fermenting fruit, occasionally made their way around, Garrett had little interest in indulging. Unless actively sought out, alcohol was not readily available within the prison walls.

Upon his release, Garrett was confronted with the omnipresence of alcohol in the outside world. It was a temptation he hadn't fully contemplated. The reality hit him when he entered a gas station to buy a soda and realized the alcoholic beverages were conveniently displayed next to the cooler where he grabbed his Pepsi. This realization catapulted him into isolation, spending most of his first month at his parents' house, afraid to venture into a world filled with reminders of drinking.

During this challenging time, Jerry called Garrett and urged him to attend a Daily Recovery meeting. Reluctantly, Garrett decided to try it, and that first meeting turned out to be a miraculous turning point for him. Although Jerry couldn't make it, Garrett felt a sense of belonging and comfort as the meeting commenced. The attendees were kind, accepting, and friendly, making him feel welcomed and understood. The meeting format was familiar, reminiscent of the ones he had attended during his time in prison. Recognizing the value of this support system, Garrett committed to attending the meeting every day for the next month.

As he continued attending the Daily Recovery meetings, Garrett formed relationships with the regular members, finding reassurance in their shared experiences. In this group, he found a sense of home and belonging. Each person had a unique story featuring different characters, circumstances, and consequences. Still, they all shared the common thread of alcohol having exacted a heavy toll on their lives. Together, they worked tirelessly to ensure they wouldn't have to pay that hefty price again. They embarked on their recovery journeys through mutual support and understanding, determined to reclaim what was precious to them in life.

Garrett noticed an attractive woman approaching their table, her presence magnetic. "Good evening. My name is Jenn, and I'll be your waitress tonight," she greeted with a warm smile. "How are the three of you doing this evening?"

Garrett returned her smile, feeling a flicker of intrigue. "Wonderful, Jenn. How about yourself?"

Jenn's eyes sparkled as she replied, "I'm fabulous. My goodness, the three of you make such a lovely group." She described the specials and answered their menu inquiries with genuine enthusiasm.

Knowing Garrett's preference for beef tenderloin, he opted for an 8-oz filet accompanied by Au gratin potatoes, asparagus, and the house salad. With an air of excitement, Jasmine chose the chicken cordon blue, served with mashed potatoes, asparagus, and a Caesar salad. Alexa followed suit, selecting the same dish but substituting the mashed potatoes with steak fries. They all decided on refreshing glasses of soda to accompany their meal.

As they waited for their food, Garrett initiated a conversation, wanting to immerse themselves in the restaurant's ambiance. "What do you guys think of this place?"

Jasmine's eyes twinkled as she took in the elegant surroundings. "It's very fancy. I like the cute lamps," she replied, her eyes drifting towards the antique lamp adorning their table, casting a soft glow.

Alexa's attention was captured by the soothing melodies emanating from the center of the room. "I love the piano music," she said, her voice filled with appreciation.

Garrett nodded, his eyes glimmering with delight. "I couldn't agree more. The lighting, the music—it all creates a magical feeling. I hope the food lives up to the overall experience," he shared, gesturing towards their enchanting surroundings.

Their meals arrived in a carefully orchestrated sequence. First came the salads, accompanied by warm garlic bread rolls.

The fresh greens and tangy dressing danced on their palates. At the same time, the aroma of the bread rolls filled the air, creating a mouthwatering symphony of flavors.

The asparagus followed suit, tender and vibrant, accompanied by a velvety butter sauce that elevated their dining experience. They savored each bite, delighting in the harmonious blend of textures and tastes.

Finally, the main course arrived, and Garrett's steak stole the show. Cooked to a perfect medium rare, it was adorned with a creamy béarnaise sauce that cascaded over the tender meat. Garrett's taste buds danced in ecstasy with every savory bite. Wanting to share the joy he offered a taste to Jasmine and Alexa, who agreed that it was a culinary masterpiece.

Nearing the end of their main course, the absence of piano music caught their attention. Garrett's gaze wandered to the vacant piano bench, and Alexa followed suit, noting the void in the room.

With a playful grin, Alexa whispered, "Maybe he had to use the bathroom."

"Good point," Garrett said after finishing his last bite.

Jenn gracefully cleared their plates, assuring them that a delicious dessert would soon arrive. As they awaited the sweet finale of their meal, a man's voice resonated through the speakers, capturing the attention of everyone in the room.

"Good evening, everyone. I hope you have had a wonderful time with us tonight. My name is Mark, and I am the General Manager of this fine restaurant. Unfortunately, our amazing piano player, Ricardo, has fallen ill and will be unable to continue performing for all of you fine people."

A murmur of disappointment rippled through the room, mingling with empathetic whispers. However, Mark's words took an unexpected turn, "But fear not! We have decided to embrace this unforeseen circumstance and turn it into an opportunity for some impromptu musical entertainment. If any of our musically inclined guests are willing to share their talent and grace us with a few songs, please raise your hand, and the stage will be yours."

Garrett and the other guests exchanged curious glances, contemplating the proposition. The room fell into a momentary silence, everyone awaiting what would come next. Then, before Garrett could locate the first volunteer, he saw Jasmine rise from her seat and gracefully walk toward Mark, determination gleaming in her eyes.

Aubrey Ellis sat across from her best friend Rachel, at Emilio's, engrossed in their conversation as they enjoyed their dinner. However, their attention was captured by the sight of a young girl approaching the General Manager. Aubrey was mesmerized by the girl's confidence, considering her tender age.

"Isn't it surprising to see someone so young volunteering to perform for this sophisticated crowd?" Aubrey whispered to Rachel.

Rachel's eyes widened with bemusement as she observed the girl's poised demeanor. "She must be quite talented. She is adorable! That dress she's wearing is exquisite," Rachel remarked, delicately dabbing the corner of her mouth with a fine linen napkin. They watched intently as the young girl approached the General Manager, exchanging a few words before taking hold of the microphone.

Aubrey's heart fluttered as Jasmine introduced herself and made an impassioned plea for her father, Garrett, to take the stage. The crowd, including Aubrey and Rachel, sat silently, anxiously awaiting Garrett's response. Aubrey felt a rush of emotion as the room erupted into applause, witnessing Garrett rise from his seat and make his way to the piano.

"Oh, this just got interesting," Rachel whispered before sipping her wine. "That man is quite a catch," she added, playfully winking.

Aubrey couldn't tear her stare away from Garrett as he strode confidently toward the center of the room. His suit, tailored to perfection, accentuated his athletic physique. His dark, combed-back hair added an air of sophistication to his youthful appearance. Aubrey found herself entranced by him. As he reached Jasmine and Mark, Aubrey noticed the warmth in his eyes as he embraced his daughter and exchanged words with Mark. Mark, in turn, raised the microphone and called out to his other daughter, Alexa, inviting her to join them.

Alexa blushed; the unexpected attention made her self-conscious, but she gathered her composure and carefully went to the center of the room. Taking a seat on a tall bar stool beside her sister, she positioned herself directly across from their father, their eyes brimming with enthusiasm as they prepared for the music to begin.

Garrett took off his suit jacket, handing it to Mark. He sat down on the piano bench, adjusting it as needed. Aubrey couldn't help but notice his muscular arms. He wore a gray sleeveless vest with a fitted, long-sleeved, white button-up shirt underneath. Rachel gave her a stunned expression, reassuring her that she was just as impressed as Aubrey.

Before Garrett's hands touched the keys, he leaned forward, his lips close to the microphone in its short stand. "Good evening. I hope you all enjoy these two songs I will be playing. I originally learned to play the piano to express my undying love for these two beautiful ladies in front of me. I love you, girls. These songs are dedicated to you."

Before he even started to play, Aubrey felt deeply touched by this father's love for his daughters. She could easily relate to his daughters' expressions, as she felt that same kind of love from her father. For her, no love ever compared to the love her father freely gave to her. At that moment, she missed her father more than anyone else.

And then he began to play.

At first, she thought her mind must have been playing tricks on her. Her ears heard what she desperately missed, not what the man was performing. But then he began to sing, and she knew it was the same song her father played and sang to her as a child. It wasn't as if her father had written the song. Paul Williams and Kenneth Ascher's, "The Rainbow Connection" was a popular song for any child. Aubrey first fell in love with the melody at the age of five. She would sing along as Kermit the Frog and Jim Henson sang it on *The Muppets*. Her father, who taught and played the piano, created his rendition, especially for her.

Feeling the tears in her eyes, she listened and watched another father play for his daughters. She was transported to an earlier time. Sitting on the living room floor of her childhood home, coloring within the lines, and her father at the piano, playing and singing like an angel from above. She could feel the safety and protection his voice carried. The unending confidence his loving eyes inspired.

She was startled to feel a warm touch and squeeze of her hand. Rachel sat beside her, knowing how much she missed her father and this song's importance. The man was extremely talented with music. His voice was deep, soft, angelic sounding. His hands moved quickly, hitting keys in perfect timing, creating a harmonious sound that seemed to calm her soul. She watched him, studying his expressions as he sang each word. She desperately wanted to seize this moment in time, keeping it with her forever.

His girls sat silently, holding each other's hands as their eyes filled with tears. They seemed to forget where they were, sitting awkwardly at the center of attention among absolute strangers. Any nervousness or embarrassment was long gone. Their faces showed the love they felt for their father. They also seemed oblivious to what was transpiring amongst the crowd. It was a world that only consisted of them, a piano, and a father who loved them dearly.

As he finished, the entire restaurant sat utterly silent. All you could hear was the occasional sniffle from someone's nose. Aubrey watched intently as he began to study his surroundings. He was surprised at how touched the people were—shocked by the tears streaming down some of their cheeks. His daughters stood, clapping loudly. One by one, everyone stood and applauded. Aubrey could barely see through her tear-soaked eyes. She wished she had a replay button to live in that beautiful moment again and again. She longed not only for her father but also to be loved again by another man.

Aubrey had lost her father in a tragic car accident. She was only fifteen years old when that dreadful call came through. The Farmington Police Department called to inform her of an accident her parents had been in. Both, she was told, were in critical condition. When Aubrey arrived at the hospital, her grandparents waited for her. Her grandfather, whom she loved dearly, walked up to her, hugging her tightly. He had a pained expression on his face. He whispered to her that her father was gone. Her mother was in the ICU, and the doctors were optimistic about her survival and recovery.

The devastating loss of her father left a void in Aubrey's heart that could never be filled. The pain she felt was indescribable, an ache that permeated every aspect of her life. Her father had been more than a parent to her—he had been her mentor, confidant, and best friend. He had given her unwavering, unconditional love that she had taken for granted. Now, she hungered for that love, for his presence, but he was forever gone.

Her father had always taught her to expect the same kind of love from her future partner and to never settle for anything less. He had been the perfect example, treating her mother like a queen and always showing her the respect she deserved. His passion had set the bar so high that, after his untimely death, no other man could measure up.

In the fifteen years that followed the accident, Aubrey struggled with long-term relationships. She entered each new connection, hopeful that it would bring the love and fulfill-ment she craved. But over time, the initial spark would fade, leaving her with a sense of emptiness and disappointment. Each goodbye chipped away at her hope of finding true love, leaving her feeling alone and disconnected. The only love she found consolation in was the fictional love she created in her best-selling novels.

Aubrey discovered her talent for writing shortly after her father's death. A therapist suggested she start journaling to help process her emotions and facilitate healing. However, she soon grew bored with writing in the first person. She was drawn to creating characters that faced similar life situations. Her diary became a collection of love, loss, and romance stories. Writing became her passion, a way to escape into the worlds she created.

After high school, Aubrey pursued a degree in journalism and creative writing at Columbia University. By age twenty-five, she had earned her master's degree and landed a position at the largest newspaper in New York State. Starting as an editor, Aubrey harbored dreams of managing a column. Simultaneously, she began writing her first book, drawing inspiration from the characters in her diary, and writing a novel felt natural to her, a familiar and cathartic process. She completed the story within a year, and a local publishing company fell in love with it. Soon after its publication, the book soared to the top of the best-sellers list.

Writing became Aubrey's refuge, a way to channel her emotions and create the love stories she craved in her own life. Through her books, she could live vicariously through her characters, experiencing the passion and romance she longed for. But deep down, she still yearned for a love that could transcend the pages of her novels, heal the wounds of her past, and fill the void left by her father's absence.

Writing had become Aubrey's full-time occupation. After achieving success with her debut book, she decided to leave her job at the newspaper and dedicate herself entirely to writing. It was a leap of faith, but she knew she had to take it. Now, her days were spent immersed in her fictional worlds, crafting stories that captured readers' hearts.

A few years earlier, Aubrey had chosen to move back to her hometown of Farmington, Connecticut. The allure of being close to her mother and childhood friends was too strong to resist. She found comfort in the familiar streets and the sense of belonging that only a hometown could provide. Farmington held a special place in her heart, and she had no desire to leave it again.

As she sat at her table, applauding the stranger, Aubrey craved to share her success with someone special. Garrett's humility was evident as he graciously accepted the crowd's applause, his smile directed at his daughter's before he began playing again.

The familiar melody of Leonard Cohen's "Hallelujah" filled the air, skillfully performed by the enigmatic Garrett. Aubrey was dazzled by his musical prowess, reminiscent of the emotions stirred by her late father. Watching Garrett, she experienced a whirlwind of feelings that she wished would linger. When he finished, she took a deep breath, returning to reality as the audience rose to give him another well-deserved standing ovation.

"Thank you all for your kindness and warm feedback. This is the largest audience I've ever played for," Garrett expressed, chuckling as he acknowledged the praise bestowed upon him.

"I love you, Jasmine and Alexa. I hope you enjoyed hearing that as much as I enjoyed performing it for you," he affectionately addressed his daughters, embracing them with a hug. Mark expressed his gratitude, and amidst the crowd's enthusiastic cheers, they returned to their table.

"Are you all right, sweetie?" Rachel asked, breaking Aubrey's attention on the man and his daughters.

"Yes. That was incredible. I have never been on such an emotional roller coaster ride. Did you think he was amazing too?"

"Oh, my! He was extraordinary, no doubt about it."

Aubrey shared Rachel's sentiment. It felt like a connection had formed between her and Garrett during his performance as if she had known him far longer than the brief encounter. Rationality told her that feeling such instant emotions and connection with a stranger was absurd. Still, she couldn't deny the intense pull she experienced. A tingling sensation coursed through her body, unfamiliar yet exhilarating. From across the room, she observed as people approached Garrett, extending their thanks and admiration for his exceptional performance. The urge to approach him, introduce herself, and confess her newfound infatuation grew within her, desperate to express what she felt inside.

"You want to talk to him, don't you?" Rachel interjected, again breaking Aubrey's focus.

"No!" Aubrey replied, her cheeks flushing. "I don't even know him. He might look amazing and sing beautifully, but he could be a complete psycho."

"Whatever, Aubrey! I know that look. I've known you for too long, honey. Do you want me to find out if he's single?" Rachel scooted her chair back, ready to investigate.

"No, Hun. If I wanted to talk to him, I would do it myself." Despite her confident tone, Aubrey felt anything but that.

"Well, it's now or never because they're coming this way."

Their table was conveniently located near the path to the elevator. Aubrey felt the room closing in on her. Her hands trembled, and her heart raced. She wanted to talk to him and learn more about this intriguing and loving individual. Her eyes met Jasmine's as they approached, and then Garrett's gaze locked onto her. It felt as though he peered into her soul. Her racing heart suddenly halted, coming to a complete stop. He flashed a smile, revealing his perfect, radiant teeth. A sense of urgency consumed her, compelling her to do or say anything to prevent him from leaving.

They passed by the table and entered the elevator—a sour feeling churned in Aubrey's stomach. Even as the doors closed, she sensed her opportunity slipping away. She knew she could still chase after him, that he was within reach. But soon, he would likely be gone forever. She looked at Rachel, vulnerability pouring out of her, and confessed, "I should have talked to him. You know me too well."

Rachel sprang up from her chair. "Hold on a minute. I might still be able to catch him."

"No, no, no! Please, don't go after him. I wish I had a better chance to meet him, that's all."

Rachel remained standing, her focus fixed on the elevator. After a few moments, she headed toward the hostess station. Aubrey followed her movements, observing as Rachel conversed with the hostess, a waitress, and eventually Mark. Finally, after what felt like an eternity, Rachel returned to the table. Her palms were sweaty, and her face was still warm.

"What in the world was that all about?" Aubrey asked as soon as Rachel sat back down.

"Tell me how much you love me."

"You know I love you more than most."

"Good enough. His name is Garrett Anderson. He lives in Boise, Idaho. His daughters live with their mom in Avon. That's the most information I could gather from the staff. Although, I know a good private detective if you want me to track him down for you?"

Garrett Anderson, Aubrey thought to herself. Hearing his last name ignited a glimmer of hope that she might have a chance to meet him again, with some effort on her part. "I appreciate the information, but I'll pass on the detective," Aubrey replied, offering Rachel a heartfelt smile. She felt blessed to have such a fantastic friend.

Later that night, as Aubrey drifted to sleep, she immersed herself in a dream about Garrett. Alone in a vast white auditorium, she watched him serenade her with his singing and piano playing. The same intense emotions she had experienced at the restaurant seized her again, listening to his velvety voice reverberate through the walls. His gaze never wavered from hers, and the love in his eyes was undeniable. Her sheer joy was boundless as if her soul was expanding, on the verge of bursting. Then, in an instant, her father replaced Garrett.

The song remained unchanged, seamlessly transitioning. She continued to watch, not seeking Garrett but entirely content with her father's presence. The intense feelings of love, joy, and happiness persisted. She closed her eyes, swaying to the music. When she opened them again, Garrett was back at the piano.

A familiar touch graced her, and she saw her father sitting beside her in the empty theater. They interlocked their fingers, his gentle squeeze comforting her. His smile radiated reassurance and pride. He momentarily averted his gaze to look at Garrett. They sat silently, watching him play, relishing in the beautiful melody he created. Aubrey turned to her father and comprehended his great pride in this man. He looked at her, leaned over, whispered in her ear, and said, "Don't ever let him slip away, sweetheart. He's a keeper worth fighting for." Then he kissed her on the cheek.

She woke up, basking in the incredible sensations from her dream. As she lay motionless in bed, the emotions faded. A longing developed as thoughts of her father's face from the dream dissipated. She heard his words echoing in her mind and sat up, retrieving a pillow and positioning it behind her lower back. Placing her laptop on her knees, she powered it on and clicked the Google icon. Once the page loaded, she entered "Garrett Anderson piano player Boise, Idaho" into the search engine. She knew the chances were slim but decided it was worth a shot.

Scanning the results, she looked for social media profiles or any pictures that could confirm it was him. A dating site caught her attention, listing a Garrett Anderson from Boise, Idaho, aged 38. She clicked the link, her heart pounding as she waited for the page to load. Thirty seconds later, she found herself again staring into those hypnotic green eyes. Holding her breath, she was paralyzed, entranced by Garrett's stunning smile.

CHAPTER

SIX

Garrett found himself back at the restaurant, pouring his heart into his music for his beloved daughters and the warm, supportive crowd. The melodies effortlessly flowed from his fingers, and the lyrics naturally resonated from his throat. Expressing his love for his girls through music felt like second nature to him. He hoped they would truly grasp his affection's depth and unwavering strength. He became utterly immersed in their presence as he performed, forgetting everyone else in the room. They were his sole focus, the only love he desired to feel, and their applause was the only acknowledgment he sought.

But suddenly, as he looked down at his hands tapping the piano keys, he was startled to find himself seated at a worn, dirty desk. His focus shifted to Jasmine and Alexa at the restaurant, only to discover five individuals seated behind elevated wooden tables. This unexpected realization made his hands tremble as he tried to make sense of the situation. Behind him, he noticed his parents, daughters, and Matt sitting on a metal bench, their expressions nervous yet supportive. Then it hit him: he was at his parole hearing, awaiting the board's decision about his future.

In the center of the panel, a lady with gray hair cropped at her shoulders sat in the highest chair, gazing sternly upon Garrett. She spoke, but her voice came across as a mere whisper, making it impossible for him to comprehend her words. Politely, he asked her to speak up, but instead of accommodating his request, she became visibly irritated and continued speaking at the same low volume. Frustrated, Garrett reiterated his difficulty in hearing her. This time, she slammed her fists on the desk and shouted, declaring that he would have to serve the remaining five years of his sentence in prison. Before he could fully process what had just occurred, two officers seized him by the arms and legs, forcefully carrying him away from the room. Amid the chaos, Jasmine and Alexa cried out, desperately pleading for their father not to leave them. As the door closed behind him, Garrett awoke abruptly, a wave of relief washing over him as he realized it had all been a nightmare.

He turned his attention to his daughters, who slept peacefully in the bed beside his, grateful to be back in the safety of reality. These recurring nightmares had haunted him since his release, bringing back the same helplessness he had experienced behind bars. But the silver lining was constantly waking up, appreciating the freedom he now possessed.

Garrett's doctor had explained that such dreams were common after enduring a traumatic experience. Post-Traumatic Stress Syndrome, or PTSD, often haunted ex-inmates, causing anxiety and fear through distressing flashbacks and recurring nightmares that transported them back to the horrors they had lived through. Garrett had already wrestled with these nightmares during his time behind bars, often dreaming of Matt being alive. Dreams of freedom were equally vivid, sometimes blurring the lines between the waking world and nightmarish reality.

While medication was an option to help manage PTSD, Garrett placed his faith in the healing power of time. He hoped that as days turned into weeks; the toxic memories in his mind would gradually fade away, allowing him to find peace again.

Grateful for the stable and blissful point he had reached in his life, he took slow, deep breaths, hoping to calm his racing heart. Glancing at the clock, he was surprised that he had slept longer than expected. The previous night had been one of the most memorable in his life, as he had finally been able to express his love for his daughters in a way that had eluded him for far too long. And though they were excited about the encounter with a music producer from New York City who had given Garrett his card, the pride and love he felt exuding from them made the night truly unforgettable.

Finding encouragement that he still had a whole week left of his visit, Garrett made plans to work from the hotel while his daughters attended school. The flexibility of his mobile office proved to be a tremendous asset, allowing him to seamlessly blend his career with this precious time he had reclaimed. In need of a revitalizing cup of coffee, he quietly dressed and headed downstairs, craving the soothing aroma to awaken his senses.

The lobby was mostly empty, devoid of Gretchen's presence. Garrett poured himself a cup of coffee, savoring its inviting scent, and added a generous splash of French vanilla cream. Making his way back to the porch where he had spent the previous morning he settled into his familiar spot, seeking inspiration in the gentle embrace of memories and the promise of a new day.

Once settled on the porch, Garrett reached for his phone, intending to call Jerry. However, his phone started ringing before he could find his contact information. Jerry's name flashed across the screen.

"Hey, Jerry, perfect timing. I just sat on the porch of this beautiful place I'm staying at. You should see the leaves; they're breathtaking."

"I wish I could be there to witness it myself, buddy. I've heard the fall foliage is truly something. I'm sorry I didn't call you yesterday. Congratulations on reaching one year! How was your dinner with the girls?" Jerry's voice brimmed with warmth and genuine interest. He had suggested the restaurant as a unique way for Garrett to celebrate his milestone with his daughters.

"It was beyond incredible!" Garrett exclaimed, his words excitedly flowing as he shared every intricate detail of the memorable evening. He held nothing back, unraveling each emotion he had experienced, painting a vivid picture of his profound connection with his daughters. Jerry had always been a great listener who understood the complexities of emotions that life could stir. As a recovering alcoholic himself, Jerry reminded Garrett of the importance of journaling and discussing these feelings in the recovery meetings he attended.

"Jerry, I don't think I've ever properly thanked you for teaching me to play the piano."

Jerry chuckled affectionately, responding, "Ha! You've thanked me plenty of times before. But you're welcome, my friend."

"This time, though, I want to thank you for a different reason. You've helped me express my love for Jasmine and Alexa in a way I never thought possible. You should've seen them last night, Jerry. Their faces were priceless."

"I can surely relate. My daughter responded the same way when I played for her. She always said it was one of her favorite things about me. I'm glad all those years of practice paid off."

As Jerry spoke, Garrett's mind drifted back to his challenges while learning to play the piano in prison. Despite being the music coordinator, Jerry's access to instruments was limited, and their lessons took place in their cell during lockdowns. With a makeshift keyboard crafted from a cardboard box and a beginner's piano lesson book sent by Garrett's mother, Diane, they diligently practiced together daily.

Months later, Jerry suggested that Garrett apply to work at the church, granting him access to a real piano at least once a week. Embracing the idea, Garrett applied and was soon hired as a maintenance manager for all church-related functions. Once his duties were complete, he could finally sit before the real wooden keys. The transition wasn't without its challenges, and Garrett dearly missed having Jerry by his side, teaching and encouraging him. However, he would always discuss his triumphs and obstacles with Jerry afterward, knowing his friend's unwavering support would guide him.

Over time, with Jerry's teaching and support, Garrett learned to read and play the music. He eventually took over as the church's piano player for all services, discovering his musical abilities and the calming effect that playing the piano and singing hymns had on his spirit. It brought him closer to God, and in those moments, he felt a deep sense of peace and contentment within the confines of his restricted world.

"Thank you for pushing me when it felt impossible in the beginning," Garrett said, noticing a figure occupying the chair beside him. It was Alexa, her radiant smile uplifting his soul. "I better let you go, Jerry. I need to get these girls ready for our big adventure today."

"Have an amazing time at the game. And one more thing, go to the audition! You have a God-given talent, Garrett. It's worth exploring all the opportunities to use it."

With those final words, Jerry ended the call. Garrett gently grasped Alexa's hand, interlacing their fingers together. "How did you sleep, sweetie?"

"I slept so well. This place is amazing. The beds are so comfortable, the breakfast is always delicious, and they even clean our room while we're out," Alexa exclaimed, her hair slightly tangled on one side. Garrett gently ran his hand through her tousled locks, kissing her forehead tenderly.

"I'm glad you're enjoying it, sweetheart. Are you excited to watch the Giants take on the Eagles today?"

Alexa's face lit up as she raised her hand in the air, clapping it hard against Garrett's, and cheerfully exclaimed, "Oh yeah! Let's go, Giants!"

Garrett had always been a die-hard Giants fan, proudly sporting the blue and white colors on game days. As a young boy growing up in Idaho, Garrett's Sunday routine involved visiting his grandparents' house. When he was about five years old, he first encountered football during one of these visits. His grandmother had the game on their giant projector television, and Garrett found himself drawn to the action unfolding on the screen. It was a matchup between the New York Giants and the San Francisco 49ers.

With wide eyes, Garrett watched as the Giants charged onto the field with unwavering confidence. Their energy fascinated him, igniting a passion for the unfamiliar sport. Curiosity got the best of him, and he nestled beside his grandmother, bombarding her with a flurry of questions about every aspect of the game.

Together, they witnessed an exhilarating battle, with the Giants emerging victorious. At that moment, two things became clear to young Garrett. First, he discovered a profound love for football, and second, his loyalty to the New York Giants was solidified.

From that day forward, Garrett's love for the game grew exponentially, as did his admiration for the Giants. He followed their triumphs and tribulations, celebrating their victories and empathizing with their defeats. Being a Giants fan wasn't just about the team's success; it represented a connection to his cherished childhood memories and his bond with his grandmother.

Now, as he prepared to take his daughters to the game, he felt a surge of nostalgia and excitement. Today, they would create another precious memory together, cheering on their beloved Giants and relishing the joy of being a father-daughter duo united by a shared love for football and unwavering support for their team. He stood up out of his chair, pulling Alexa up with him. "We better go get your sister up. We need to eat, and then get ready to catch our train."

Being just a few hours away from the Giants stadium in East Rutherford, New Jersey, Garrett and his daughters took advantage of the special train services available on game days. They boarded the train at Fairfield Metro, excitedly anticipating the thrilling experience ahead. The train ride was filled with a buzz of anticipation shared by fellow fans, all dressed in their team colors.

Arriving at the stadium, the atmosphere and comradery between fans began to grow. Garrett had secured seats that were a dream come true for any Giants fan. The view was impeccable, located ten rows up from the field on the forty-yard line. He had gone the extra mile by purchasing matching blue jerseys for himself and his daughters. Each jersey proudly displayed the number ten and "MANNING" on the back, paying homage to their favorite player.

At their respective schools, Jasmine and Alexa were surrounded by a mix of fans supporting various northeastern teams. While the Patriots had a strong following among their peers, the girls had chosen to rally behind the Giants. Garrett felt a deep sense of pride, knowing their decision was a testament to their love as a family.

As they settled into their seats, Garrett couldn't help but feel a swell of joy and gratitude. The weather was on their side, with clear skies, a vibrant blue expanse overhead, and the sun's warm glow. The temperature was seventy-two degrees, accompanied by a gentle breeze that added to the pleasant atmosphere. Garrett sat between his two daughters, his arm draped lovingly around each of their shoulders.

Eager to soak in the action, Garrett asked his girls, "What do you think of these seats?"

Jasmine's face lit up with a wide grin as she gazed at the field while Alexa turned around to admire the sea of fans behind them. "Very nice, Dad!" Jasmine exclaimed.

"We have the best seats in the place!" Alexa chimed in, a beaming smile adorning her face.

Garrett agreed, relishing the enchanting ambiance surrounding them. However, he couldn't shake the desire for the ultimate perfection—a victory for their beloved team. Sharing his sentiment, both girls raised their hands for a high five, their cheers blending with the anticipation of the home team's imminent appearance from the tunnel.

Aubrey was immersed in a mix of nervousness and excitement as she explored Garrett's dating profile. Although she had been hesitant about signing up for the dating site, the anticipation in her chest grew with each click. She had taken Rachel's advice and used photos that were not readily recognizable to maintain anonymity.

As Garrett's profile loaded onto the screen, Aubrey's heart raced, evoking a sense of teenage anticipation. She clicked on the photo icon, her eyes drawn to the first picture. In the image, Garrett stood alongside another man, appearing younger with a captivating gaze. His eyes, a unique shade of green, seemed to hold her captive, intensifying her pounding heart. She found it difficult to look away from those mesmerizing eyes, her cheeks flushing with warmth when she noticed the NY Giants cap, he wore. The Giants had been her favorite team since childhood, a connection she shared with her father.

Moving on to the next photo, Aubrey stared into a scenic backdrop of towering pine trees and a rushing river with white-capped rapids. The caption explained that it was a picture of Garrett and his brother during a white-water rafting trip. As she stared at the image of a shirtless Garrett, her cheeks blazed with heat, and an unexpected sensation fluttered in her stomach. Her body's visceral response took her aback. Garrett's physique resembled a Greek god, with well-defined muscles and an impressive tone. His perfectly proportioned body stirred a deep appreciation within Aubrey, aligning with her value for physical fitness.

Aubrey's gaze shifted to the third picture, revealing Garrett and his daughters donning snow skiing equipment at a picturesque ski resort. The towering mountain behind them contrasted with the smaller hills she was accustomed to skiing down. Their smiles were utterly delightful, radiating warmth and affection. Even in a frozen moment captured in a still photograph, the evident love they shared resonated deeply within Aubrey. She was drawn to their adorable bond, the image tugging at her heartstrings.

Moving on to the next photo, Aubrey's eyes were fixed on Garrett swinging a golf club. His body was positioned to send the ball soaring, his gaze averted from the camera. The side profile highlighted his strong jaw line, adorned with a well-groomed dark beard. Aubrey was drawn to this rugged look, finding it more appealing than his formal attire at the restaurant. She couldn't deny the sheer attractiveness Garrett exuded, whether dressed up or in more casual attire. His appeal seemed to transcend external appearances.

With excitement and suspense, Aubrey clicked on the last photo. She instantly knew that taking the risk of signing up for the dating site had been worthwhile. The image showcased Garrett playing the piano, his black hair cascading straight, extending past his ears. Clad in a snug white T-shirt that accentuated his well-defined chest and arms, he was completely immersed in the music; his gaze focused on his hands dancing across the keys. The photo, captured in timeless black and white, exuded a passion and love for music. Aubrey's heart swelled with joy as she envisioned herself in that cherished moment, the connection between them palpable even through a mere photograph. She couldn't tear her eyes away, savoring the sensations the image evoked.

In that single moment, Aubrey's attraction to Garrett deepened, fueled by their shared interests, his captivating presence, and the evident passion he carried within. The prospect of getting to know him held a fascination she couldn't resist.

Aubrey clicked on the written description about himself and the type of woman and relationship he sought. It read:

"Hello, ladies! This is my first time on a dating site. I decided to try it since it is the most sensible option at my age. The days of finding someone at bars and indulging in drinking are not my cup of tea, which leaves limited opportunities to meet fun and exciting people. If you're reading this, I assume you've at least enjoyed my pictures. Allow me to tell you about myself.

I was born and raised in the Boise area and graduated with a business degree from Boise State University. I have two beautiful teenage daughters and have been divorced for five years. My daughters live with their mother in Avon, CT, and I spend as much time with them as possible. They bring meaning and purpose to my life. Eventually, I plan to relocate closer to them.

I have a wide range of hobbies. I enjoy outdoor activities such as golfing, rafting, fly fishing, camping, and snow skiing. I also have a passion for traveling and discovering new places. Fitness is important to me, and I maintain a regular workout routine and a healthy diet. I was heavily involved in mixed martial arts for fifteen years, but my interest has waned. Instead, I've developed a newfound love for music and have been playing the piano for about four years. It has brought me immense joy.

When finding a future partner, I must admit that I am highly selective. I'm in no rush and believe in practicing patience when building a meaningful relationship. However, I do have some basic criteria. I prefer not to date anyone under thirty, as there can be significant maturity differences when there is an age gap. Physical fitness is a must, and I don't expect anything more than what I am willing to give. Successful, independent, active, and humorous women are attractive. If you reside in the Northeast, that's a huge plus. If you're still interested after reading this, don't hesitate to message me. While unsure if I'll find true love here, I hope to meet new and intriguing people and form friendships. Good luck in your search for love!"

Aubrey took in the details, noting his preferences and requirements in a partner. She admired his thoughtful approach and honesty. It seemed he was genuinely looking for meaningful connections. With each piece of information she gathered, Aubrey's attraction to Garrett grew more substantial, and her decision to sign up for the dating site felt increasingly justified. She contemplated reaching out to him; her heart filled with excitement and hope for what the future might hold.

Aubrey took a deep breath and gathered her thoughts as she prepared to send Garrett a message. She understood that this could be a tremendous turning point in her life. With Rachel's support and guidance, she drafted a short but sincere message.

As she pressed the send button, she reminded herself to remain cautious and not let her expectations soar too high, considering her past experiences. She had learned the hard way about the disappointment that can come with building up unrealistic expectations.

Aubrey decided to trust the process and maintain a level-headed approach. She knew that patience would be essential and that she couldn't control the outcome. All she could do now was wait for Garrett's response, praying that he would still be in town and open to getting to know her better.

In the meantime, Aubrey vowed to stay positive and focus on other aspects of her life. She had taken a leap of faith, and it was up to fate to unfold its course. If things didn't work out with Garrett, there were plenty of opportunities for happiness and love in her future.

Garrett couldn't contain his excitement as the Giants pulled off a thrilling victory in the game's final moments. The adrenaline rush and the electric atmosphere in the stadium were indescribable. He looked over at his daughters, Jasmine and Alexa, who were jumping up and down, caught up in the wave of celebration.

The crowd's roar was deafening as the fans erupted in cheers and applause. Garrett joined in the jubilation, cheering alongside his fellow Giants supporters. He felt a sense of pride as he witnessed the joy and awe on his daughters' faces. This was their first Giants game, a momentous occasion he hoped they would never forget.

As the crowd settled down and the celebration gradually subsided, Garrett turned to his girls and said, "What a game, huh? I'm so glad we got to experience this together. This is what being a Giants fan is all about—the highs, the lows, and moments like this that make it all worth it."

Jasmine and Alexa nodded eagerly, "Dad that was incredible!" Jasmine exclaimed. "I can't believe we saw them win like that!"

Alexa chimed in, grinning from ear to ear. "Yeah, it was amazing! I'll never forget this day."

Garrett's heart swelled as he soaked in the happiness radiating from his girls. He knew these shared experiences would create lasting memories and deepen their bond. At that moment, he couldn't have asked for anything more.

As the game ended, they exited the stadium, joining the throngs of satisfied fans towards the train station. The energy was still palpable in the air, and Garrett could feel a sense of camaraderie with his fellow fans.

Boarding the train, they found seats together and settled in. Garrett wrapped his arms around his daughters, trying to memorize the sensation their presence evoked.

As the train rumbled back towards their home, Garrett felt a renewed sense of optimism. The game reminded him of the power of shared passions and the joy of embracing life's thrilling moments. He looked forward to what the future held, both as a Giants fan and as a father.

CHAPTER

SEVEN

Garrett's senses jarred awake as his alarm pierced through the morning silence. Mindful to avoid disturbing Jasmine and Alexa in the bustling bathroom, he marveled at their effort to perfect their appearance. From meticulously styled hair to flawless makeup, they strived for nothing less than perfection before stepping outside. Miraculously, he managed to drop them off on time, a small victory.

Due to their age difference, they attended different schools. Jasmine, a sophomore at Avon High School, and Alexa, a seventh grader at Avon Middle School, were exceptional students who seldom received anything less than an A on their report cards. Garrett fervently hoped that boys wouldn't distract them from their educational pursuits. While Jasmine had experienced a couple of short-lived relationships, none had endured beyond a few months. On the other hand, Alexa was beginning to dip her toes into the realm of romantic interests, with new crushes blooming every other day. Their striking beauty brought about a mix of pride and concern for Garrett as he navigated the challenges of watching his daughters grow older. Nevertheless, he remained committed to fostering open lines of communication, valuing their trust and willingness to share any aspect of their lives.

Before the stock market opened at nine-thirty, Garrett carved out time for his physical well-being. He stepped into the nearby weight room, grateful to find it devoid of other visitors. Deciding to focus on his chest, he selected a pair of substantial seventy-five-pound dumbbells and a sturdy bench. With focused determination, he performed ten sets of dumbbell presses and an equal number of clap push-ups, feeling the strain and satisfaction with each repetition. Concluding his workout, he dedicated fifteen minutes to strengthening his core before returning to the B&B. A quick shower refreshed his body, preparing him for the day ahead.

Settling into the corner of his room, Garrett positioned himself at the wooden desk overlooking the front of the property through a window adorned with delicate white curtains. The vibrant hues of autumn painted a picturesque scene beyond the glass pane. As he awaited the awakening of his computer, his attention wandered to the mesmerizing dance of purple leaves swaying gracefully in the wind across the lawn. A glance at his phone confirmed that he still had half an hour before the market opened, providing him with a precious reflection window.

Having conducted extensive research the preceding week, Garrett felt well-prepared for a relatively light workload. He perused the stocks he intended to invest in, mentally preparing himself for the choices ahead. His work demanded unwavering attention to detail. Each investment he made was accompanied by signing up for news alerts, recognizing the influence of current events on the trajectory of the stocks. Positive news could propel them to soaring heights, while adverse developments could lead to their downfall.

Most of Garrett's day revolved around delving into articles published about the companies he had invested in. The fast-paced nature of his work provided an exhilarating rush that appealed to his inner adrenaline junkie.

As his computer sprung to life, he sifted through his emails for relevant information. Amidst the sea of alerts, he noticed notifications from a dating website he had joined a few months earlier. Though he hadn't been actively seeking a relationship, he felt nervous about online dating because it was uncharted territory. A friend from Daily Recovery's recommendation led him to this site, prompting him to take a leap of faith and explore new possibilities.

Having ventured into online dating, Garrett was surprised by the caliber of women he encountered. The digital landscape drew individuals of great courage, as evidenced by the mul-titude of messages flooding his inbox daily. He realized that responding to each request was an unrealistic feat. Drawing from his professional approach, he devised a screening process to discern potential matches.

The initial test revolved around physical attraction. While he didn't expect the women to be supermodels, he sought a spark of desire when perusing their photos. He evaluated their age, location, and hobbies to see if their images interested him. Garrett set his sights on a dating range of women aged thirty to forty-five, believing that this bracket aligned with the maturity and life experiences he sought. Given his reservations about long-distance relationships, he narrowed his search to women within a fifty-mile radius of Boise. Although he yearned for a connection near Avon, he hadn't discovered anyone who allured his interest from that locale. Women who exhibited independence, educational attainment, or promising careers enticed him most. Engaging in intellectually stimulating conversations held significant value to Garrett, and he believed that such women would serve as remarkable role models for his daughters. Lastly, he longed for a companion who shared his hobbies and possessed a lighthearted sense of humor.

With a few spare minutes, he logged into the dating site to peruse his messages. Having neglected it for a couple of days, he discovered thirty-two new messages. Fortunately, the advantage of the platform was that each message displayed the woman's profile picture, age, and location, allowing Garrett to focus solely on those he felt had potential.

After deleting several messages, Garrett's eyes froze, fixated on the center of his screen. He rubbed his eyes, questioning if his vision was playing tricks on him. "Wow," he exclaimed aloud, unable to contain his astonishment. "This woman is stunning." Noting her age and location sparked a wildfire of excitement within him. He clicked on her message with a trembling finger, eager to explore the connection.

The message began with a friendly greeting, expressing how

the sender had stumbled upon Garrett's page and instantly noticed the striking number of shared interests. She emphasized a high standard of living, mirroring his own. The message closed with a compliment, describing Garrett as "gorgeous."

"Interesting," he murmured, continuing to converse with himself. Intrigued, he clicked on the hyperlink that led him to her profile page.

To his disappointment, he discovered only a few pictures and a concise description of her profile. The first picture featured her and another woman seated at a table in a restaurant, which felt oddly familiar to him. He admired her beauty— her dark, flowing hair cascading past her shoulders and her enchanting blue eyes reminiscent of clear skies reflecting the Caribbean Ocean. Her appearance exuded an exotic allure, with her rich complexion, dark hair, and those adorable dimples adorning both sides of her cheeks. Her perfect, white teeth framed by luscious, full lips invited warm and fuzzy feelings running from head to toe.

The next and final picture showcased her in a challenging yoga pose at a gym, dressed in black yoga pants and a snug yellow tank top. The pose highlighted her toned, muscular physique. Her sleek, black hair was pulled back in a ponytail, reaching her shoulders. In this particular shot, she looked away from the camera, revealing an attractive side view of her face and body. The attraction Garrett felt for her surpassed anything he had ever experienced. In her prime, not even Julie had stirred such intense longing within him.

He proceeded to read the brief description she had posted, which went as follows:

"Hey, guys!

I am new to this site and online dating in general. A friend of mine has had great luck on here, so I decided to try it. I enjoy lots of hobbies and interests in life. My favorites include fitness, yoga, mountain biking, theater, arts, dancing, traveling, and snow skiing.

I have a master's degree in journalism and am an editor for a local newspaper. I have never been married and have no kids. I am looking for someone who shares similar hobbies and interests. I love the stereotypical tall, dark, and handsome. If you want to know more about me, ask."

Direct and to the point, her words portrayed a sense of maturity beyond her years. Garrett found her straightforwardness appealing. He was drawn to her and felt compelled to respond immediately. With another week left on his trip, he hoped they could arrange a meeting before he headed back home.

He quickly typed up a simple yet heartfelt message.

"Hi, Bri!

I'm Garrett. It's a pleasure to meet you. Thank you for reaching out to me and for the sweet compliment. Speaking of gorgeous, you are stunning! I'm in Simsbury visiting my daughters for the week, and I would love to meet up for coffee if you have some free time. Let me know if this is possible. If not, we can stick to the slow, tedious online dating process to get to know each other. Just kidding. I eagerly await your response, Bri!

Garrett"

He reread his message several times, ensuring it conveyed his genuine interest before hitting the send button. Unable to resist, he stared at her pictures, savoring the orchestra of emotions they elicited.

With the dating site momentarily put aside, Garrett turned his attention to the start of his day. The imaginary bell rang, signaling the beginning of his work routine. As he embarked on his daily tasks, a sense of giddiness lingered. The possibility of a new romance had ignited a spark of excitement that he hadn't felt in a long time. He reminded himself to remain cautious and not let his hopes soar too high, but the mere presence of hope brought a renewed sense of optimism. Now, all that was left for him to do was to continue with his day and patiently await Bri's response, wondering where this potential connection might lead.

Aubrey's office was a haven of creativity and productivity within the expansive walls of her home. The room emanated an air of sophistication and warmth, with its dark hardwood floors that echoed the house's historic charm. Gray walls provided a neutral backdrop, allowing the white wood trim to stand out elegantly.

The centerpiece of the office was Aubrey's large mahogany desk, where she spent countless hours writing her novels and managing her business affairs. The desk was meticulously organized, adorned with pens, notepads, and a sleek laptop. A comfortable mahogany chair accompanied the desk, providing style and comfort during long work hours.

Along three walls, built-in bookshelves showcased Aubrey's extensive collection of books, ranging from literary classics to contemporary works. The shelves overflowed with knowledge and experience, inviting Aubrey to immerse herself in a world of words and ideas.

Natural light streamed through the large windows, offering a picturesque view of lush greenery. Aubrey often found solace in gazing outside, drawing inspiration from the beauty of nature that enveloped her home.

With its combination of timeless charm and modern amenities, Aubrey's office reflected her taste for sophistication and her dedication to her craft. It was a space where her creativity thrived, and she could fully immerse herself in the world of storytelling.

There, she sat on a conference call with Rachel, her editor and best friend, and Georgia, her publishing agent. They were discussing her newest book, "Night and Day," which was scheduled to be released in early October.

"We have five hundred thousand copies ready to be shipped tomorrow. We expect most of those copies to be sold by the end of next week. This could be one of your top-selling books, Aubrey," Georgia said enthusiastically.

"I hope you're right and that the critics agree. This book has been my favorite to write so far."

The book marked a departure from Aubrey's usual teen

romance novels. It delved into deeper emotions and personal experiences, drawing insights from her relationship with her father as a young girl. The book's characters mirrored her feelings and provided a therapeutic outlet for her grief.

"I'm certain that readers will love it just as much as I do," Georgia added, her southern accent becoming more pronounced.

"You've truly outdone yourself, Bri. Your fans, the critics, and the whole world will adore it. Get ready for the spotlight, girl! This book will catapult your celebrity status," Rachel, always a loyal supporter, said.

Aubrey smiled and replied, "Ah, thanks! I couldn't have achieved this without you two by my side."

"So, has your mystery man responded to your message?" Rachel asked, reminding Aubrey of her new crush.

"As of nine this morning, nope," Aubrey replied, her disappointment evident in her voice. "Every other man in the world seems to be interested. I have over a hundred messages in basically twenty-four hours."

She glanced at her inbox again, now filled with even more new messages. She hadn't bothered to read any of them; her interest solely focused on Garrett. And then, there it was. He had finally replied. Aubrey realized she had stopped breathing.

"Aubrey, are you still there?" Rachel's voice came through the phone's speaker.

"Yes, sorry. I just rechecked my inbox, and guess who finally replied!"

"I told you he would reply, girl. Why wouldn't he? I mean, look at you!" Rachel chimed in.

Georgia joined in, saying, "She's right, Aubrey. You are a doll!"

"What does it say?" Rachel asked impatiently.

Aubrey clicked on the message and began to read it aloud. As she read his words, her soul melted, bit by bit.

Rachel was the first to speak up when she finished reading, "Yay! He's still in town. He seems great. I love his sense of humor. Are you going to meet up with him?"

Aubrey pondered what she had read along with Rachel's question and panic suddenly overrode her previous excitement.

"I don't know. Maybe I should take it slow and message him for a few days," she said, feeling dizzy.

"Come on, Bri, don't be a prude. He's only in town for a week. You'll regret it later if you lose the opportunity to spend time with him. This is the quickest way to find out if you two are a match," Rachel urged persuasively.

Aubrey had a fleeting thought that she held onto tightly. "Oh my goodness, what if he recognizes me from the restaurant? What would I say or do then?" Meeting him had become a reality, and this possibility hadn't crossed her mind.

Georgia offered her perspective, trying to be the voice of reason, "If that happens, just tells him the truth. At that point, what do you have to lose? You're not fully invested in each other yet. It might be the best time to be honest, anyway."

Aubrey let this advice sink in. Part of her wanted to be upfront about their initial encounter, while another part wanted to stick to the dating site story, which seemed to involve less vulnerability and embarrassment.

"Georgia is right. If he seems to recognize you, then come

clean. Otherwise, keep that information between us. There's nothing wrong with being honest later after he's fallen in love with you," Rachel's words felt unsettling and wrong. Still, the idea of immediate disclosure did seem like a surefire way to sabotage any potential connection.

"I have to admit, I agree with both of you. I'll see how it plays out. But first, I need to respond and let him know I'm ready to meet. Are you sure it isn't too soon?"

"It's just coffee, sweetie. I think a coffee date is brilliant for a first meeting. It's casual, and the date can last as long as you want. It takes away the pressure that more formal dates often bring. If this date goes well, you can plan a more formal one later," Georgia answered, appreciating Garrett's approach.

"She's right. Coffee is the easiest and quickest way to gauge if there's a connection. If there isn't, you could be done within twenty minutes," Rachel added.

"All right, all right! I'll respond and let him know I can meet for coffee. I better go, in case he wants to meet today. I need to get myself ready."

"Yay! Text me as soon as you find out when and where," Rachel exclaimed.

"Me too, please!" Georgia added.

"I'll give you both the play-by-play. Bye!"

She clicked on the reply button, her fingers trembling slightly with nerves. Taking a deep breath, she mustered up some courage and typed her response:

"Hi, Garrett,

I appreciate the compliment, although I'm still determining if you're being sincere. It's hard to trust words on a screen. However, I will take a chance and get to know you better. Coffee sounds like a good idea. I'm free today if that works for you.

Let's move this conversation to text. It'll be easier for me to communicate that way. I am looking forward to hearing from you.

Take care,

Bri"

She proofread the message before adding her number, ensuring it conveyed the right balance of interest and caution. After a moment of hesitation, she hit the send button, knowing that her response could change everything.

Garrett sat in his room, staring at the glow of his computer screen displaying stock charts and news articles. He had already made significant investments in various companies when the market opened that morning, and now he was scouring the internet for potential new opportunities.

As he refreshed his inbox, his heart skipped a beat. The nervous energy surged through his body as he hastily clicked on the message, eager to read what she had written. It amazed him how someone he had never met in person could evoke such a strong reaction within him. His hands trembled slightly as he tried to steady himself.

"What is happening to me?" he wondered, bemused by his nervousness. "I've spoken to countless people, but this is different. She has me feeling like a teenager again." The feeling was both exhilarating and unsettling, but he couldn't deny the thrill of it.

As he read Bri's message, he realized his initial forwardness had paid off. She had taken the bait and expressed her willingness to meet for coffee, even suggesting today as a possible option. A mix of excitement and panic erupted within. He hadn't anticipated meeting so soon. His mind raced as he considered his schedule.

Glancing at the time in the corner of his computer screen, he realized it was already five minutes past ten. His daughters needed to be picked up at two forty-five and he had a Daily Recovery meeting in Avon at one o'clock. The timing seemed tight, but he couldn't let this opportunity slip away.

His mind became consumed by thoughts of the upcoming coffee date. He was feeling overwhelmed by the situation, his anxiety getting the best of him. Just as he was lost in his thoughts, his phone rang, startling him out of his reverie.

"Hey, Jerry. You have perfect timing, my friend."

"Good morning! How was the game?" Jerry asked, his cheerful voice bursting through the phone.

"Amazing! It was one of the greatest games of my life."

"I bet it had something to do with the two ladies you were with, huh?" Jerry teased.

"Absolutely! The seats were incredible, the weather was perfect, and the game ended just as we wanted. Did you manage to catch it on TV?"

Jerry chuckled. "You know I wouldn't miss a game. It was too close for comfort, but I'm glad we pulled off the win."

"You and me both."

Jerry continued, "So, what's happening this morning?"

Garrett's stomach churned, his voice trembling slightly, "Well, I met a woman ..."

"Huh? Where did you meet her? At the game?"

Garrett laughed nervously. "No, no, on the dating site. She's from Farmington, Connecticut, just a few miles away. And she's beautiful."

Jerry seemed to grasp the underlying concern in Garrett's voice, his tone shifting to a more paternal one, "I see. So why does this feel like an issue rather than an opportunity?"

Garrett sighed, struggling to articulate his feelings, "I don't know ... she's thirty, has never been married, and has no kids. It's making me nervous. We've only exchanged messages, but I asked her for a coffee date, and she agreed. She's asking if today would work, and now I'm freaking out."

Jerry chuckled. "Take a deep breath, my friend. Being a little nervous is a good thing. It means you genuinely care about her thoughts, even if you don't fully understand why. I felt the same way when I met my wife for the first time."

Garrett attempted to calm himself, but Jerry's words made him even more jittery. He felt like he had consumed too much caffeine.

"Maybe it's too soon," Garrett suggested, trying to regain control of his emotions. "I could ask if tomorrow works instead. That way, we could text back and forth to get to know each other better. She gave me her phone number."

"Sure, that's an option. But remember, the reason you chose coffee dates in the first place was to keep things casual and low-pressure. It gives you the flexibility to end the date early if it's not going well, or if you like her, it gives you an extra day to get to know each other. Plus, you can always text in the meantime."

Garrett felt a sense of relief as he considered Jerry's perspective. Coffee dates were meant to be informal and offered an opportunity to gauge compatibility.

"You're right," Garrett finally agreed. "I'm going to message her and let her know today works. I should start getting ready now."

"Have a great time, Garrett, and remember, you're an amazing catch. Let me know how it goes," Jerry encouraged before ending the call.

CHAPTER

EIGHT

Garrett quickly typed a reply to Bri's message, "Hi Bri, its Garrett. Thank you for your number and flexibility. I'm excited to meet you. I have a meeting in Avon at 1:00. Would it be a problem to meet at the Flying Cup around 11:30?"

The Flying Cup was known for its excellent coffee and pastries, making it an ideal location for their first meeting. He hesitated momentarily, rereading his message to ensure it conveyed the right tone before finally hitting the send button.

As he awaited Bri's reply, Garrett's mind raced with thoughts of the upcoming coffee date. He glanced at the clothes hanging in his closet, considering the weather for the day. With cloud-covered skies and a peak temperature of sixty-six degrees, he decided on a flannel button-up shirt over his white t-shirt, paired with faded jeans. To complete the look, he grabbed a plain black baseball cap and added a touch of cologne. Standing in front of the mirror, he evaluated his appearance and felt satisfied.

Returning to his computer, Garrett's attention was quickly drawn to the sound of his phone chiming. His heart skipped a beat as he saw Bri's name on the screen. Opening the message, he read, "Hi, Garrett. Thanks for the quick response. 11:30 at the Flying Cup works perfectly for me. I will text you when I arrive. I'm excited to meet you, too!" A smile spread across Garrett's face, relieved and thrilled that their plans were coming together.

Glancing at the time, Garrett realized he needed to leave soon. He shut down his computer, grabbed his black jacket, and headed toward the lobby. He heard Gretchen's distinctive laughter, finding her in conversation with some guests. He made his way over to her.

"Well, hello, handsome! Where are you off to today?" Gretchen greeted him, raising her eyebrows mischievously.

"Good morning, Gretchen. I'm heading to Avon for a coffee date," Garrett replied, appreciating the boost of confidence Gretchen always provided.

"A date, huh? When do I get a turn?" she teased, winking at him. "You smell fabulous, by the way, and look incredible. Whoever the lucky girl is, she'll surely be impressed."

"Thank you, Gretchen. You're a sweetheart. I'm meeting her soon, just heading out the door. The girls and I won't be back until later this afternoon. Maybe you can tell them some more ghost stories tonight. They're very intrigued by them," Garrett suggested, knowing his daughters enjoyed Gretchen's company.

"You've got it. If I'm not up and about, knock on my door. Have fun!"

"Thanks, Gretchen," Garrett said gratefully as he walked out the front entrance toward his rental car.

He arrived at the coffee shop with fifteen minutes to spare, grateful for the light traffic that granted him extra time. Seated in his rental car, he calmed his nerves and prepared for her arrival. A sleek black luxury SUV pulled into the vacant spot beside him, catching his attention. An attractive woman, Bri, emerged from the vehicle, unaware of his presence. His heart seemed to stop beating as he looked at her, leaving him breathless and stunned. She possessed a beauty akin to a movie star, enthralling him with her presence. He observed her graceful stride and waited for her to walk through the entrance doors before leaving his car.

Inside, he spotted her sitting in a booth along the far wall, engrossed in typing a message on her phone.

"Hi, Bri," he said, startling her a bit.

"Oh, hi! I was texting you to let you know I was inside." She rose and hugged him quickly, her delightful fragrance reminiscent of wildflowers in an idyllic meadow. Her touch sent a wave of electricity through him as her breasts pressed against his chest.

She embodied elegance, wearing white jeans accentuating her long legs and a tight black blouse showcasing her slim waist and toned arms. Taking their seats across from each other, Garrett removed his jacket and placed it beside him.

"Have you ordered anything yet?"

"Not yet. I decided to wait for you," she replied, fumbling with the small menu. A waitress approached them, ready to take their orders.

"So, when did you open your account on Absolutely Single?" Garrett asked after the waitress left with their orders.

"Just yesterday," she responded, gracing him with the most adorable smile. He had a similar effect on her as she did on him.

"Really? Well, I'm glad you found me so quickly. I've heard it can be quite overwhelming for beautiful women like you, receiving countless messages from all sorts of men." He remarked, removing his hat and placing it on his jacket.

With her enchanting blue eyes fixed upon him, it felt like she could peer into his soul. "It has been overwhelming. I haven't even responded to any of the messages I've received. You're the only one who caught my attention."

"Lucky me," he responded with a smile.

"And how about you? How long have you been a member?"

"Just a few months. I wasn't actively seeking a relationship, but I thought it wouldn't hurt to try it," he answered, momentarily breaking eye contact to acknowledge the arrival of their coffee and scones.

"Mm," she murmured, sipping her caramel mocha. "This is one of my favorite coffee shops in the area."

Garrett nodded in agreement after tasting his mocha. "I agree. I wish they had locations in Boise."

As a noisy car passed outside the window, Bri glanced to her left. Garrett admired her straight, silky black hair, which kept escaping from behind her ears. He fought the temptation to reach across the table and tuck those wayward strands back into place.

"I have to tell you, you're even more beautiful in person," he confessed, feeling his cheeks ache from the permanent smile on his face. Watching her cheeks flush, he reveled in the reaction he elicited.

"Awe, you're too sweet. Thank you for saying that. You are gorgeous, by the way." she replied, briefly placing her hand on his arm. Although the touch was fleeting, a tingling sensation lingered on his skin.

Garrett blushed slightly at Bri's compliment, as a warm energy grew within his chest. "Thank you," he replied, trying to regain his composure. He took another sip of his drink, savoring the moment.

Bri looked at him with genuine curiosity. "Have you been on many dates before?"

"I've been on a few," Garrett replied, taking a small bite from his scone. Bri followed suit, cutting through a corner of her pastry with her fork. "I've met some fun and interesting people, but nothing has progressed beyond a few dates. The timing or connection wasn't right, I suppose."

Bri leaned in, intrigued. "If you don't mind me asking, what didn't work out with those women?"

Garrett thought for a moment, careful to choose his words. "It's not that there was anything necessarily wrong with them. They were both wonderful in their ways. But they seemed too eager to rush into a serious commitment. I value independence and taking things slow, so their approach didn't align with what I sought."

Before Garrett could further explain, Bri asked another question, her eyes locked with his. "You mentioned being patient for a relationship. Does that mean you're not looking for one right now?"

Garrett felt worried, not wanting to give the wrong impression. He wanted to be honest and open with Bri, knowing she seemed the perfect match for him. He took a deep breath, gathering his thoughts.

"That's a good question," he said, sitting up straighter and placing both hands on the table. "Honestly, a relationship isn't my top priority at the moment. I have two incredible ladies who take up most of my time."

Bri's eyes widened with curiosity. "Oh? Who are they?"

A smile played at the corners of Garrett's lips, his heart swelling with pride. "They're my daughters. Jasmine is fifteen, and Alexa is thirteen. Being their father keeps me incredibly busy, especially now that they're teenagers."

Bri's smile matched his, her eyes sparkling with warmth. "I saw pictures of them online. They're adorable."

Garrett chuckled, a mixture of joy and exasperation in his voice. "Thank you, but I can't decide if it's a blessing or a curse. It seems like all the boys in their school are falling head over heels for them."

Bri's laugh was a sweet and melodic sound that filled the air. "Well, they must have gotten their charm from their father."

Garrett blushed again, grateful for the dim lighting in the café. "Thank you. They're amazing girls. They are good, well-mannered students and have such a zest for life. I couldn't be prouder of them."

"You seem like a wonderful father. I have respect for that. I had a great relationship with mine."

Garrett noticed her fidgeting in her seat, sensing there was more she wanted to share. However, he didn't want to push, deciding to let her open up when she was ready.

Changing the topic, Garrett asked, "Are you originally from Farmington?"

A smile spread across Bri's face. "Yes, I was born and raised here. I moved away to New York City for school and stayed for a few years after graduating when I got my first job with a newspaper company. But recently, I transferred back to Farmington, and I honestly have no desire to leave."

"I love this area too. I plan on moving here when the time is right," Garrett confessed, his words hinting at longing. He knew there was more to his story, but he wasn't ready to reveal his past. Fear of judgment held him back, and he believed it was fair to disclose everything after a few dates if the connection grew more robust and had the potential for a lasting relationship.

Bri took another delicate bite of her scone, contemplating his words. "And your daughters live with their mother in Avon?"

"Yes, they moved here about five years ago after their mother, Julie, and I divorced. Julie's father lives in this area, so she decided to start her new life here. I approved of the move since the public school system is rated so highly and the crime rate is insanely low."

He sensed his explanation might not make complete sense, but he decided not to delve into further details. "Where did you attend college?"

Bri's eyes sparkled with pride as she replied, "I went to

Columbia University. I graduated with a master's degree in journalism."

Columbia was renowned as one of the most prestigious schools in the country. He wondered why someone as incredible as Bri was still single. Insecurities crept into his mind, gnawing at his confidence, and reminding him of his past mistakes.

"Columbia, that is very impressive," he said, his fears casting a slight shadow over his words. "And you work for a local newspaper?"

"Yes," Bri nodded modestly. "I'm an editor for some of the columns in the local Farmington Newspaper. I've also written a few books."

Garrett's insecurities heightened as she mentioned her books. He sensed she didn't want to delve deeper into the topic, and an awkward silence hung between them. After a few moments, Bri spoke up again, her warm smile melting away his self-doubt.

"How about I make you a deal? I'll give you a copy of my books if we go on more than two dates."

Her offer brought a genuine smile to Garrett's face, instantly connecting them on a deeper level. "Sounds like a great deal to me," he responded, enjoying the profound connection building between them.

As the conversation shifted, Bri turned the attention to him. "How about you? What do you do for work?" she inquired, pushing her empty plate aside.

Garrett mirrored her actions, stacking his plate on top of hers, before answering. "I'm a stock day trader. I was a corporate director for a wireless phone company, but I recently transitioned to day trading for more flexibility with my time and work location."

"Day trading … is that like a stockbroker? I don't know much about stocks besides having some in an account for my retirement," Bri admitted with the most adorable chuckle Garrett had ever heard.

He finished his mocha, placing the empty cup near the plates. He understood that explaining his work could be complex, but he welcomed the opportunity to share it with her. "That's okay, Bri," he reassured her, his gaze locked with her vibrant blue eyes. "Most people don't fully understand how it works. All publicly traded companies have stocks representing ownership and value. Every business day, stocks are bought and sold in large volumes. As a day trader, I find undervalued stocks to buy through a plethora of research and information. Once they reach what I consider to be a fair price, I sell them."

Bri's dimples formed on her cheeks as she absorbed his explanation. "That's wonderful. It sounds like an interesting line of work. So, as long as you have your computer and an internet connection, you can work from wherever you want?"

"Exactly. I bought shares from several companies in my rented room just this morning." His phone chimed, alerting him that his Daily Recovery meeting started in thirty minutes. Time seemed to have flown by, and as much as he didn't want to leave her, he knew he had to attend the meeting.

"Do you need to get going?"

"I'm afraid so," he replied with a hint of disappointment. He wished the date didn't have to end just yet. "I had an amazing time with you. I'll be here until Sunday, and if you're up for it, I would love to see you again."

Her smile quickly vanished from her face, her cheeks rising, eyes squinting in a pained expression. Garrett's anxiety and a dull ache in his heart resurfaced. He cared deeply about her response.

But then her smile returned. "I'm just kidding, Garrett," she said, letting out a delightful laugh. It was infectious, and he couldn't help but join in. "You mentioned wanting someone with a sense of humor. Well, here you go!"

"Wow, you got me," he admitted, "I want to see you again."

"Good! I would love to see you again, too." Bri rested her elbows on the table, her chin resting in her hands. They locked eyes, comfortable in the silence between them. He felt an overwhelming desire to kiss her, to feel her soft, inviting lips against his.

Before he could act on that impulse, the moment passed. He had hesitated for too long, watching as she grabbed her jacket. "What are you doing tomorrow?"

"Let me check," she said, pulling out her phone. "Luckily, my schedule is flexible. I work from home and have a light workload this week. What do you have in mind?"

Garrett had planned to call Tom, the talent agent from New York City, to confirm his audition for the following day. Suddenly, the idea of having Bri along for the experience seemed enticing.

"I have an appointment in New York City tomorrow. If you're not too busy, maybe you could come with me?" he suggested as they both put on their jackets and prepared to leave.

"What kind of appointment?" she asked as they approached the cashier.

"It's a long story, but I can fill you in on the way there. In short, I'll be playing some music for a talent agent," he explained, expecting her to express more surprise. Instead, she tucked her loose strands of hair behind her ears.

"I'd love to go with you. Text me later and let me know when to be ready."

They exchanged a warm hug before parting ways. A whirlwind of emotions stirred within him as he waited for the receipt. He knew one thing for sure: he liked her. But she seemed too good to be true. As he drove to the recovery meeting, he looked forward to connecting with fellow alcoholics who understood the struggle of navigating intense emotions and confronting lingering insecurities. He recognized the importance of addressing these feelings to avoid relapse and maintain sobriety.

On his way to the meeting, Garrett called Tom, and they arranged to meet at Tom's office the following day at one in the afternoon. Pulling into the church parking lot where the meeting was held, visions of past meetings flashed through Garrett's mind. He had been to this meeting before and was excited to reconnect with familiar faces.

Entering the designated room, Garrett spotted an empty chair along one of the walls and made himself comfortable. Across the room, he noticed an older couple who had become his friends during previous visits. Their warm smiles and handholding always brought him joy. They were living proof that sobriety could bring happiness and fulfillment.

The meeting was well attended, with around thirty people sitting throughout the room. Recognizing a few more familiar faces helped Garrett to relax even more. Lori, a woman he met during a previous meeting, served as the chairperson for the day. She went through the customary rules and guidelines before announcing that the topic for discussion would be relapse triggers.

Lori opened the floor for discussion, inviting anyone to share their thoughts. Without hesitation, Garrett decided to speak up. This was the perfect opportunity.

"Good afternoon. My name is Garrett, and I am an alcoholic," he began, receiving warm greetings from the group. "Some of you already know me, but I'm visiting from Boise, Idaho, for those who don't. Whenever I'm in town, this meeting feels like a home away from home. I've been sober for six years."

Applause and words of support filled the room. "Thank you all," Garrett continued as the room fell silent. "I spent five years in prison because of my addiction. Although I cherish my freedom now, this past year has been one of the most challenging of my life. I'm incredibly grateful for finding this program while I was incarcerated. The program, and the people in it, has helped me navigate the temptations to drink. Sobriety has created countless blessings in my life. I have a thriving business, a loving relationship with my daughters, and the opportunity to pursue hobbies I enjoy. So, when Lori mentioned the topic of relapse triggers, I knew I had come to the right place."

Members of the group nodded in agreement.

"This visit has stirred up emotions I'm still not accustomed to. Fear, insecurities, and vulnerability have been extreme. I recently started dating again and navigating the world of sober dating is fascinating and challenging. I used to think I was a social person when I drank, but now I see that it was the false courage provided by alcohol. I wouldn't say I like feeling awkward or uncomfortable. These situations were always the perfect excuse to reach for a drink in my drinking days. Now, I'm learning how to face these emotions in a more positive and healthy manner. I know this room has a wealth of knowledge, experience, and sobriety, and I would appreciate any insights or feedback you can offer."

Smiles and expressions of gratitude filled the room as members thanked Garrett for sharing his experience. They knew their collective wisdom and support could help him navigate the challenges of sober dating and cope with the emotions that came with it.For the remainder of the meeting, Garrett listened attentively as others shared their struggles and offered him feedback and advice. It was comforting to know he wasn't alone in facing these challenges. The program's power was evident as he felt a sense of belonging, like being part of a second family where everyone shared a common problem: alcoholism.

As the meeting neared its end, Lori expressed gratitude to those who had shared and asked if any new members were in attendance. A man, whom Garrett estimated to be around his age, timidly raised his hand. He seemed nervous and uncomfortable with the attention. Lori invited him to introduce himself to the group, and he began after a moment of hesitation.

"Hi, my name is Dave. This is my first meeting. A family member recommended that I come here. I can relate to what Garrett and others have shared about struggling with the emotions that come with sobriety and freedom. I found this meeting helpful, and I think I'll continue coming. Thank you." The room filled with applause and smiles directed at Dave.

Service to others was essential in the program, and mentoring fellow alcoholics was encouraged for long-term sobriety. Garrett had received such support from others when he first started attending, and he felt compelled to extend that same kindness to Dave.

After the meeting ended, Garrett approached Dave, extending his hand and introducing himself. Dave shook it, and they exchanged pleasantries.

"Are you from Avon?" Garrett inquired.

"Yeah, born and raised here," Dave replied, briefly making eye contact before glancing toward the exit.

"That's great. I love this place. As mentioned, my daughters live here with their mother, so I visit every few months. I plan on moving here once I find a place to stay. My parole officer won't approve the transfer until then."

Dave made eye contact again, hinting that he wanted to say something but hesitated. He stuffed his hands into his pockets and looked away toward the door. Garrett realized he should respect Dave's boundaries and not push him too much.

"I'm glad you came today, Dave. Staying sober can be tough,

but these meetings and the support from fellow members make it a little easier. I want to give you my phone number. I'm in town for the rest of the week, so if you ever want to join a meeting together or need someone to talk to, feel free to call me anytime."

Dave's face visibly relaxed as he exhaled, and his tense shoulders dropped. He took out his phone from his back pocket. "Thanks, Garrett. I appreciate that."

After exchanging numbers, Garrett watched as Dave hurried toward the exit. He reflected on the delicate nature of early sobriety. He understood the importance of giving newcomers space to find their way and make their own decisions. It was a painful truth that only a tiny fraction of those who walked through the doors would genuinely commit to the program and experience the transformative power of recovery.

Yet, despite the challenges and frustrations, Garrett knew that witnessing someone embrace the program and see the positive changes it brought to their life was worth every moment. The joy and fulfillment from helping others find their path to sobriety made the arduous journey worthwhile. It was a reminder of the program's profound impact, not just on individuals but on the collective strength of the recovery community.

Garrett took a deep breath, recognizing the responsibility that came with being a member of the program. He knew he had to tread lightly with newcomers like Dave, offering support and guidance without overwhelming them. The journey to sobriety was personal and unique for each individual, and he respected that.

While parked outside of Alexa's school, Garrett sent a message to Bri, expressing his gratitude for their time together and his anticipation for their upcoming trip. He felt giddy as he thought about their plans for the following day.

As Alexa joined him in the car, he decided to keep the details about Bri to himself. Before sharing the news with his daughters, he wanted to gauge how things would unfold. He needed to approach the situation cautiously and ensure his relationship with Bri was progressing positively.

With Jasmine and Alexa settled in their seats, Garrett shifted his focus to enjoying the afternoon with his girls. As they chatted and caught up on each other's lives, he was grateful for his progress with recovery and the precious moments he could share with them.

At the 1818 Estate, Garrett looked through emails while the girls studied and completed their homework. Knowing their shared love for horror films, he had promised to take them to a new scary movie that evening. One of the benefits of their teenage years was finding common interests that brought them closer together.

"Before we head to dinner and the movie, how about we find Gretchen to tell us a couple more ghost stories?" Garrett asked.

"Yes!" Jasmine shouted from the bathroom.

He waited for Jasmine to finish while Alexa joined him on the bed, her hair straightened and a touch of makeup enhancing her features.

"You look stunning as always," Garrett said, putting his arm around her shoulders and squeezing her tightly.

"I like Gretchen, Dad. We should stay here every time you visit," Alexa commented.

"You've mentioned that a few times now. I'm glad you enjoy it here. I do, too," Garrett replied, a smile forming.

As they went downstairs to find Gretchen, Garrett's phone rang, surprising him. He glanced at the screen and was delighted to see it was Bri calling—the suspense of their upcoming day trip made his heart skip a beat.

"Hey girls, I need to take this. I will meet you in the lobby." He walked in the opposite direction, toward the back exit, ensuring privacy before answering.

"Hi, Bri. How are you?" he greeted, his voice filled with genuine interest.

"Hi, Garrett. Is this a good time to talk?" Bri asked, her voice warm and inviting.

Garrett hesitated momentarily, his mind briefly entertaining the fear that she might be calling to cancel their plans. "Of course. My girls and I are getting ready to hear scary ghost stories before heading out for dinner and a movie. I am staying at the Simsbury 1818 Estate, and the super swears it is haunted," he shared, hoping to lighten the conversation with humor.

He could hear Bri laughing on the other end, her laughter music to his ears. It was a sound he could easily get used to.

"Jasmine and Alexa went to get her, so I have a few minutes. You're not calling to cancel on me, are you?" Garrett asked teasingly, although nervous energy began twirling within his stomach.

"No, not at all. I enjoyed meeting you and look forward

to our day trip to the city tomorrow. I'm calling to talk about the logistics. I wanted to let you know that I wouldn't mind driving. Would that be all right with you?" Bri's words reassured him, erasing any concerns he had.

Garrett had yet to consider driving into the city, always deterred by heavy traffic and scarce parking. He was fortunate to get his license reinstated upon release to community supervision. The Judge had originally ordered his license to be suspended for one year but that sentence ran concurrently with his prison time. The additional one-year requirement for the interlock device in his vehicle also ran concurrently. Serving five years satisfied some of the consequences that were ruled that day.

"Honestly, I never drive into the city. Not only because parking stinks, but the traffic makes me nervous."

"I understand. I feel immune to it all after living there for nearly eight years. My friend has a prime parking spot we can use in Midtown. From there, we can walk or take a cab to your appointment."

"That sounds wonderful. Where would you like to meet in the morning? I should be ready to go at nine."

"How about I come to pick you up at nine? I am familiar with where you are staying. I will text you when I arrive," Bri offered, her thoughtfulness warming his heart.

"Sounds great. Thanks for offering to drive, Bri. I look forward to seeing you again."

"No problem, Garrett. I look forward to seeing you too. Bye," Bri bid farewell, and Garrett ended the call, feeling a weight lift off his shoulders. The tension he had carried moments ago had evaporated completely. He was overflowing with happiness, his emotions running deep. His connection with Bri was unlike anything he had ever experienced.

A realization dawned on him as he put his phone back in his pocket. This woman, whom he had only recently met, could bring him tears of joy and an unyielding smile. She profoundly affected him, something he had never expected to encounter. What was this woman doing to him?

Garrett headed to the lobby and settled into a seat, joining his daughters, who were engrossed in Gretchen's storytelling. He tried his best to immerse himself in the atmosphere, listening to Gretchen's words, observing her animated facial expressions, and witnessing his daughters' reactions to the spooky tale. However, his mind wandered, unable to resist the allure of thoughts about Bri and the possibilities ahead for them.

As Gretchen weaved her narrative, Garrett's gaze drifted, lost in his reverie. He envisioned future moments with Bri, their shared adventures, and their deepening connection. A wave of anticipation washed over him, tinged with a hint of uncertainty. This new chapter unfolding in his life was both exhilarating and unsettling.

Trying to refocus, Garrett reminded himself to cherish the present moment. He glanced at Jasmine and Alexa, their expressions a mix of fascination and delight, and a swelling of love filled his soul. They were his priority, and he was determined to create beautiful memories with them now and forever.

CHAPTER

NINE

Over in Farmington, Aubrey pulled into her garage after her weekly yoga session. She loved the flexibility and inner peace that yoga provided. It helped her today when she called to speak with Garrett regarding their upcoming date. She entered her house, heading directly upstairs to wash off her sweaty body.

As she showered, her mind wandered to Garrett—his genuine smile, charming personality, and captivating presence. He seemed too good to be true. Some of her expected their first date to be underwhelming, but she was pleasantly surprised. He exceeded her expectations and made her feel at ease. There was a spark, a connection that she hadn't felt in a long time.

Turning off the shower, she grabbed a towel from the rack. After drying herself off, she wrapped the towel around her chest and stood in front of the mirror. Her vision traced the small wrinkles forming near the corners of her eyes, evidence of the passage of time. She smiled at her reflection, thinking of how Garrett's gaze lit up whenever he looked at her. It was a feeling she adored that made her feel desired and beautiful.

While blow-drying her hair, she heard her cell phone ringing from the bedroom. She turned off the dryer and rushed over to the phone. She was relieved to find it was Rachel.

"Hey, sis. How's your night going?" she asked, sinking onto the edge of her bed.

"Great. I just sat down for dinner. I have a few minutes before the drinks arrive, so I'm checking on you. How was the coffee date?"

Aubrey could hear the faint sounds of laughter and chatter in the background, reminding her of the city's vibrant energy.

"Oh, Rachel, it was incredible! Garrett is everything I could have hoped for and more. We have a natural connection, and he invited me to join him for an audition in New York City tomorrow!"

Rachel chuckled, a sound that resonated with Aubrey, making her feel supported and understood. "That's amazing, girl! I'm so happy for you. But remember, don't put too much pressure on yourself or him. Love has a way of surprising us when we least expect it. Just enjoy the process."

Aubrey nodded, her thoughts turning to her past relationships and the disappointment they brought. She longed for a connection beyond surface-level attraction, something deeper and more meaningful. She wanted a love that could withstand the tests of time and adversity, a love like the ones she read about in her favorite novels.

"I know, Rachel. I'll try to keep my expectations in check. But sis, I do hope for something extraordinary. Who knows, maybe this could be the beginning of my beautiful love story."

Rachel's voice softened, filled with warmth and affection. "You deserve nothing less, Aubrey. Embrace the possibilities but remember to love and value yourself. I'm rooting for you, always."

Aubrey smiled, feeling a sense of peace from hearing her best friend's words. With Garrett by her side, she felt her heart was in good hands. She lay down on her comfortable, California king-sized bed, her mind drifting into a blissful sleep filled with dreams of love, adventure, and a future that held the promise of a love story worthy of a Nicholas Sparks novel.

She awoke the following day to the sound of her blaring alarm. Groggily, she sat up, realizing she had slept through the night with her towel still wrapped around her body. Yoga always had a way of lulling her into a deep slumber, especially after the long hours she had dedicated to her new book. She chuckled at the thought of her friend Georgia's remark about popularity as an author, jokingly linking it to shorter deadlines. Perhaps there was some truth to it.

Rubbing the sleep from her eyes, she reached for her phone and pulled up the weather app. The forecast promised a beautiful sunny day in the city, with a high of seventy-five degrees. The excitement for the upcoming day began building as she rummaged through her walk-in closet, selecting a comfortable yet stylish outfit.

In the bathroom, she combed through her long, dark hair, relishing the soothing sensation of the bristles against her scalp. She left her hair down, allowing it to frame her face naturally. She highlighted her favorite features with a light makeup touch, accentuating her eyes and lips.

As she finished getting ready, the weight of the day's events settled upon her. Nervous energy created a flurry of butterflies in her stomach. She glanced at the fruit smoothie she had prepared for breakfast, taking a few bites before deciding her excitement overwhelmed her appetite. She dumped the rest down the drain and opted for a quick cup of coffee instead.

Grabbing her light jacket, purse, and coffee mug, she exited the garage door, stepping into the fresh morning air. She estimated her arrival a little before nine, giving her enough time to settle her nerves. Luck was on her side as she encountered light traffic on her way to the meeting point, arriving ten minutes early. Parking her SUV, she sent Garrett a message, letting him know she had arrived and was waiting out front. The anticipation grew with each passing moment as she wondered how their conversation would flow. She hoped for an easy and natural connection devoid of any awkwardness.

A knock on her window startled her, causing her body to flinch. Garrett stood there, wearing a smile that nearly took her breath away. She quickly rolled down the window, allowing the sweet sound of his laughter to fill the car.

"I'm so sorry, Bri. I didn't mean to frighten you," he apologized, his gorgeous green eyes melting away her fears. They seemed to have transformed overnight, appearing even more vibrant and beautiful. "I was wondering if you ate breakfast. They have coffee and snacks I can get for you."

She smiled, still entranced by his stare. "I did eat before I came and brought some coffee. Thank you, though." Garrett walked to the passenger side, sliding into the seat beside her. He placed his jacket on the back seat and positioned his coffee mug next to hers.

"I appreciate you driving today. And I love this car by the way. Very nice!" he complimented, causing a blush to her cheeks. This was not a normal reaction for her, but she found herself enjoying every moment of it.

"Ah, thanks, Garrett. It's great to have a handsome man sitting next to me. The car feels even more luxurious," she replied, her voice filled with playful banter. And he was undeniably handsome; she had no doubts about that.

He wore faded designer jeans, perfectly worn in all the right places. His white V-neck T-shirt hugged his well-defined chest and arms. His tanned skin was flawless, without any signs of aging. If she hadn't known his age, she would have easily guessed him to be in his late twenties or early thirties. His jet-black hair was neatly tucked behind his ears, partially hidden under a solid black baseball cap. A whiff of his cologne reached her, sending a delightful shiver down her spine. What is this man doing to me...?

"Thanks, Bri."

"All right, I'm ready if you are."

"I've got everything I need, even more now that you're here."

"Ah, that's so sweet," she said, placing her hand on his for a brief second. The touch caused a pleasurable flinch in her abdomen, an unexpected sensation she was eager to explore further.

She backed out of her parking spot and headed toward the interstate that led to the city. The drive would take over two hours, allowing them ample time to enjoy lunch before his one o'clock appointment. She assumed that Garrett's ex-wife would be picking up his daughters from school since they would not return until late afternoon or early evening.

"All right, now I want to hear all about this audition. Did I meet you right before you became rich and famous?" she asked playfully, feeling at ease with him.

"From what I gathered yesterday, you beat me to the rich and famous status," he replied, raising his eyebrows with a mischievous grin.

"Ha-ha, hardly." She laughed, trying to play it off. "Just because I've written books doesn't make me rich and famous. I'm working on it, though."

Garrett waited, intrigued and wanting to hear more. When she didn't offer any additional information, he proceeded to answer her question. He explained that a good friend had taught him to play the piano a few years earlier, speaking highly of this mentor who played a significant role in his musical journey. Garrett shared how he initially turned to music to express his emotions and recounted the night at Emilio's when he played for his daughters, a memory Aubrey vividly recalled. However, she had to feign surprise at certain moments. She admired his humility, downplaying his performance and acting as if Tom, the talent manager, was crazy for extending an invitation.

"You must have made a great impression. I doubt they invite anyone to play for their talent scout. I'm excited to hear you play today."

"I hope you enjoy my performance. I have to admit; I'm nervous."

"It's normal to be nervous, even if you're not actively pursuing a music career. This is a once-in-a-lifetime opportunity."

"I'm not nervous because of that, Bri. I care more about what you think than some random talent manager in New York City," he confessed, his words causing her heart to flutter.

Grateful for his sweet compliment, she looked at him sincerely and replied, "Thank you. You're too kind."

Their conversation flowed effortlessly from that point onward, as comfortable and natural as Aubrey had ever experienced. They delved into discussions about her books, where she revealed that her father's death in a car accident had significantly ignited her passion for storytelling through writing in her diary. She shared how therapeutic it had been for her and admitted that her real name was Aubrey, explaining her fears regarding her fans and the public domain of the dating platform. Garrett took it all in stride, not seeming bothered by her little fib.

As they continued their conversation, they explored various topics, ranging from childhood memories to funny college experiences. He shared his perspective on growing up and living in the Northwest, while she painted a picture of life on the opposite end of the country. Despite living in seemingly different worlds, they found common ground in their likes and dislikes.

Aubrey's excitement peaked when she learned Garrett shared her passion for traveling. They excitedly discussed the places they had been, sharing their favorite destinations and recounting memorable experiences. Bali, Indonesia, emerged as a top choice on their dream vacation lists.

As they neared the city, the tall skyscrapers began to come into view, signaling their arrival.

"I can't believe we're already here," Aubrey remarked, glancing at the clock in her car to note the hour and a half they had to spare.

"I know. It went by much quicker than I expected," Garrett replied, his gaze fixed on the cityscape.

"Oh, really? Were you expecting this to be boring and torturous?" Aubrey playfully slapped his leg and wrinkled her face.

"No, not at all," he responded, his tone innocent. "I knew I would enjoy being with you. I'm just not a huge fan of driving long distances."

"Really? Well, lucky for you, I love to drive," she teased, looking at him and winking.

"Yes, I agree. Lucky for me!" he exclaimed, staring at her with longing and desire. Contentment emanated from his beautiful eyes, causing her to blush again.

"So, I have a friend who rents an apartment in Manhattan. That's how I have a perfect parking spot for us."

"Do they not use the parking spot?"

"My friend is like you. She hates driving, so she doesn't even own a car. The parking spot is included in her apartment fees, a huge perk for all her friends."

"How do you know it's available? What if some of her other friends visited the city today?"

"Well, that could have been a problem if I hadn't already texted her yesterday and asked, silly boy."

"Well done, Aubrey. Again, thank you for chauffeuring me. Not only are you the most gorgeous driver I've ever had, but you're also the most fun and interesting."

"Thanks, Garrett. I enjoy being your driver. I could get used to this."

Driving through the bustling city was as chaotic as ever, but Garrett proved to be a great help, alerting Aubrey to the presence of impatient and aggressive drivers. They eventually arrived at her friend's designated spot in a garage beneath a tall brownstone apartment building. When Aubrey turned off the engine, she noticed it was a quarter till noon. Garrett pulled up Tom's office on his GPS app, revealing it was only a ten-minute walk away.

"So, I know of a yummy Italian sandwich shop around the corner from here. Would you like to stop and eat before heading to meet Tom?" Aubrey's stomach rumbled softly.

"Sounds good to me. I love Italian subs. You lead the way," Garrett agreed, and they exited the car, making their way toward the exit to the ground level. Vinnie's, a local restaurant, was bustling with customers, and Aubrey and Garrett had inadvertently chosen a busy time and place to grab a quick bite.

"Don't worry. It's always like this. They do a great job of moving people through the line," Aubrey assured Garrett, their shoulders brushing against each other in the crowded space. She caught another whiff of his enticing scent, feeling butterflies fluttering in her stomach.

"I trust you. I have no worries at all."

They waited for another fifteen minutes before it was their turn to order. Collecting their sandwiches and water, they found an empty table. Sitting across from each other, they dug into their delicious meals. The restaurant buzzed with the chatter of customers, but Aubrey and Garrett sat in comfortable silence, savoring both the food and each other's presence. Aubrey appreciated how at ease she felt with him, how there was no pressure to fill every moment with conversation. She liked the fact that he was content to enjoy the quiet moments.

After finishing their meals and tidying up the table, they left the restaurant, walking toward their destination. Aubrey didn't need Garrett's phone for directions since she knew the location. The building was near Madison Square Garden, and one of her friends worked there. As they strolled through the busy and vibrant city, Aubrey realized the significance of this meeting and how it could potentially change his life. Despite the weight of the occasion, Garrett remained calm, collected, and seemingly unfazed.

"You don't seem nervous about this audition," Aubrey observed.

"I guess I'm not," Garrett replied casually.

"Why do you think that is?" she inquired, curious about his mindset.

"I'm not worried about the outcome. It has never crossed my mind that I may be good enough to pursue music as a career."

As they reached a busy intersection near their destination, the bustling streets of Midtown were filled with diverse people. Business professionals hurriedly went from one street to another, blending into the usual crowd.

As they began crossing the street, Garrett extended his arm, offering it to Aubrey as an escort. She gladly interlocked her arm with his, feeling an explosion of heat and desire as his strong muscles pressed against her. Together, they made their way toward the building. Upon reaching the front entrance, Garrett stopped near a metal bench and motioned for Aubrey to sit.

"Sorry, it was too noisy to finish what I was saying. So, anyway, I guess not having unrealistic expectations for this meeting has helped me stay calm and casual about it."

Aubrey listened attentively, realizing the importance of this opportunity. He briefly broke eye contact, gazing at the towering buildings and the sky above, seemingly taking in the moment's significance.

"Don't worry, Aubrey. Just because I'm not nervous doesn't mean I'll squander this opportunity. I'm taking it seriously and plan to give an unforgettable performance."

"I can't wait to hear you play. What songs did you choose?"

Garrett pulled out his phone checking the time. "Well, you'll find out soon enough," he replied, standing up and offering his hand. She took it, expecting him to let go after helping her up, but he didn't. Instead, they laced their fingers together, and Aubrey focused on the electrifying sensation that rushed up her arm. With their hands intertwined, they walked towards the entrance of the building, ready to face whatever awaited them inside.

After checking in at the front desk, they were directed to take the elevator to the thirteenth floor. The electric connection between Aubrey and Garrett coursed through her body as they entered. Garrett pressed the button for the thirteenth floor, and the elevator doors closed, enveloping them in silence. Aubrey watched the digital LED lights illuminate one by one as they ascended, marking each passing level.

"Here goes nothing," Garrett uttered as the elevator stopped. A man in a black suit and blue tie appeared as the doors opened.

"Hi, Garrett! I'm so glad you could make it today," the man exclaimed, rushing over to shake Garrett's hand.

"Hi, Tom. Thanks for the invitation. This is my friend, Aubrey," Garrett introduced, gesturing towards Aubrey.

"It's a pleasure to meet you, Aubrey. You look very familiar. Have we met before?" Tom asked, furrowing his brow as he studied her intently. Aubrey wasn't in the mood for the attention, preferring to keep the spotlight on Garrett.

"I don't believe so, Tom. I do get that a lot, though," Aubrey responded, sensing that Garrett wanted to say something. She firmly held his hand, giving him a silent message to let it go. A heart-stopping smile graced Garrett's face.

"All right then, Garrett. Are you ready to play us a few songs?"

"Absolutely," Garrett replied confidently.

"Perfect. We're all excited to have you here," Tom expressed, leading them through two double glass doors that prominently displayed the name, "Mansfield Productions." The floor was filled with scattered cubicles in the center and spacious offices lining the perimeter. Aubrey estimated that they employed at least a hundred people. She was familiar with the production company but had never been invited for a visit.

As they walked through the office, Aubrey's mind was invaded with thoughts. This was the moment that could change Garrett's life. She hoped his performance would enthrall everyone, including Tom, and open the door to a bright future in the music industry.

As they arrived at the large wooden door labeled, "Recording Studio," Tom swiped a key card, unlocking it with a distinct clicking sound. The front section of the room displayed an array of musical instruments, while the back showcased a collection of electronics and gadgets behind a glass partitioned wall. A young man with dark brown hair and black-rimmed glasses sat inside the room, and he quickly stood up from his chair upon their entrance. He walked towards the glass door that separated the two areas.

Dressed in khaki pants, black loafers, and a black button-up long-sleeved shirt, he extended his right hand towards their group. "You must be Garrett. My name is Dale. I'm the head of talent acquisition here at Mansfield Productions. It's a pleasure to meet you," Dale greeted Garrett enthusiastically, shaking his hand.

"Nice to meet you too, Dale. Thanks for the incredible opportunity. This is my friend, Aubrey," Garrett introduced, and Dale turned towards Aubrey, taking her hand in his.

"Hello, Aubrey. I'm glad you could join us today."

"Thanks for allowing me to be here with this stud."

Over the next thirty minutes, Tom and Dale explained the history and operations of Mansfield Productions and their respective roles within the company. They discussed the audition process and explored scenarios that could unfold if the audition went well. Throughout the conversation, Garrett's grip on Aubrey's hand tightened, indicating his growing anxiety and nerves.

Finally, Tom and Dale concluded their explanations, seating Garrett at a large white grand piano while they positioned themselves on the other side of the glass wall. Tom offered a chair for Aubrey to sit in, and Dale took a seat beside Tom. Dale put on oversized headphones, pressed a red button, and spoke into a tiny microphone.

"Okay, Garrett. As Tom explained, play the two songs you performed at the restaurant. Take your time, and don't worry about making any mistakes. We will be recording, so if you want to start over at any point, feel free," Tom instructed.

Garrett nodded in understanding, reassuringly smiling before adjusting the piano bench to his liking. With his eyes closed, he took a moment to gather his thoughts and steady his nerves. The room fell into a hushed silence.

CHAPTER

TEN

As Garrett's fingers glided effortlessly over the keys, he held his daughters in his thoughts. Jerry had taught him the power of recalling beloved memories and moments in time, and with Jasmine and Alexa in mind, he played with a newfound passion. Memories of their younger years played like a home video, transporting him back to the cozy moments they shared on the couch, watching their favorite show together.

His girls were well-behaved and delightful in those memories. The only difference in their current relationship was the shifting dynamics. Garrett used to be the center of their world and relied upon for everything. Now, he knew they still needed him, but in different ways. The clarity of his role in their hectic lives wasn't always as apparent as it once was.

As Garrett transitioned into the second half of the melody, his focus shifted from the past to the present. He observed his audience, taking in Tom's swaying motions and Dale's intense gaze. The weight of the invitation and the moment's significance struck him with a sudden realization.

Anxiety gripped him. His breathing became labored as if a vice was constricting his chest. The room seemed to close on him, and his body temperature rose. Beads of sweat formed on his forehead, and his palms grew damp with perspiration. His voice cracked, amplifying his inner turmoil, while his insecurities screamed at him, urging him to give up.

Just as Garrett was on the verge of succumbing to his negative thoughts, he deliberately shifted his attention to Aubrey. The chaotic sea of thoughts within him calmed, and a sense of tranquility washed over him. The clouds of doubt parted, and he was enveloped in the warm rays of sunshine emanating from Aubrey's tear-stained face. Their eyes locked, and her smile held a multitude of meanings—encouragement, faith, and passion. As he neared the song's end, he fixed his gaze on her as if she were the sole audience he played for. Time seemed to stand still, and her beauty fueled a new motivation within him, igniting a burning desire to give his absolute best performance.

As the final notes of "The Rainbow Connection" resonated, Garrett seamlessly transitioned into "Hallelujah." His fingers moved flawlessly over the keys, losing himself in the music once again. With closed eyes, he immersed himself in the beautiful words he sang, his thoughts directed toward a higher power—God. He felt the spirit of God uplifting him, embracing him with warmth and love, and the intensity of the moment brought tears streaming down his face, mingling with the music.

When Garrett eventually opened his eyes, he noticed tears streaming down his three spectators' cheeks. He attributed these emotions not to his performance but to the presence of God in the room. The song evoked a range of feelings within each person, and for Garrett, it served as a joyous reminder of God's boundless love for him and his profound love for God. The room felt thick with the spirit, His presence tangible.

As he continued playing with unwavering intensity and passion, it felt like he was offering his music as a gift to God Himself. The song reached its conclusion, and in the wake of its final note, a complete silence descended upon the room. Garrett wiped the tears from his face and slowly surveyed his surroundings. His audience remained motionless and silent, leaving him uncertain of their reaction. His mind raced, questioning whether his performance had been so terrible that they were at a loss for words. Or perhaps the song's emotional resonance had stirred painful memories and emotions they had long wished to forget. With every passing second of silence, his chest tightened, and his heart rate accelerated, fear and self-doubt raging within.

A voice sounded from above, startling him at first. "Garrett, that was impressive. One of the finest auditions I've witnessed," the voice exclaimed. The three of them began to applaud, their applause filling the room. They rose from their chairs and exited the inner chamber. He stood, shaking Tom and Dale's hands as they expressed appreciation. Aubrey embraced him gently, momentarily transporting Garrett to another world.

"That was beautiful, Garrett," she whispered, her eyes slightly puffy and red from shedding tears. He was deeply touched by her response, knowing that her opinion mattered most to him.

Dale shared his intention to recommend Garrett for the next step in the process, assuring him that his boss would review the recording they had made. Garrett felt a glimmer of hope emerging as he began believing in his potential. Dale's positive feedback ignited a newfound aspiration within him, birthing a fresh sense of purpose.

Dale and Tom walked them to the elevator. Dale assured Garrett that he would reach out after his boss had reviewed the recording. After thanking them again, Garrett and Aubrey bid their farewells, their minds filled with endless possibilities.

Once the elevator doors were closed, Aubrey pushed the button for the lobby floor. She still held his hand firmly in hers, and the warmth of her touch sent pleasant sensations coursing through Garrett's body. He leaned back against the elevator wall, relishing in the gentle touch as they descended toward the ground floor. Aubrey positioned herself before him and intertwined her fingers with his free hand.

"Thank you for allowing me to be a part of this," Aubrey said, her eyes locked with his, illuminated by the bright overhead lights.

Garrett stood a little taller, drawing himself closer to her. Their faces were inches apart as he gently guided her arms around his neck, releasing her hands. His hands settled around her waist, pulling her closer, meeting her waiting lips. Their kiss began tenderly, gradually intensifying as the passion between them ignited. Her lips were soft and inviting, surpassing all his expectations. It awakened a deep yearning within him, a craving, a hunger that needed satisfied.

As the elevator doors opened with a cheerful chime, Aubrey stepped back, her eyes sparkling mischievously. She took Garrett's hand and led him onto the bustling city streets. The warm sun bathed everything in a golden glow, casting a magical aura over the surroundings. The symphony of car horns and the city's vibrant pulse filled the air, reminding them that they were part of something bigger, something extraordinary.

Pausing near the edge of the street, Aubrey reached into her purse and pulled out her phone. "What time do you need to be back for your daughters?" she asked. Garrett retrieved his phone from his pocket, checking the time.

"Their mom is picking them up from school, and I promised to join them for dinner at their house around seven."

Aubrey's brow furrowed slightly; her lips pursed in thought. "You're having dinner with your ex-wife?"

A warm smile spread across Garrett's face as he gently squeezed her hand. "I understand if it seems unusual, but we've managed to build a friendship over the years. Julie, my ex-wife, has remarried an amazing man named Ben. We've found a way to coexist and put our children's well-being first."

Aubrey's eyes softened with understanding, her expression filled with admiration. "That's incredibly mature and beautiful, Garrett. It's refreshing to see divorced parents prioritizing their children's happiness above all else."

He nodded, appreciating her understanding. "It wasn't always easy. We went through our fair share of challenges and heartache. But in the end, we realized that nurturing a positive environment for our girls was far more important than holding onto resentments."

Glancing at her phone and then back at Garrett, Aubrey's lips curved into a playful smile. "We still have a couple of hours before we need to head back. Would you like to take a stroll through Central Park with me?"

"That sounds wonderful; I'd love to walk the park with you."

They hailed a cab, grateful for its convenience in navigating the busy streets of New York City. The yellow taxi whisked them away, weaving through the bustling traffic with a sense of urgency. Garrett compared the exhilaration of riding in a New York City cab to that of a thrilling roller coaster; his stomach filled with excitement and butterflies. With a thick foreign accent, the cab driver focused on the road ahead, seemingly uninterested in his passengers.

As they sped through the streets, the cab driver accelerated after each intersection, only slowing down when pedestrians stepped onto the crosswalk. It was a constant battle between the cab drivers and the pedestrians, with tensions simmering beneath the surface. Each group vied for its space, determined to assert dominance whenever the opportunity arose.

Finally, the cab screeched to a halt near their destination. Garrett released his tight grip on Aubrey's hand, realizing how tense he had been during the wild ride. He paid the driver, and they made their way toward the park entrance. Following winding paths that led them deeper into the lush greenery and towering trees, they discovered a small, unoccupied hill of grass that offered a picturesque view of the surrounding landscape.

They settled down on the soft grass, finding comfort in each other's presence. They lay side by side, gazing up at the clear blue sky and feeling the gentle caress of the cool breeze on their faces. The park's serenity provided a welcome escape from the bustling city, allowing them to be in the moment. Hand in hand, they embraced the tranquility, cherishing the stillness amidst a world that never seemed to stop.

As they basked in the peacefulness, Garrett propped himself on his elbow and turned to face Aubrey. Her radiant blue eyes met his, and she offered him a smile that stirred something deep within him. He marveled at the connection they shared, grateful for the ease with which they had found comfort in each other's company. With a sense of curiosity, he couldn't help but ask her a question lingering in his mind.

"Why are you single, Aubrey? You're an incredible catch, and I can't understand why no one has swept you off your feet yet."

Aubrey mirrored his posture, propping herself on her side to face him. Her face drew closer to his, their eyes locked in an intimate exchange.

"That's a good question. I'm quite picky. I've had a few serious relationships, but in the end, the spark faded away."

Garrett could relate to the notion of being selective, especially regarding matters of the heart. Though their relationship was still in its infancy, he understood the importance of finding the right partner. With a gentle touch, he brushed a stray strand of hair behind her ear, marveling at its softness and the way it caught the sunlight.

"Tell me about your books," he urged, his curiosity piqued. He wanted to delve deeper into her world to understand the passion that fueled her creative endeavors.

Aubrey met his gaze, a thoughtful pause preceding her response. She began to share how her first novel came to be, describing the characters she had created in her diary to process the powerful emotions that losing her father had evoked. She spoke of her best-selling trilogy, the "First Love" series, and how the characters had captured readers' hearts.

She revealed that writing was her main occupation, primarily focusing on fictional novels. While she occasionally edited columns, her passion lay in crafting captivating stories. Aubrey spoke excitedly about her upcoming book, "Night and Day," which was set to be released the following week. She explained how her father's love, life, and eventual passing had inspired the novel, infusing it with deep meaning and heartfelt emotion.

A Frisbee landed near their feet, drawing their attention away from their conversation. They paused their discussion and greeted the young teenage boy, who hurriedly retrieved it. With a nod, he tossed the Frisbee to another boy and darted away to continue their game. Garrett admired Aubrey's friendly and approachable nature, recognizing it as an exceptional quality.

Curiosity burning, Garrett cautiously broached a more personal topic. "You mentioned that your father passed away in a car accident. How old were you when it happened?" he asked, hoping not to pry too much into her past.

Aubrey lay back down, her focus fixed on the expansive blue sky above. "I was fifteen years old on that fateful day when I received the call. An officer informed me that my parents had been involved in a serious accident. When I arrived at the hospital, my grandfather had to deliver the devastating news. They were hit by a drunk driver, barely old enough to consume alcohol legally."

Garrett's stomach churned as he listened to Aubrey's heartbreaking story. Suddenly, a vivid image of Matt's bloodied face on his car's airbag flashed through his mind, catching him off guard and filling him with mixed emotions. He felt as though Matt's presence was trying to communicate with him, unsettling him for a moment.

"Garrett, are you all right? You look pale," Aubrey's concerned voice broke through his thoughts.

"I'm fine. Just felt a wave of nausea, but it's passed," he reassured her, pushing aside the unsettling memory for now. He knew he needed to share his story with her, including his time in prison and the tragedy involving Matt. But he also understood it wasn't the appropriate time to reveal it all. Perhaps, he thought, before he left for Idaho.

"I'm so sorry about your father, Aubrey," Garrett said sincerely, lying down on his back beside her. She reached for his hand, infusing him with a comforting energy that replaced his unease. The flashback he experienced would have to wait for another time for a more suitable setting.

Lying there, side by side, their eyes gazing up at the vast expanse of the universe, they listened to the melodic songs of nearby birds filling the tranquil afternoon. In Aubrey's presence, Garrett found peace that soothed his naturally restless spirit. She acted as a calming force, akin to a sedative for his anxious mind.

"It's all right, Garrett," she spoke softly, carrying warmth and reassurance. "One of the reasons I'm attracted to you is because you're a wonderful father. I know my father's importance to me, and I can see your immense love for your daughters. I'm certain they feel incredibly fortunate to have you in their lives."

"I truly hope so. Being so far away is difficult, but I do my best to show them how much I love them, even from a distance."

Aubrey squeezed his hand gently, turning her head to face him. Her breath brushed against his nose, creating an intimate closeness. "I can see it in their smiles. They feel your love."

Turning his head toward hers, their faces now inches apart, Garrett's heart swelled with affection. "Thank you for saying that" he whispered, their lips meeting for their second kiss. It was a tender exchange, each savoring the touch of their lips and the taste of the other. Their tongues met in a delicate dance, accompanied by the gentle caress of his hand on the side of her cheek. Her skin felt incredibly soft, unlike any woman he had been with. As their kiss deepened, her hand found its way to his hair, pulling him closer.

The laughter of a group of teenage girls shattered the intimate bubble they had created, bringing them back to reality. Both blushed, their connection momentarily interrupted by the outside world. Aubrey checked her phone and realized it was time to leave.

They were hand in hand during the trip back to Simsbury, with Garrett sharing stories and anecdotes about his daughters. Aubrey listened attentively, relating to his experiences and offering genuinely respected and appreciated advice. He could already envision his girls adoring her; she embodied the qualities he hoped they would develop—success, independence, confidence, education, and intelligence. Meeting her had made him feel incredibly fortunate.

After briefly discussing his daughters, Garrett turned the conversation toward Aubrey's father. She shared cherished childhood memories and revealed that "The Rainbow Connection" was their song. Hearing him sing it had brought tears to her eyes, and he hoped his girls would feel that same special connection with him. Aubrey spoke lovingly about her father, describing all the little gestures of love he had shown her and her mother. Hearing her story, Garrett felt happiness and sadness, realizing the depth of her longing for that kind of love again. Her loss still haunted her.

"Was it difficult for you to hear me playing your song today?"

She briefly glanced at him before refocusing on the road. "It was beautiful. The way you play, the way you sing—it all reminded me of him. The tears I shed were tears of joy, not sorrow. Like an angel, it felt like he sent you from above to sing in his place."

He studied her carefully, searching for any trace of sarcasm, but found none. "That is one of the most meaningful compliments I have ever received. Thank you for saying that."

"No, Garrett, thank you for being you."

When they arrived at the 1818 Estate, Aubrey stepped out

of the car and hugged him tightly. Garrett didn't want her to leave and asked, "When can I see you again?"

She contemplated for a moment before responding, "What are your plans for tomorrow?"

"I have some work to do in the morning while the girls are at school, and I plan to work out. How about you?"

"I have a few things to take care of as well. Would you like to work out together?"

"Absolutely!"

"I had such an amazing time with you today. You are truly exceptional and incredibly talented. Thank you again for letting me share that experience with you."

"Thank you, sweetheart, for driving me. That was incredibly sweet of you, and I genuinely enjoyed your company today. You helped me with that audition more than you'll ever know."

He kissed her softly before bidding her goodnight. Garrett watched as she drove off, her taillights gradually disappearing into the distance, filled with a longing for their next meeting.

Garrett arrived at Ben and Julie's house a little after seven that evening. Their home was situated in a middle-class neighborhood. Ben and Julie worked for a large financial corporation specializing in asset management and mortgage lending. They had met at work a few years after Julie and the girls had moved to Avon. Initially, it had been challenging for Garrett to accept that Julie was dating someone new, but over time, he had come to respect their relationship.

Now, he was grateful for Ben's presence in his daughters' lives. Ben had given them love, support, and protection as a father figure when Garrett couldn't be there for them.

Ben had never had children and had gone through a failed marriage. Despite that, he had earned Jasmine and Alexa's respect and love, which brought immense joy to Garrett's heart. Over time, Garrett and Ben developed a friendship based on mutual respect.

Garrett also felt grateful for Julie and the incredible job she had done in raising their girls to become the strong young women they are today. He understood the difficulty she had faced when he was incarcerated and knew that Julie had made the right decision by moving to Avon. The girls thrived in their new environment, excelling in a top-ranked public school system. Everything felt right in their world, and the only thing that could make it better was if Garrett could secure a transfer of his parole.

Sitting around the dining room table, they enjoyed a delicious meal prepared by Julie, her special sweet and sour chicken. As they ate, they took turns questioning Garrett about his audition, their curiosity resembling detectives at a crime scene. Garrett shared the details of his trip without mentioning his special guest, explaining the possibilities and potential outcomes that Tom and Dale had highlighted. Jasmine and Alexa hung onto his every word, their interest and pride evident. Deep down, he doubted he would achieve the success they hoped for, but he knew it didn't matter. Regardless of the outcome, he knew they would be proud of his small accomplishment.

The evening continued with laughter and family conversations, reinforcing their bond. Garrett was grateful for the support and love from Ben, Julie, and his daughters. They made him feel like he belonged and had a second chance at building a meaningful life.

After bidding his daughters goodnight and tucking them into bed at the B&B, Garrett settled down at the desk and retrieved his phone from his jacket pocket. To his pleasant surprise, he found a message from Dave, asking about a meeting and suggesting lunch beforehand. Garrett adored any opportunity to help others. He blinked back tears and began composing his response, expressing his enthusiasm for the lunch meeting. Content with his message, he hit send.

Seated at the desk, he took a moment to meditate and reflect on the state of his life. Gratitude filled his heart as he recognized the blessings that had come his way. Engaging in quiet prayer, he thanked God for continuously showering gifts and pledged to remain humble, peaceful, grateful, and sober regardless of life's challenges. After concluding his prayer, he checked his email, acknowledging that although he had neglected his business that day, he had made significant investments in his future, particularly with Aubrey. Buying and selling stocks could come and go, but meeting someone like Aubrey was an unparalleled opportunity—a once-in-a-lifetime chance. He deemed it priceless.

A smile tugged at the corners of his mouth as he reminisced about his time with her. The memory of her scent and appearance resurfaced effortlessly in his mind. He recalled how gracefully she walked the city streets, turning heads wherever they went. Seeing other men admiring her didn't trigger insecurity or jealousy. Instead, walking beside this stunning woman, he felt an enormous amount of pride.

Aubrey seemed oblivious to the attention other men gave her, perhaps accustomed to it. Or, he hoped, she treasured the attention he bestowed upon her.

Closing his computer, he attended to his nightly routine of brushing his teeth before settling his head onto the soft pillow. Drifting into the realm of slumber, he couldn't shake the feeling that he was falling deeply for Aubrey. He reminded himself that their relationship was still in its early stages, but it did little to quell the flood of emotions raging through him. Having long ago surrendered his will to the care of God, Garrett accepted that whatever unfolded with Aubrey, whether positive or negative, was exactly as it was meant to be. He succumbed to a deep and peaceful sleep with this serene thought.

CHAPTER

ELEVEN

Garrett awaited Aubrey's arrival in his car, parked outside the gym. Aubrey's SUV zoomed into the parking lot and parked in the spot beside his. Stepping out of his vehicle, he grabbed his bag, and Aubrey greeted him with a radiant smile. Her smile sent a shiver down his spine, even in the warm weather. Dressed in a fitted pink tank top and black yoga pants, she looked more stunning in her workout clothes than anyone he had ever taken to a fancy restaurant.

"Good morning, handsome," she said, approaching him. He opened his arms, and she cuddled up to his chest.

"Good morning to you, beautiful," he whispered, savoring the fragrance of her shampoo.

"How was your evening with the girls?" she asked as they approached the gym entrance.

He held the door for her, appreciating how she moved gracefully through it. He wore gray sweatpants, a snug white athletic t-shirt, and multicolored running shoes, catching Aubrey's admiring gaze.

"It was peaceful and relaxing. Julie made one of my favorite dishes, sweet and sour chicken."

Aubrey made a mental note to remember his favorite dish. "Sounds like a lovely evening," she said as they went to the weight room.

"What's on your workout agenda today?"

"I was thinking of doing some full-body circuit exercises."

"That sounds perfect—no wonder you look incredible. Circuit training is an excellent way to stay fit," Garrett said, stashing his gym bag in a designated cubby.

Aubrey smiled, grateful that he understood her workout routine. She couldn't recall ever working out with any of her previous partners. Uncertain about what to expect from a workout date, she knew one thing for sure – she loved spending time with him. Yesterday had been a magical day for her, from their effortless conversations to the intensity of their connection. She knew he was talented, and his performance at the studio had touched her deeply. She did not doubt that he would make a mark in the music industry. Tom and Dale had practically fawned over him as they left the office.

"Thank you, Garrett. I put in effort to maintain my body," she replied, striking a pose with one hand on her hip and the other behind her head, exuding confidence.

Feeling the warmth spread within him, he was amazed by his attraction to her. "I'll let you lead the routine."

Aubrey guided him to a corner of the gym where a pull-up

bar stood on blue gym mats. They both stretched their muscles, preparing for the workout.

"How about some burpee pull-ups? I learned about them in my weekly cross-fit training class."

Burpee pull-ups brought on a vivid flashback for Garrett, a flashback he wished he could forget. Garrett had spent six months at a medium-security prison before his transfer to the Idaho State Correctional Center, a medium/high-security facility. This institution was known among the inmates as the Gladiator School due to the high gang activity and the population mainly being violent offenders.

A month after his transfer, he struggled to fit in with his fellow inmates in his unit. He had been assigned to one of the toughest and most political units within the prison walls. Eighty felons lived in the "K" pod he called home. His roommates had charges that ranged from armed robbery to murder. The top-ranking gang members of the three most powerful prison gangs resided there.

A pull-up bar sat in the southeast corner of the room where Garrett was only ten minutes into his thirty-minute burpee pull-up routine when a stocky white man interrupted him. "Hey, bro, my boys and I need to use this area. Can you wrap it up?"

Garrett recognized the man as John, a member of a white gang that was known as SHFL. They were one of the most respected gang members due to their high level of violent behavior. John had prison tattoos running up and down each arm, and on his neck, he had SHFL blasted across it. He was in excellent shape, someone the ordinary prisoner would not want to mess with.

Garrett's feelings were still numbed by the anger and rage that consumed his mind and body. He did his own time and rarely spoke to or associated with anyone other than his cellmate. He just did his thing without issues until now. Garrett wiped the sweat from his forehead with his shirt. "I am not even halfway done. Give me about twenty minutes, and then I will be out of your way."

John's eyebrows quickly furrowed, and his lips formed a straight line. "No, you are done now. Get your ass out of here," he said through gritted teeth.

Garret noticed a few other SHFL members watching and inching closer as the situation escalated. When there was drama in the units or the prison yard, the prison code was not to make a scene. No one was supposed to attract attention to the Correctional Officers. If it had to be done, getting away with fighting and violence was the ultimate goal. His buddies were in range to attack if needed.

Garrett gave John a cold stare before resuming his routine. Ignoring the threat, John spit in his direction. Garrett observed the other gang members form a circle that would block the vision from the officer's station. Garrett knew the cameras would still expose the scene. He continued his workout even though John was closing the distance between them. Once John was within a few feet, he pulled his right foot back while Garrett was in the push-up position.

Garrett rolled to his right, avoiding the blow directly

approaching his face. He jumped to his feet in a fluid motion, standing toe to toe with his assailant.

"Trust me, you don't want to do this," Garrett warned.

John stood ready to strike, positioned in a fighting stance. He attacked, throwing a right hook toward Garrett's face. He ducked, shuffling his feet to the left, placing himself behind John. Before John could turn around, Garrett swept his left leg out from underneath him. John landed with a loud thump on the concrete floor. The other gang members started to close the gap between them.

John got up slowly, clearly injured by the harsh fall. When he rushed at Garrett again, he threw a right haymaker, wanting to end this with one punch. Garrett quickly put his left arm at the side of his face in a flexed position. He guided his elbow to connect with John's incoming fist. The sound of bones breaking echoed from the walls. John winced loudly in pain, holding his hand out in front of him.

Because of the injury, another member stepped forward while John backed away. Garrett barely noticed the guy coming from his peripheral vision. He turned and ducked to avoid the punch, and then swiftly shot up with an open hand that met his attacker in the middle of his throat. This was a lethal punch, given enough force behind it. Garrett's experience ensured it was enough to take the wind from his pipes. The man put both hands to his throat, desperately trying to catch his breath; fear of death riddled his face.

Since he easily defeated his first two attackers, the SHFL leader called upon his best weapon, Peter. He stood over six feet, five inches tall, and had bulging muscles from every area of his body. He easily weighed over two-eighty with maybe five percent body fat. He was by far the most intimidating inmate within the unit.

Garrett squared up with him, waiting for the assault to begin. He kept his breathing steady, not wanting his adrenaline to spike out of control. This kept everything in slow motion, giving him an advantage over less experienced fighters. Garrett could see Peter getting caught up in that moment, his body trembling with rage. Peter threw a jab with his left, making Garrett shift to his left while simultaneously jabbing upwards toward Peter's nose, his open hand connecting with its target.

This did not stop him from squaring up again with Garrett. Blood gushed from his disfigured nose, rapidly dripping the dark red liquid onto the concrete. He closed in on him, throwing a hard right hook in his direction. Garrett quickly went into a squatting position, placing him right in front of Peter's stomach. He threw a powerful punch into the center of his abdomen, pushing the breath out of his lungs. While Peter bent over, gasping for air, Garrett threw an uppercut at Peter's chin. It connected and threw him backward violently onto the hard floor.

At this point, even the top gang leaders, including the shot caller of SHFL, watched in awe at what they witnessed. Garrett could tell by their expressions that this was something they had never seen before. Garrett had had enough of this and was ready to put Peter out of commission. Peter lunged at Garrett with everything he had, trying to take him to the ground. Garrett threw his knee directly into Peter's incoming forehead, connecting right in the center, otherwise known as the "sweet spot." Peter fell to the floor unconscious, blood covering most of his face.

Garrett expected to be jumped at this point, but no one stepped forward. Instead, they all stared at the man who had just annihilated some of the most brutal inmates they knew.

"Garrett," Aubrey's voice snapped him out of his thoughts. "Are you okay?"

Garrett shook his head, trying to clear his mind. "Yeah, sorry about that. Those words brought back a memory I had forgotten. Burpee pull-ups are impressive," Garrett said, stretching his body. "I've done them before, but it's been a while. Lately, I've been focusing more on weight training. Maybe I should incorporate endurance training, too."

"I try to stay away from weights. I prefer to keep my body toned without being overly muscular." She felt heat rush to her face as she admired Garrett's physique. Quickly averting her gaze, she looked away, hoping to hide her slight blush.

They made their way to the pull-up bar, and Aubrey suggested they do ten sets of pull-ups and burpees each before rotating. They pushed themselves for forty-five minutes, alternating between exertion and rest. By the end, they were both sweaty and decided to take a few laps around the track.

"That was intense," Garrett commented, wiping the sweat off his forehead. He loved the exhilarating feeling that came after a good workout. However, he also felt self-conscious, aware of his sweaty appearance. Thankfully, the gym had its distinct scent that helped mask his own.

"I agree. You're in great shape," Aubrey said sincerely. She was genuinely impressed by his endurance.

"What are your plans for the rest of the day?" she asked, gently squeezing his hand. Garrett pondered how much to share, not yet ready to reveal his struggles with alcoholism.

"Well, I'm meeting a friend for lunch and have some work to take care of before picking up my daughters from school. Then, I thought I'd take them out for a nice dinner. How about you?" he asked, noticing a jogger passing by.

"I have some work to do as well. Tonight, I promised my mom I'd have dinner at her place." Aubrey felt a twinge of curiosity, wondering about Garrett's lunch companion. She reminded herself to be patient, knowing they were still in the early stages of getting to know each other.

"You haven't told me much about your mom."

"She's wonderful. We have a close bond. She's been there for me during the toughest times in my life. She's one of the reasons I moved back to Farmington."

After cooling down, they gathered their bags and walked toward their cars. Garrett paused and pulled Aubrey closer to him. "When can I see you again?" His heart raced as they embraced.

Aubrey smiled, feeling the warmth of his touch. "I'm available tomorrow."

Garrett's smile grew wider. "Tomorrow sounds great. I'll text you later tonight and we can figure out the details."

"That sounds perfect," Aubrey replied, giving him an affectionate kiss before they reluctantly parted ways.

Dave had responded to Garrett's text the night before, suggesting they meet at Friendly's around eleven-thirty. It was a familiar spot for Garrett, having taken his girls there. Despite being a few minutes late, Garrett hurried inside and spotted Dave sitting on a cushioned bench near the entrance. They exchanged a friendly handshake and followed the hostess to their booth. As they settled in, Garrett noticed the faint scent of fresh-cut lumber emanating from Dave.

Almost as if he could read Garrett's thoughts, Dave spoke up, apologizing for his casual attire. He explained that he worked for his uncle's construction company and that taking time off for meetings didn't sit well with him, though his uncle remained supportive of his recovery. It was his uncle who had referred him to the program in the first place. Garrett listened attentively, appreciating Dave's openness.

Their waiter approached, swiftly taking their orders before disappearing. Sensing the opportunity to delve into the heart of the matter, Garrett asked Dave how long he had been sober, his curiosity guiding the conversation.

Dave took a deep breath, hesitating momentarily as he contemplated how much to share with this relative stranger. Garrett sensed Dave's dilemma and decided to take a different approach. "I'm sorry, Dave. I understand that we barely know each other. Let me begin by telling you a bit about myself. Would that be all right with you?"

Dave nodded, visibly easing into the conversation. Both were startled by a loud crash coming from the kitchen area.

After scanning the area for any potential danger, Garrett controlled his breathing and focused on calming his racing heart. PTSD was a daily struggle.

For the next half-hour, Garrett shared his history with Dave. He spoke of his early years and how his relationship with alcohol started normally, much like that of others. But as time passed, the signs of alcoholism began to surface, gradually consuming his life. He openly discussed the toll it took on his marriage, the nights of drunken embarrassment that pained Julie in the company of friends and guests. Then, he bravely shared the devastating impact of the car accident that claimed the life of his best friend and led to his imprisonment.

Tears welled up in Garrett's eyes when he mentioned his dear friend's loss. The ache of missing him so profoundly resonated within his soul. He longed to have his friend back by his side, yearning for their connection.

Garrett recounted how he found Daily Recovery, attributing his sobriety to the program and his unwavering faith in God. He spoke of the challenges he faced upon his release and how, through divine guidance, he stumbled upon the program in the streets. Garrett marveled at the miracles he witnessed through the eight steps, emphasizing the profound transformation in his life through small daily efforts. Lastly, he stressed the significance of helping others, underscoring that his long-term sobriety relied on supporting people like Dave.

Dave listened intently, his gaze fixed on Garrett as he shared his story. He nodded in understanding, absorbing every word with gratitude and vulnerability. Even the loud screaming from the toddler in the booth next to them did nothing to break his undivided attention.

When Garrett finished speaking, Dave cleared his throat, breaking the silence between them. "Thank you for sharing that incredible story with me," Dave said, his voice filled with genuine appreciation. He fidgeted in his seat, searching for the right words to express himself. "I can relate to so much of what you just said. I, too, was recently released from prison because of an alcohol-related accident. Staying clean and sober was a struggle for me at first. But I put together over two years of sobriety over the last few years. I didn't attend meetings; I relied on my determination never to drink again. But I didn't realize how hard it would be to resist once I got out."

Garrett nodded, his eyes conveying understanding and empathy. He could sense the weight of Dave's experience, the battles fought, and the fears faced. Dave struggled to make eye contact as he continued. He described his initial fear and anxiety upon leaving prison. How he hid away at his parents' house, seeking refuge from the temptations that lurked outside. But eventually, he had to confront the world again, gradually rebuilding his self-confidence and finding moments of happiness.

Dave recounted a pivotal moment of weakness when he questioned his resolve and decided to experiment with drinking again. The consequences were swift and harsh, leaving him with intense cravings and a realization of the depths of his addiction. It was after this episode that his uncle recommended Daily Recovery as a lifeline.

As Dave finished speaking, Garrett delved into the importance of understanding cravings as a symptom of alcoholic disease. He stressed his powerlessness over the first drink and the role of a higher power in his sobriety. He emphasized the transformative power of step work, allowing him to move past the weight of guilt, shame, and past mistakes. Dave's face softened with understanding and his eyes twinkled with hope.

Garrett sensed it was time to address the path forward. Aware of their limited time before the meeting, he leaned in and spoke with sincerity. "It's quite simple, Dave. To maintain your sobriety, you must do three essential things: First, be willing to wholeheartedly work through all eight steps, with God at the forefront of your thoughts. Second, attend as many meetings as necessary, ideally at least ninety meetings in your first ninety days. And finally, share your story with others and be there to help them stay sober."

Pausing, Garrett assessed Dave's response. He wanted to ensure Dave's commitment was genuine, his determination unwavering. After contemplating, Dave looked back at Garrett with a newfound resolve. "I want what you have, Garrett. I am willing to do whatever it takes."

Joy filled Garrett's soul, a profound connection to the divine. He knew this moment began a meaningful friendship built on trust and shared experiences. To explain the program's first step, Garrett assigned Dave homework, encouraging him to complete the first ten pages of the program's workbook. He offered to buy the book for Dave at the meeting.

With their meals paid for, they left the diner and headed to the familiar church where their paths had crossed two days earlier. As they drove together, a sense of hope and possibility enveloped them, paving the way for a future filled with support, growth, and sober living.

Aubrey sat comfortably in her leather chair, enjoying the picturesque view of the national forest behind her home through the large windows of her office. The beautiful weather outside promised a delightful weekend ahead. Her gaze wandered to the trees, where squirrels played and chased each other among the ancient sycamores.

Returning her focus to the computer screen, Aubrey realized she had been neglecting her work over the past few days. She had a lot to catch up on, especially since she planned to spend the day with Garrett tomorrow. As thoughts of him in his sweaty workout clothes flashed through her mind, she couldn't help but feel a delightful shiver run down her spine. She couldn't deny her attraction towards him, appreciating his rugged charm.

Her train of thought was interrupted by a new email from her agent, Michael Donnelly. Excitement filled her as she opened the message, knowing it pertained to her latest book and its upcoming tour.

Michael expressed his confidence in the book's success, anticipating that sales would surpass those of her previous three books combined within the first year. He conveyed the pride he and the team felt for Aubrey's achievements, emphasizing the positive and glowing reviews received from preliminary responses. He assured her he expected the upcoming nationally publicized reviews to be just as favorable.

The email included the itinerary for Aubrey's four-week national book tour, divided into two two-week segments with a one-week break in between. Michael mentioned being open to feedback and any changes she might want. Aubrey perused the list of cities she would be visiting, starting with several major cities in the Northeast and then going to the West Coast, beginning in Seattle and traveling down the Pacific Ocean.

An idea sparked as she considered her trip to Seattle and the West Coast. She pondered the possibility of persuading Michael to include a short visit to Boise in her itinerary. The thought of spending time with Garrett in his hometown excited her. She had never been to Idaho but knew of Boise's unique blue football field and reputation for growing the best, most giant potatoes.

Deciding to take a chance, Aubrey quickly emailed Michael, suggesting they add a one-night stop in Boise. She explained her desire to visit a friend in that area and hoped it would be easy to rearrange the schedule.

Aubrey hit the send button, hoping her request would be met with understanding and the opportunity to explore a new place and deepen her connection with Garrett.

Garrett and Dave found themselves in the parking lot, bidding farewell to the members of their recovery meeting. The focus of the meeting had been on the various symptoms of their alcoholism, and Dave had shown genuine interest as each person shared their experiences with these symptoms. When it was Dave's turn to speak, he surprised Garrett by opening up about his recent relapse. He spoke openly about the intense cravings he had been plagued with and how they lingered until the meeting on Monday. Dave expressed his commitment to the program and his desire to stay sober.

After the meeting, many attendees congratulated Dave on his courage and honesty. Garrett emphasized the importance of connecting with these fellow members, as they could be a valuable source of support. He handed Dave a phone list that had been circulated, containing the contact information of the male members. Garrett explained the significance of this list, highlighting the power of talking to another alcoholic in times of temptation and cravings. He stressed that seeking support from non-alcoholic friends or family members often led to relapse, whereas engaging with fellow members could help prevent it. Garrett observed Dave's expression, hoping to see comprehension in his eyes.

Dave held the list, carefully examining the names and numbers before responding to Garrett's instructions. He acknowledged the importance of working with other alcoholics, realizing that his discussions with Garrett about their shared disease had already been more beneficial than years of mere abstinence during his time incarcerated. Dave promised himself and Garrett that he would reach out to the people on the list, building relationships that could save his life.

Before parting ways, Garrett and Dave committed to maintaining regular communication. They agreed to talk at least once a day, ensuring that Dave had a consistent source of guidance, encouragement, and accountability. These conversations would serve as opportunities to discuss Dave's progress in working through the steps, celebrate his achievements along the way, and provide unwavering support during the inevitable challenges that would arise.

With newfound determination and the knowledge that he had a caring ally in Garrett, Dave set off on his path to a healthier and sober life. He knew that, with the support of his fellow alcoholics, he had the strength and resilience to overcome the obstacles that awaited him.

Garrett treasured the time spent with his daughters as they drove home from school, sharing the latest updates on school gossip. Upon reaching their temporary residence, Garrett informed them they had a few hours of free time to relax and complete their homework. The decision to go bowling instead of dining out for the evening was a testament to the simple pleasures they enjoyed as a family. They found a nearby bowling alley that offered a range of activities, including a diner and a laser tag arena. It was a perfect choice for an evening of fun and togetherness.

As they sat in their room at the end of the evening, their minds focused on different subjects, Garrett couldn't shake the feeling that something was missing. He yearned to move to Avon, be there for his daughters consistently, and create a permanent home where they could continue to grow and thrive as a family. The energy and love they shared fueled his resolve to find a way to make this dream a reality.

CHAPTER

TWELVE

Aubrey parked her car in the familiar driveway of her childhood home, submerged by a wave of nostalgia. Her mother, Jenny Ellis, had managed to pay off the house with the money from a life insurance policy her father had taken out decades ago. Aubrey was enveloped in a delightful symphony of delicious aromas from the kitchen as she stepped through the front door. Jenny, renowned for her culinary skills, always went above and beyond when they had dinner together. Aubrey knew she would leave with abundant leftovers that would sustain her for a week.

Jenny stood by the stove in the kitchen, deftly stirring something in a pan.

"Smells divine, Mom," Aubrey commented, planting a soft kiss on her mother's cheek. Sitting at the nearby kitchen table, she observed her mother's graceful movements while beloved memories of their time in this kitchen flooded her mind.

Aubrey had inherited her mother's striking features—dark hair, blue eyes, a petite frame, and luscious lips—a testament to their shared gene pool.

"It should be ready in about an hour," Jenny said, going over to Aubrey. "How about we enjoy this gorgeous weather on the back patio?" She removed her pink apron, draping it over an empty chair.

"A wonderful idea," Aubrey replied, eager to soak in the sun's warm rays.

"Would you like a glass of wine, dear?" Jenny offered as Aubrey approached the back door leading to the inviting concrete patio.

"Sure. Do you need any help?" Aubrey asked, pausing at the doorway.

"No, I've got it covered. I'll join you shortly."

The back patio boasted intricate epoxy stamp work, with pinkish-brown hues and artful designs that embodied a modern vibe. Unlike Aubrey's home, her mother's house resided in a mature middle-class subdivision on the outskirts of Farmington. Aubrey's parents had been esteemed professors at a local university, with Jenny still imparting knowledge at fifty-five. Teaching was her lifelong passion, one she had no intention of relinquishing.

Aubrey settled into a cushioned metal chair surrounding a circular patio table. A large umbrella adorned the table's center, casting a welcoming shade. Jenny emerged from the doorway, gracefully balancing two glasses of red wine in her hands. She took the seat closest to Aubrey, presenting her with one of the generous, bulbous glasses. With effortless grace, they indulged in the rich flavor of the wine, savoring each sip.

"Now, tell me about this mystery man, Aubrey. You've kept me waiting long enough," Jenny exclaimed, her face radiating impatience.

Aubrey offered a playful smirk, fully comprehending her mother's anticipation. She proceeded to narrate the whirlwind events of the past few days, describing Garrett's captivating allure and sharing the pictures from his profile on Absolutely Single. Jenny appeared duly impressed by his striking features and youthful exuberance. She wholeheartedly agreed with Aubrey, affirming that his two adorable daughters possessed the same mesmerizing smiles. Aubrey confessed to her mother how utterly smitten she was, how her emotions had taken on a life of their own, with blushing, nervousness, and trembling becoming constant companions. Jenny chuckled knowingly, empathizing with these inexplicable reactions on a deeper level.

Jenny reached out, tenderly holding her daughter's hand, a smile gracing her face. "He seems like a real keeper. I've never seen you this excited about a man before."

Aubrey raised her glass, taking in the rustic aroma from the deep purple liquid. She savored the final sip, feeling its warm embrace as it cascaded down her throat. It made her lightheaded, as she was not accustomed to the effects of alcohol, having never been much of a drinker.

"He is undeniably unique. I can honestly say I've never felt this way before," she responded, gently placing her empty glass on the table.

Jenny studied her daughter, a quizzical expression adorning her face. Setting her glass down, she held Aubrey's hand, looking into her eyes as she asked, "Do you have any doubts yet?" Aubrey met her mother's intense stare, aware she would offer a cautionary lecture about not sabotaging a potentially fulfilling relationship.

Receiving feedback from her mother in matters of the heart was always challenging for Aubrey. Jenny had never remarried after her father's tragic accident, which had occurred when she was only forty. The incident left her widowed and nearly claimed her own life, resulting in severe injuries, broken bones, and traumatic head injury. She had spent months in the hospital, and it took her a whole year to physically recover.

However, the emotional wounds were far more profound. Her one true love had been ripped away, leaving a shattered heart. Jenny battled depression and anxiety, relying on medication to cope with the relentless pain that gripped her daily existence. Eventually, she found peace in returning to teaching, her most potent remedy for healing her fractured soul.

Throughout the years, Aubrey had urged her mother to date, to seek companionship and a fresh start with someone new. Although Jenny had occasionally gone out with other men, she always found flaws or excuses to cut ties, especially when things seemed to be getting serious. Aubrey, too, shared her mother's condition, finding it difficult for anyone to measure up to the boundless love her father had showered upon them.

Feeling her mother's thumb gently caressing the back of her hand, Aubrey was brought back to the present moment.

She contemplated the question again before responding, her voice sincere. "So far, no doubts. It's still new, so we'll see what unfolds. He lives in Idaho, and I'm unsure how a long-distance relationship would work."

Jenny, brushing away a few loose strands of her dark hair, acknowledged her daughter's valid concern. "Didn't you mention that he would be willing to relocate here eventually?"

Aubrey's face brightened with a smile at the recollection. "Yes, he did mention that as a strong possibility."

Her body flushed with emotions, baffling her with inexplicable reactions. Her mother giggled upon noticing her daughter's rosy cheeks. "Oh, come on, Mom!" Aubrey playfully protested, feigning hurt. "I have no idea why my body is reacting like this."

Jenny's laughter resonated, and Aubrey joined in. After a few moments, their laughter faded, and they sat in comfortable silence, enjoying each other's company and the tranquil ambiance of the patio. Aubrey closed her eyes, basking in the warmth of the sun's gentle caress, feeling blessed to have her mother's unwavering support.

Garrett and his girls were snuggled up on the bed, enjoying the simple pleasure of watching TV. The evening had been filled with laughter, tasty fried foods, and exciting activities like bowling and laser tag. Among all the thrilling experiences they shared, the unlimited laser tag stood out as the highlight of the night. They had fearlessly faced off against strangers who dared to test their skills. As they ran tirelessly throughout the laser tag arena, their shirts became soaked with sweat, a testament to their dedication and competitive spirit.

The soft glow from the television spread across the room as they watched an episode of *Impractical Jokers*. Amid the light-hearted comedy, their exhausted bodies began to unwind and relax. Garrett's jacket pocket emitted a muffled ring, catching his attention. Rolling off the bed, he reached for the phone and answered it on the fourth ring.

"This is Garrett," he greeted, unaware of the caller's identity.

"Hey Garrett," Jerry's familiar and friendly voice boomed through the phone. "Did I catch you at a bad time?"

"Not at all, Jerry," Garrett replied, slipping into his shoes and grabbing his jacket. He motioned to Jasmine and Alexa that he would be back shortly before disappearing into the hallway. As he went to the back door, he asked, "How have you been?"

"Oh, you know. Busy as usual. But I didn't call to talk about me, now did I? Tell me about your week."

A smile danced across Garrett's face. To have someone who cared for him as deeply as Jerry did made him feel accepted and like he belonged. He proceeded to recount the details of his week, starting with meeting Dave and assuming the role of his mentor. The significance of Garrett's contribution to Dave's recovery was a topic of discussion, with Jerry sharing his mentoring experiences and offering valuable advice to enhance Garrett's abilities.

Eventually, Garrett delved into his audition, explaining the feedback he had received and the possible outcomes that could result from it. Jerry applauded Garrett for having the courage to step outside his comfort zone and follow through with the appointment. And then, with heartfelt sincerity, Garrett spoke of Aubrey—of their time together, the depth of his feelings, and the attention he showered upon her. Throughout Garrett's heartfelt monologue, Jerry remained silent, allowing Garrett's emotions to pour through the phone's receiver.

When Garrett finally finished speaking, he wondered if he had lost the connection. Glancing at his phone, he realized the call was still active. "Are you still there?" he asked, surprised at his friend's absence of immediate response.

"Yes," Jerry answered quietly. "Just digesting everything you told me. She sounds like an amazing woman."

Garrett smiled, wholeheartedly agreeing with Jerry's assessment. "She is, Jerry. The emotions can sometimes be overwhelming," he confessed, yearning for Jerry's wisdom on managing his swirling feelings.

Jerry's chuckle resonated through the phone's speaker. "Well, love is a funny thing, my friend. It has a way of igniting feelings and emotions we never knew existed. Sometimes, we have to accept those feelings for what they are. There's no better advice than that, Garrett," he said, surprising Garrett with his use of the "L-word." While Garrett was undoubtedly fond of Aubrey, he questioned if it was too early to declare it as love. Interrupting Garrett's thoughts, Jerry spoke again. "When are you seeing her again?"

"We made plans to go golfing in the morning."

"That sounds like fun but do me a favor. If you go out on

Friday, take her to the beach. Women adore strolling along the waterline. It's a place where romance thrives, and opportunities to create lasting impressions exist."

"Will do. Thanks for the advice."

"You're very welcome. I'm thrilled to hear about all the wonderful things unfolding in your life. Remember to keep God your number one priority and your recovery as number two. I promise that by doing so, everything will continue to fall into place and find order in your life. I'm proud of you, Garrett." With those parting words, Jerry disconnected the call.

As Garrett glanced at his phone's screen, his attention was drawn to an unopened message from Aubrey. He tapped on it, revealing a picture message. It displayed Aubrey standing alongside a woman who bore a striking resemblance to her, albeit with a touch of age. The statement below the photo read, "Hello from the Ellis's." The image showcased the undeniable beauty of both Aubrey and her mother, highlighting the remarkable genes they shared.

Inspired by Aubrey's gesture, Garrett reciprocated by capturing a snapshot of himself with Alexa and Jasmine. Sitting between the two girls, he requested a quick pose, knowing their photogenic nature. They were well-versed in the art of selfies, spending a significant amount of their leisure time capturing moments and sharing them on various social media platforms. After a couple of attempts, Garrett managed to capture the perfect shot. With a message accompanying the photo that read, "Hello from the Andersons," he tapped the send button, watching as the image disappeared into the vast telecommunications network carried by lightning-fast technology.

THIRTEEN

The following day, Garrett sat in front of his computer, making last-minute purchases before Aubrey arrived. That morning, he sold stock from two companies, which netted him a total profit of seven hundred and thirty dollars. He had found an extremely undervalued company that he quickly reinvested his earnings into. As soon as his transaction was complete, he heard his phone ringing. He answered it as he shut down his laptop.

"Good morning, beautiful," he said, feeling his body tingle with the thought of seeing Aubrey for the fourth straight day.

"Good morning to you, handsome."

"I am on my way down. See you in a second." He hung up the phone, headed out of his room, and down the stairs to the front door.

Aubrey's body emitted a pleasurable tingling sensation when she saw Garrett emerge from the front entrance. He wore a black snugly fit polo shirt, jeans, and running sneakers.

His hair was hidden under a white hat with a prominent blue NY logo on the center front. He opened the passenger door to her Audi SUV and slid in next to her.

"Hi," he said, winking his left eye. "Thank you for offering to drive again. I feel very spoiled."

She laughed, feeling a warm affection for him. "You're welcome. It's my pleasure since you're a visitor to Connecticut."

Garrett watched her as she put the vehicle into gear, exited the parking lot, and headed towards the main road. She wore a white polo shirt, light blue shorts, and white ankle socks. For the first time, Garrett glimpsed her long, toned, silky bare legs. They were flawless, and he had to resist the urge to reach over and touch them. They looked so soft and inviting. She wore a blue visor to the middle of her forehead, and her clean, healthy-looking hair was pulled back into a ponytail.

"You look extremely hot this morning," he complimented her with desire raging from within.

"Thank you. I can say the same about you!" She gave him a shy smile that accelerated his heartbeat. She held his hand in hers but pulled it towards her leg. The back of his hand rested on her exposed inner thigh, sending a jolt of electricity up his arm and throughout his body.

Aubrey watched as Garrett blushed, feeling her cheeks flush as well. The touch of his hand on her leg sent shivers running up and down her spine.

They made small talk on the short drive to the Farmington Hills Country Club, where Aubrey was a member. Garrett paid for his club rentals, golf balls, and tees. They decided to use a cart instead of walking the course. At the first hole, Garrett politely let Aubrey tee off first. He watched in awe as Aubrey made a perfect connection with the ball, driving it straight down the fairway and landing about two hundred yards away.

"Great shot!" Garrett exclaimed, his eyes wide open and his eyebrows raised.

Aubrey loved seeing Garrett's impressed reaction to her golf game. It made her feel accomplished. Garrett then teed up his ball and prepared for his shot. He could feel Aubrey's gaze following his every movement. After several practice swings, he positioned himself and focused on the exact spot he wanted to hit. With a swing, the ball sailed away in a seemingly perfect line before unexpectedly slicing near the tree line to his left.

Garrett let a few inappropriate words slip from his throat. Aubrey laughed, finding Garrett's frustration to be cute and comical. His frustration melted away as he heard her angelic laughter. "You think that's funny?" he asked, playfully.

Aubrey embraced Garrett, touched his face, and kissed him softly. They felt an intense passion building between them, their bodies trembling with desire. Aubrey pulled away, her body still on fire. "I'm sorry for laughing, Baby. I've never heard you cuss before, and I understand how frustrating it is to slice the ball like that. But don't worry; I'm sure you'll have a chance to laugh at me too!"

Garrett pulled her close, kissing her soft, luscious lips again. They were lost in the moment's intensity until the sound of another golf cart approaching snapped them back to reality.

"We better focus on golf again, mister," Aubrey said, giving him one last kiss before hopping back into the golf cart.

She dropped him off near his ball and parked the cart on the path. Garrett watched as she hit a perfect shot with her eight-iron. He admired her graceful swing and physical features. Her talent and beauty left him mesmerized.

With his pitching wedge in hand, Garrett approached his ball and took a few practice strokes. He reminded himself to keep his head down and focused on making a clean stroke.

After connecting with the ball, Aubrey's sweet voice reached his ears. "Great shot, Garrett!"

To his delight, Garrett's ball stopped a few feet away from Aubrey's. It was becoming evident that he was a better golfer than he had let on. Aubrey found herself impressed by his many talents, wondering if there was anything he couldn't do well.

"Ladies first?" Garrett offered, swapping his wedge for a putter.

"Sure," she responded with a smile. Aubrey skillfully two-putted for par, while Garrett nearly achieved a one-putt for birdie. He ended up with a well-earned par as well. The remaining eight holes continued similarly.

Aubrey impressed Garrett with her golfing skills, while Garrett showcased his talents in different areas of the game. By the end of the nine holes, Aubrey finished three over par, and Garrett finished five over par.

After parking the cart and removing their golf bags, Garrett's phone rang. "Private number" was displayed on his phone's screen. He apologized to Aubrey, who mentioned that she didn't mind.

"Hello, this is Garrett," he spoke into his phone, trying to steady his voice. On the other end, he recognized the familiar voice of Dale Carter from Mansfield Productions.

"Hi, Garrett. This is Dale Carter. Do you have a minute to chat?"

Garrett took a deep breath, his anxiety building. "Absolutely, Dale," he managed to respond, his body trembling with nervous energy.

Aubrey, realizing the significance of the call, watched Garrett intently. She remembered Dale's name from the audition. Garrett's anxious smile mirrored his excitement and apprehension as if he were a child on the first day of school. Setting his golf bag down, he propped it up on its legs, and Aubrey placed her bag beside his, reaching out to hold his hand for support. The touch of her thumb caressing the back of his hand helped to settle his racing heart.

Garrett listened attentively as Dale relayed the purpose of the call. Dale had already informed his boss about Garrett's demo, which was well-received. Now, they were discussing the possibility of arranging a meeting for Garrett to perform another song in person. While Dale checked his boss's calendar, Garrett pondered the logistics, trying to find a reasonable solution.

"Hey, Dale. I'll be leaving early Sunday morning to go back to Idaho. It will be challenging for me to make it into the city again during this trip. Perhaps I could plan on coming back in two or three weeks. Would that be too long?" Garrett proposed, hopeful for a positive outcome.

Dale paused momentarily, considering Garrett's suggestion. "Well, Garrett, my boss is excited about you, and I'd hate to keep him waiting too long. You're staying in Simsbury, right?"

Garrett's curiosity was piqued. "Yes, I am," he replied, eager to find out where the conversation was heading.

Aubrey's anxiety grew as she felt her sweaty hands caressing the back of Garrett's hand. She couldn't shake off the nagging feeling that waiting a few weeks might not be the best course of action. Opportunities like these are rare, especially in such a fiercely competitive industry. She understood the significance of being discovered and recognized how fortunate he was to be in this position.

Listening closely, Aubrey observed Garrett agreeing to whatever Dale was proposing. Finally, Garrett bid farewell to Dale and shifted his focus back to her. Their eyes met, and Aubrey could see the excitement and uncertainty in his expression. She wanted to voice her concerns but hesitated, not wanting to dampen his spirits.

He spoke softly as he stared into Aubrey's stunning blue eyes. "His boss, Walter, has a weekend home in Avon," Garrett revealed. "He wants me to stop by and meet him Saturday night. He owns a grand piano and wants me to play for him."

Aubrey's expression transformed from tense to pure joy in an instant. She wrapped her arms around Garrett's neck and kissed him passionately. This ignited a fire, and they lost themselves in each other's arms. Time ceased to exist, and the world around them faded away.

When their lips finally parted, Garrett slowly opened his eyes. Aubrey's eyes remained closed as if she was suspended in a state of bliss. The intensity of their kiss had left them both breathless. It was a moment of pure magic, an experience unlike any other. As her eyes fluttered open, Garrett noticed they were a deepening shade of blue.

Blushing, they realized that others had been observing their passionate display. Aubrey giggled, breaking the spell, and collected her belongings, urging Garrett to meet her at the car. She tossed her golf clubs into the trunk and swiftly changed into more comfortable shoes. Garrett joined her in the car as she started the engine.

She stole a glance at him, enamored by his striking features. His hat was off, allowing his dark hair to cascade over his ears. "I'm proud of you, Garrett," she expressed, intertwining her fingers with his. "You're an extraordinary man, and I'm grateful you chose to spend your free time with me."

As she spoke, Garrett felt a surge of warmth and affection. Their connection was undeniably unique, and he sensed that Aubrey also recognized it. Memories of Jerry's advice from the previous night surfaced as he watched the air conditioner gently tousle Aubrey's hair.

"Can I see you tomorrow? It'll probably be the last time I see you during this trip."

"Of course," Aubrey replied, a smile forming. She didn't want him to leave; she had just found him, and the thought of being separated weighed on her. A glimmer of hope crossed her mind, however. Michael, her agent, had agreed to give her one night in Boise. She hadn't shared this news with Garrett yet, hoping it wouldn't clash with any plans he had already made. She decided to reveal it the next day.

Garrett wanted to keep their plans for the following day a surprise. He informed Aubrey that he would pick her up the next morning at nine sharp. She gave him her address, playfully warning him about her colossal home. With one final magical goodnight kiss, Garrett entered the 1818 Estate.

That night, Garrett returned to his prison cell. His dream picked up right where his flashback had left off. He stood there, anxiously watching as everyone's eyes bore into him, sensing an imminent assault. But instead of facing gang members, the unit door swung open with a resounding bang, and correctional officers flooded in, yelling for everyone to get down.

While the rest of the inmates obediently dropped to the floor, Garrett remained standing, defying the orders. Five guards rushed toward him, their voices growing more desperate. Ignoring their commands, he resumed his original workout routine, impervious to their attempts to bring him down. It took all five guards and a lot of mace to subdue him. Eventually, they cuffed him and escorted him to the dreaded hole—solitary confinement.

Garrett took the blame for the incident, but the head correctional officer was skeptical of his story. The unit was notorious for gang activity and he had witnessed Garrett's reclusive behavior. Reviewing the fragmented video footage, which showed only glimpses of the altercation obscured by other inmates, the officer sought to pressure Garrett into signing a statement that would implicate his attackers.

Refusing to cooperate, Garrett endured a thirty-day sentence in solitary confinement. Upon his return to the original unit, tension hung in the air, heavy as the sweltering heat of a

Florida summer day. He went to his cell, stowed away his few belongings, and braced himself for the next wave of violence.

Surprisingly, Garrett enjoyed inflicting pain on his three assailants more than he expected. Each punch, kick, elbow, and knee connecting with bone and flesh evoked exhilarating rage. It became almost therapeutic as if it were mending or masking his inner turmoil. He craved more of it, leading him back to the unit where it all began. Returning to the lion's den seemed like an invitation for further confrontations.

It didn't take long for members of the SHFL gang to appear at Garrett's cell door. They requested his presence, stating that Ty, their leader, wished to speak with him. Surprisingly, they showed him respect instead of aggression. Respect, or rather power, was a newfound sensation that Garrett appreciated.

Guided by the four members, Garrett walked to the day room where Ty sat alone at a small metal table in the center. Garrett sat across from him while the others positioned themselves nearby, ready to offer protection.

Ty bore prison tattoos, marked by their distinctive pea-green color. Inmates fashioned makeshift tattoo guns using melted plastic, with guitar strings as needles. Ty's head was shaved, and a well-groomed brown beard framed his face. A prominent scar ran across his left cheekbone.

Rumors circulated among inmates about Ty's charges. They whispered that he had been convicted of first-degree murder for killing his wife and her lover in a fit of rage after discovering their infidelity. They claimed that he found them naked in his very own bed, and with his bare hands and feet, he had beaten them so brutally that their hearts ceased to beat.

Ty locked eyes with Garrett, emanating an intimidating glare that would make others tremble in fear. Unfazed, Garrett maintained eye contact, refusing to be intimidated by this stranger. He was ready to engage in another dance of violence, longing for the opportunity to harm another human being. After a minute of tense silence, Ty finally spoke.

"Do you know who I am?" Ty asked with authority.

Garrett smirked, feigning annoyance. "No, I don't. Why don't you enlighten me?"

"My name is Ty, and I lead the SHFL gang, also known as 'Skinheads for Life.' Last month, you assaulted three of my members. They ended up in the infirmary for weeks."

Garrett's cold heart stirred. "You've got it all wrong," he retorted. "I didn't attack them. They got in the way of my workout and came at me. Don't act ignorant, Ty. You know exactly how it went down."

Ty's eyes twitched with anger, his face contorting. He glanced at his soldiers, a silent signal passing between them.

"Let's get one thing straight, homie. If you ever disrespect me like that again, I'll send every one of my boys after you. You may fight well, but I promise you, your body will be beaten and battered so badly that the infirmary may become your permanent home. And even if you survive, you'll likely be a vegetable for the rest of your pathetic life. Understand?"

Garrett knew deep down that Ty was right. These men fought dirty and showed no mercy. They would likely resort to weapons if they needed to overwhelm him with sheer numbers. Ambushing others was an everyday activity among gang members.

"Understood," Garrett replied, choosing to show respect rather than defiance to the man who held the keys to such a robust prison enterprise.

"Good. Now, we can talk like men. I'm not happy with what happened. Normally, you'd be in a body bag by now. But I heard about what you did, how you refused to spill the truth to those filthy pigs. You spent extra time in the hole for that, right?"

"I did."

"And you requested to be placed back in this unit despite the COs advising against it?"

"Absolutely."

"You've got balls, my friend. Most men wouldn't dare to do what you've done. I'm also impressed by your fighting skills. Where did you learn to fight like that?"

As Garrett sat across from Ty, memories of Matt flooded his mind. They had been inseparable, studying martial arts together since childhood and forging a deep friendship. Their weekly sparring sessions had been intense, pushing each other to their limits. As they grew older, they made a pact to explore more lethal and defensive techniques to enhance their skills and protect themselves. While they had earned black belts in Kung Fu at sixteen, they felt that commercialized martial arts fell short of their aspirations.

Instead, they embarked on a journey, attending various martial arts schools to learn different styles and absorb as much knowledge as possible. Together, they would practice and refine what they had learned, pushing each other until they mastered each technique.

The thought of Matt sent a sharp pang of sorrow through Garrett's chest, quickly transforming into a fit of burning anger. It was a defense mechanism, a coping tool his body had developed to shield him from pain.

"I have studied martial arts and practiced the skills I learned most of my life," Garrett responded, acknowledging Ty's observation.

Ty offered Garrett a place within the SHFL group, emphasizing its power and influence inside and outside the prison walls. Despite his lack of interest in joining, Garrett couldn't deny his curiosity about the potential for violence that came with such an offer.

Garrett replied respectfully, suppressing his amusement, "Ty, I genuinely appreciate your offer and respect your position. However, I have no desire to be part of any gang, including yours."

Ty's disappointment was evident, but before he could express his thoughts, Garrett interjected, wanting to learn more. "I am curious about the expectations and requirements for your members."

This piqued Ty's interest, and he explained, "We prioritize the well-being of our own. As a group, we ensure that the prison runs smoothly. Anyone who disrespects us, or non-members we protect, faces consequences. We give them a green light as a symbol that designates them as a target for any member. If no one volunteers, we assign the mission to the newest recruits. They must complete three missions before officially joining the gang. However, considering what I witnessed, I wouldn't require that for you."

Garrett had heard rumors and whispers about the concept of green lights and missions among inmates, and an idea began to take shape in his mind—an idea that could serve both of their interests.

"Ty, I won't join your gang, but I have a proposition for you," Garrett declared. Ty's eyes pleaded for him to continue. "I want to unleash hell on those who truly deserve it—men with questionable charges, poor behavior, or a lack of respect for others. These individuals should not be allowed to live in our homes. I will be your right-hand man, handling your most significant issues. I'll take care of any missions you assign. I do this for myself alone, but exclusively for SHFL. However, I must clarify one thing: I'm out when I decide to stop, just like that. If you agree, we can start taking care of business."

Ty's face contorted into a wicked grin, clearly pleased with Garrett's proposition. He reached out his hand across the table, sealing the agreement, and said, "You're one crazy son of a bitch; we've got a deal!"

Garrett took a deep breath, trying to calm his racing heart. The vividness of the nightmare clung to his mind, refusing to let go. He reached for a glass of water on his bedside table and took a sip, hoping to soothe his parched throat.

He gained control of his breathing as he glanced at the peaceful faces of his daughters sleeping soundly. They were his anchor, source of strength, and motivation to overcome the haunting memories that plagued him. They represented his freedom, his sanctuary from the prison walls that still haunted his dreams.

PTSD was a relentless companion, a constant reminder of his trauma. The nightmares and flashbacks were like phantom chains, attempting to pull him back into the darkness of his past. But he refused to succumb to their grip. He had come too far to let his demons control him.

In the quiet of the early morning, he made a silent promise to himself. He would continue to face his demons head-on, to confront the nightmares and memories that threatened to consume him. For the sake of his girls and his well-being, he would keep working through the symptoms of his PTSD, one day at a time.

Garrett closed his eyes, allowing the warmth of his daughters' presence to guide his thoughts. Today was a new day, another opportunity to embrace the freedom he had fought so hard to reclaim. As he drifted back to sleep, he held onto the hope that the nightmares would gradually fade, replaced by the serenity of peaceful dreams.

FOURTEEN

The following day, Garrett used the navigation app on his smartphone to find Aubrey's home. He followed the narrow, tree-lined road up the mountain, marveling at the gigantic houses he passed along the way. Finally, his GPS announced that his destination was on the right, and he spotted Aubrey's house number on a square stone mailbox next to a long cement driveway.

As Garrett parked his silver four-door rental car, he couldn't help but feel insecure staring at Aubrey's impressive home. Her books had achieved more success than she had let on. Just as he was about to follow the path to the large wooden door, Aubrey suddenly was visible and seemed to float like an angel in his direction.

She looked breathtaking in her tight ankle-length jeans accentuating her long, sculpted legs and a black cashmere sweater that hugged her trim upper body. Her black leather sandals and straight, radiant hair completed the picture-perfect image. As she approached with a smile, Garrett felt his breath catch in his throat.

"Good morning, Sunshine!" Garrett greeted her, his heart racing as she stopped and hugged him before getting into the passenger seat.

She could smell his unique scent—a mixture of body wash, cologne, and his natural smell—which stirred a wild desire within her. Garrett shut the door and walked around the front of the car to the driver's side. Aubrey admired how his jeans perfectly fit his hips and how his zip-up black hooded sweatshirt and white and black hat complemented each other, showcasing his fashionable yet understated style.

As Garrett got into the car, she couldn't contain her excitement. "So, where are we headed?" she asked, grabbing his free hand and placing it on her thigh.

"I'm taking you to Mystic Beach," Garrett replied, a proud smile on his face. Spending time together at the beach felt incredibly romantic to him.

Aubrey's heart skipped a beat at the mention of the beach. "That sounds lovely."

"I'm glad you approve!" Garrett replied, reversing out of Aubrey's driveway. "Nice house, by the way!" He raised his eyebrows, gesturing towards her grand colonial home.

Feeling slightly embarrassed about the extravagant expenditure, Aubrey asked, "Do you think it's too much? Like maybe I'm overcompensating for something?" She surprised herself with her vulnerability, as she rarely opened up like this.

"Not at all, Aubrey. You've worked hard to achieve your

goals, and your success is well-deserved. If a big, beautiful home is your way of rewarding yourself, congratulations! I love it. And I hope someday I'll get a tour of it."

Aubrey's cheeks flushed as she squeezed his hand, feeling the familiar energy between them intensify. "I would like that," she replied. She knew that sharing her home with him would be a special moment.

"Tell me about it." He wanted to understand the significance of her home, not just because he had seen it, but because he wanted to know what it meant to her.

Aubrey began describing every intricate detail, leaving nothing out. She spoke passionately about the luxurious cook's kitchen, the elegant crown molding, and the overall design and ambiance of the house. Garrett listened intently, asking questions when he needed clarification, genuinely interested in understanding her world.

When Aubrey finished, it was Garrett's turn to share. He spoke of his fondness for large, modern homes and shared stories of his previous experiences, including the home he shared with Julie. They discovered a commonality in their taste for interior design, deepening their connection. Garrett expressed his desire to own a home again someday once he found a place to settle down, and he described his apartment in downtown Boise, highlighting the breathtaking views it offered. Aubrey's excitement to visit Boise the following weekend grew stronger as she listened.

Not long after, they arrived at the empty parking lot near their destination. Hand in hand, they strolled along the beach for over an hour, sharing their future goals and dreams. As hunger set in, Garrett retrieved a blanket and a large grocery bag from the trunk of his rental car. He spread the blanket on the sand near the water's edge and pulled out two wrapped sandwiches.

"I have smoked turkey with cheddar or ham and provolone," Garrett offered, holding up the subs in each hand.

"I'll take the turkey, please," Aubrey replied, unwrapping the paper and placing it neatly in front of her. Garrett handed her a personal-sized bag of potato chips, a napkin, and bottled water.

"I have a surprise for you once we're finished," Garrett declared.

They sat together, savoring their food and reveling in each other's company. The crashing waves and the calls of seagulls filled the air around them. A cool ocean breeze created a shiver in Aubrey's arms and legs. She marveled at how Garrett seemed to know her love for the ocean, even though she had never mentioned it to him. His romantic gestures left her mesmerized. After they finished their lunch, Garrett handed her a champagne flute and pulled out a bottle of sparkling cider.

Seeing the surprise on her face, he quickly spoke up. "I know real champagne would have been more romantic," he admitted, his cheeks reddening. "But I don't drink. I'm in recovery from alcoholism." He braced himself, hoping this revelation wouldn't be a deal breaker for her. He held the bottle, fumbling with the foil covering the corkscrew, feeling the weight of his confession.

Aubrey looked at him with genuine appreciation in her eyes. "I admire your honesty, Garrett," she said softly. "Opening up about our weaknesses is never easy. It takes much courage.

I respect you even more for sharing one of yours." Her smile dissolved the insecurities that had crept into Garrett's mind.

"My father was an alcoholic," Aubrey revealed, holding Garrett's hand tightly. "He was very involved in a program called Daily Recovery. Have you heard of it?"

"Yes, that program has helped me maintain my sobriety. It has truly saved my life in so many ways."

Aubrey watched Garrett remove the foil and uncork the bottle, producing a satisfying pop sound and a misty release. He poured her half a glass, mirroring the action for himself.

"Here's a toast to us, Aubrey. I don't know what the future may hold, but if this week was any indication of what it could be, I've never been more excited for it to unfold," Garrett raised his glass. "To living one day at a time."

Their glasses clinked together, producing a delightful sound. "One day at a time," Aubrey responded, and they both tilted their glasses, savoring the effervescent, amber liquid.

Garrett gently took her glass and set them both aside near the edge of the blanket.

"Thank you for all of this," Aubrey said, gesturing toward the ocean, the beach, the blanket, and the remnants of their picnic.

"You're welcome," Garrett said, rising to his feet and extending his hand to Aubrey. She accepted his offer, allowing him to help her, their hands interlocking. A flicker of fire danced in his eyes as he spoke softly, "Come with me; I have one more surprise."

Hand in hand, they strolled towards the weathered wooden dock, its grayish hue tinged with a hint of dark green. Stretching thirty feet into the water, it led them to a circular wooden structure enclosed by three-foot plank walls, creating an intimate sanctuary.

As they reached the end of the dock, the scent of saltwater filled Aubrey's nostrils. Garrett reached into his pocket, retrieving a pair of earbuds. Skillfully, he plugged them into his phone, placing one blue and white earpiece in Aubrey's right ear, the other in his own. Tapping on his phone's screen, a soft and exquisite melody began to flow into her ears, its familiar tune elusive.

"What song is this?" Aubrey inquired. They swayed together, their bodies moving in sync, guided by the music and the symphony of ocean waves.

Garrett's lips brushed against her ear as he whispered, "It's 'Viva La Vida' by Coldplay, but The Two Cellos perform this version." Aubrey had never heard of the duo before, yet their harmonious melody resonated with the atmosphere perfectly. The cellos danced harmoniously above the dark gray water, encapsulating the moment's magic.

In their close embrace, Aubrey felt the warmth radiating from Garrett's body. Resting her head against his chest, she wrapped her arms around him, appreciating the moment of togetherness. It was a bond that continued to astound her, surpassing every boundary and stirring a storm of emotions within.

When the song reached its final notes, Aubrey looked into Garrett's eyes, noticing the subtle shifts in their hue, reflecting his ever-changing moods. He cupped her face gently with both hands, caressing her cheeks, and leaned in, their eyes closing as their lips met. Raging desire coursed through Aubrey's veins, her muscles tightening with longing. Her hands roamed his body, reaching the back of his head, entangling in his hair. Their kiss deepened, their tongues entwining, igniting a firestorm of passion that consumed them both.

Reluctantly, they broke apart, their hands still clasped as Aubrey held onto Garrett's neck. Her voice quivered as she revealed her deepest fears, tears brimming in her eyes. "I don't want you to go, Garrett," she confessed, struggling to hold back her emotions, a reservoir of tears ready to spill at any moment. His gaze held a newfound intensity, his warmth unwavering.

"I don't want to leave either," Garrett replied, pulling her closer and seeking comfort in their embrace. Unable to contain her emotions any longer, Aubrey's tears flowed freely as she sought consolation against his chest.

Garrett held her tenderly, his touch soothing, his fingers gently caressing her back and running through her hair. Inhaling deeply, he committed her scent to memory, cherishing every remaining moment they had left. He yearned for this instant to stretch into eternity, nurturing the hope that they could overcome any obstacles that lay ahead.

Taking a deep breath, Aubrey composed herself, attempting to regain control over her emotions. It was the opportune moment to discuss her upcoming travel plans. She glanced at Garrett shyly, wiping away the remaining tears from her face. Sensing her unease, he reached into his jacket, retrieved a napkin, and handed it to her. She gratefully accepted it, using it to dab at her tears and blow her nose, gathering the courage to share her news.

"I have something to ask you," Aubrey said, gripping his hands tightly. "My new book, 'Night and Day,' will be released on Monday. I'll embark on a four-week promotional tour on the East Coast next week. But here's the exciting part—I can make a quick trip to Boise next Saturday night. Would you like that?"

She studied Garrett's expression, hoping to decipher his thoughts from the subtle cues. At first, he seemed enigmatic, his emotions veiled. But then, his eyes lit up, and a broad smile spread across his face.

"Oh, baby, that's incredible news!" he exclaimed enthusiastically. Cupping her face with his hands, he leaned in, planting a soft kiss on her lips. "So, we'll have two days and a night together?"

"Yes," Aubrey replied, her previous sadness replaced by pure joy at his reaction. "I'll arrive around noon and won't leave until eight the following evening."

"I can't wait to show you Idaho," Garrett said, retrieving the dangling earbuds and tucking them back into his pocket.

"Where do you suggest I rent a room?" Aubrey inquired, feeling a blush warm her cheeks uncontrollably.

Garrett pondered for a moment, a mischievous glint in his eyes, before responding, "I highly recommend the old Owyhee Plaza Hotel. Don't worry; I'll take care of your reservations." His playful nature added a touch of lightheartedness to the conversation.

"That sounds lovely," Aubrey replied, savoring his playful spirit. She walked alongside him, their steps carrying them back towards the beach where their picnic supplies awaited. The coming week couldn't come soon enough, she thought, her heart brimming with joy for the moments they would share in the enchanting city of Boise.

On the drive home, Garrett and Aubrey excitedly discussed the possibilities that awaited them in Boise. They delved into the attractions, scenic spots, and local favorites, imagining the memories they would create together in the vibrant city. Their conversation effortlessly flowed, devoid of any need to assert control or talk over each other. It was as if they had been together for years, their connection defying the short time they had spent in each other's lives.

As the clock ticked, they finally arrived at Aubrey's house a little after four. Aubrey turned towards Garrett, a jaw-dropping smile lighting up her face. "Do you have time to tour the house with me?"

"I would love to, Aubrey. Unfortunately, I need to pick up the girls and their friends for our big 'Frightmares' expedition," Garrett explained, disappointment evident in his tone.

Aubrey understood the situation, realizing he hadn't yet shared their new romance with his daughters. She respected his decision and knew they would have their time together in the future.

"I understand," she whispered. "Wait here; I have a going-away present for you." With that, she quickly left the car and entered her house. Aubrey headed straight to her office, where she had stored the special gift. She retrieved a small gray bag from the top of her desk, filled with something she knew he would appreciate.

Returning to the front drive, Aubrey handed Garrett the bag. Curious, he looked at her as he accepted the gift, not knowing what to expect. With a smile, he opened the bag and pulled out four books, sifting through them. Recognition dawned on his face, and he held the books before him. "Your books!"

"I promised I would give you copies if we made it past two dates," she reminded him, winking playfully. Moving closer to him, she added, "I hope you enjoy them."

Garrett placed the books back in the bag, keeping them on the passenger seat. He looked at Aubrey with gratitude. "Thank you, Aubrey. I am excited to read them," he expressed, genuinely intrigued by the opportunity to explore her talents and gain a deeper understanding of her world through her writing.

Aubrey nestled closer to Garrett, savoring their final moments together. "You have a copy of my new book before it has even been released. Hopefully, that helps you understand how special you are to me."

Garrett's heart swelled as her words resonated within him. He held her tightly. "You mean so much to me, too, baby. I can't wait to see you again."

They shared a slow, tender kiss, relishing each lingering moment. Aubrey stood at the driveway's edge, watching as Garrett backed out and eventually disappeared from her view. As she walked back into her large, empty home, she remembered his touch, the taste of his kiss, and his scent on her skin. She knew it would be a challenging week ahead, longing for the time when they could be together again.

Jasmine, Alexa, Maddy, and Isabelle waited for Garrett's arrival at Julie's house, excited for the evening's festivities. After quickly stopping at the 1818 Estate to pick up supplies, they hit the road toward their destination. The reviews had hailed it as one of the scariest places in New England, and the girls were thrilled to experience it for themselves.

Jasmine took her place in the front seat, assuming the role of the "DJ." The car was filled with the sounds of music as she carefully selected songs to set the mood. The four girls sang along enthusiastically, their voices blending in a harmonious chorus. Laughter filled the air as they shared jokes and gossip about boys they liked in their grade. It was a carefree and spirited atmosphere that Garrett loved, enjoying the sight of his daughters in their element, surrounded by their friends.

As the miles passed, the conversation veered into unexpected territories, revealing the interests and passions of the girls that Garrett hadn't been aware of before. Time seemed to fly as they traveled together, engrossed in the music, laughter, and conversations. Before they knew it, they arrived at their destination, ready to face the frights that awaited them at the haunted venue. The girls and Garrett stepped out of the car with fear and excitement.

As they waited in line to enter the haunted building, the atmosphere grew more eerie and suspenseful. Employees dressed in terrifying costumes roamed the area, intentionally startling the guests with unexpected scares. One particular encounter with a little girl covered in white makeup, her face adorned with gory wounds, sent a collective scream through the group, including Garrett. The girl's appearance and the unexpected screams gave him the chills, making him question whether the girl's costume or the startled reaction unnerved him the most.

Amid the crowd, Garrett noticed that many people around them were closer in age to Jasmine, Alexa, and their friends than his own. The girls caught the attention of a group of young boys, and the flirtatious exchange began. Feeling somewhat protective of his little angels, Garrett stepped in and introduced himself to the boys, wanting to ensure they treated his daughters and their friends respectfully.

He shook the boys' hands, engaging them in polite conversation and introducing them to the girls. Nervousness and shyness seemed to take hold as they exchanged pleasantries, discussing their origins and expressing excitement about the haunted building they were about to explore. After the initial introductions, Garrett observed as the boys and girls retreated to their respective groups, but now with raised voices, attempting to communicate indirectly with each other.

At that moment, Garrett experienced a bittersweet realization. It was his first time witnessing his daughters' interest in boys firsthand. A well of sadness emerged from an unfamiliar place, acknowledging the passage of time and the realization that his girls had grown up faster than he had anticipated. Reflecting on his lost years while in prison, he understood the significance of the moments he had missed and the realization that Jasmine and Alexa had blossomed into young women before his eyes.

Finally, after waiting almost an hour, it was their turn to enter the haunted playground. The group stepped inside, and the door closed behind them, immersing them in darkness and suspense. The rooms they entered were intricately themed, each designed to raise the hairs on the back of your neck. At every turn, costumed employees lurked, ready to pounce and startle the unsuspecting guests.

Jump scares and spine-chilling surprises awaited them at every corner, eliciting screams and gasps from the girls. The adrenaline rushed through their veins as their hearts pounded in their chests. The fear was short-lived but intense, creating an exhilarating experience that left them both terrified and thrilled.

Despite the sheer fright, Garrett and the girls emerged from the haunted playground with impressed smiles. They appreciated the attention to detail and the efforts put into creating a truly immersive and memorable experience. It was a brief but intense adventure that brought them closer together, filled with shared screams and laughter that would be remembered for years.

On returning to Connecticut, Garrett and the four girls stopped at a restaurant. They settled into an oversized booth, and Garrett observed as the girls pulled out their smartphones, capturing moments and uploading them to an app called Click. Each photo was met with laughter and quick evaluations before being shared with their virtual audience.

Garrett chuckled as their laughter occasionally startled nearby guests, prompting him to remind them to keep the noise level down. He was amazed at how seamlessly they navigated the world of social media, effortlessly capturing and sharing.

As the girls chatted, their conversation revolved around the boys they liked and disliked, and Garrett listened attentively. They seemed to have an encyclopedic knowledge of their classmates, enthusiastically discussing details and opinions about each one. Garrett mistakenly asked if they could name every classmate, which sparked a determined mission for the girls to prove their knowledge. Throughout the rest of the evening, Garrett listened as they rattled off random names, realizing the extent of their social connections.

After dropping Maddy and Isabelle off at their homes, Garrett returned to the 1818 Estate with Jasmine and Alexa. Exhausted from the long drive and eventful evening, they quickly prepared for bed. As Garrett lay down, thoughts of Aubrey filled his mind, and he yearned to see her one last time before he left. Determined to make it happen, he invited her to the audition at Walter's house the following evening. With that comforting thought, Garrett drifted to sleep, anticipating the coming days.

CHAPTER

FIFTEEN

The following day passed by in a whirlwind of activities. After a satisfying breakfast, Garrett and the girls shopped at a nearby mall. They had their hearts set on getting new sneakers, so they visited several shoe stores until they found the perfect pairs that matched their tastes. Garrett was delighted to support their choices and made sure they left with their desired brands.

Not stopping at footwear, they also explored a clothing store to update their winter wardrobes. Together, they picked out cozy sweaters, jackets, and accessories to keep them warm during the upcoming colder months. Trying on different outfits and seeking Garrett's opinion, the girls found great joy in finding stylish and comfortable clothes for the winter season.

After their shopping spree, it was time for lunch. They opted for sushi, a shared favorite, and indulged in various sushi rolls while engaging in lively conversations. The girls shared stories from school and giggled over the latest gossip among their friends.

With satisfied appetites, they made their way to the nearby movie theater. They chose to watch a popular romantic comedy, immersing themselves in the film's lighthearted humor and heartfelt moments. The laughter echoed through the theater as they leaned in close, savoring the simple pleasures of being together.

After the movie ended, Garrett led his girls to a round white table in the foyer of the movie theater. They sat down, their excitement still fresh from the enjoyable movie they had watched.

Garrett cleared his throat, ready to share his secret with them. "I have something important to tell you, girls," he began, his voice plagued with anxiety. Jasmine and Alexa exchanged curious glances, waiting for him to continue.

"I've recently started dating someone," he said, his eyes meeting theirs, searching for their reactions. Their faces lit up with surprise, their smiles growing wider.

"That's fantastic, Dad!" Jasmine exclaimed, her eyes shining with joy.

Alexa nodded enthusiastically. "It's about time you found someone special!"

Garrett felt a rush of emotions. His daughters' support meant the world to him. He continued, telling them about Aubrey, her profession as an author, and the connection they had formed.

"Her name is Aubrey Ellis. We've spent a good amount of time together this week while you two were attending school."

Jasmine and Alexa's eyes widened. "Wait, you're dating Aubrey Ellis?" Jasmine asked, her voice filled with awe.

Alexa nodded a big smile on her face. "Wow, Dad! She's one of my favorite authors. I can't believe you're dating her!"

Garrett smiled, relieved and thrilled that his daughters already had a positive impression of her. He knew this would make their meeting even more special.

"I'm glad you both know and admire her work. As you already know, we are headed to Walter's house, and you'll have a chance to meet her in person."

They exchanged excited looks, their curiosity piqued. "We can't wait to meet her, Dad!"

They left the theater and the girls were prepared to meet the woman who had captured their father's heart and their imagination through her books.

Garrett drove his daughters to a beautiful colonial-style home owned by Walter. The exterior boasted a white and blue facade on a spacious lot. As Garrett rang the doorbell, a distinguished man in his early sixties greeted them with a warm smile. Walter wore a neatly pressed white button-up shirt, gray slacks, and polished black shoes. His silver hair added an air of sophistication as it glistened in the evening sun.

"Hello there, Garrett," Walter said, extending his hand. "And who do we have here? These must be your lovely daughters, Jasmine and Alexa."

The girls shook Walter's hand one by one, their eyes filled with curiosity. "Nice to meet you, Walter," Jasmine said politely.

Garrett thanked Walter for his hospitality, expressing his

gratitude for making this gathering possible. Walter assured him it was his pleasure and led them inside the house.

The interior revealed a modern yet cozy theme. Dark wood floors graced the spacious rooms, while the walls were adorned with muted, neutral colors. In the kitchen, a group of well-dressed individuals conversed, their voices blending with the clinking of glasses and soft music playing in the background.

Walter cleared his throat, gaining everyone's attention. "May I have your attention, please? Our special guests, Garrett, Jasmine, and Alexa Anderson, have arrived."

Warm smiles and nods welcomed them, embracing their presence among the attendees. Garrett observed that the gathering consisted of Walter's close friends, all sharing a similar age range and refined elegance.

"Thank you for the warm welcome. I'm grateful to be here tonight. I look forward to sharing some music with all of you." He turned to Walter. "Thanks, Walter," Garrett's voice quivered with nervous energy. "I have a friend joining us shortly," he explained, not wanting to begin without Aubrey. Just as he finished speaking, a sweet melody floated down from above.

"That must be your friend," Walter commented, excusing himself to greet Aubrey at the door. Within moments, Aubrey's radiant presence filled the room. The fluttering butterflies in Garrett's stomach transformed into a warm sensation in his chest, a feeling he only experienced when she was near.

"Hi, Garrett," she greeted him. He admired her stunning appearance from head to toe. She wore an elegant black cashmere sweater that hugged her body down to her mid-thighs, gray leggings, and knee-high boots. Diamond-studded earrings adorned her ears, and a silver diamond pendant hung delicately from her neck.

"Thank you for coming, Aubrey," Garrett expressed gratefully. "I'd like you to meet my daughters, Jasmine and Alexa." The girls embraced her enthusiastically, and Aubrey was enraptured by their beauty in person. Their pictures had only hinted at the full extent of their charm. As they released their hugs, Jasmine and Alexa showered Aubrey with heartfelt compliments about her beauty, style, and books.

Walter had tactfully stepped aside, allowing the girls and Aubrey to become acquainted. He reappeared upon hearing their discussion about her books.

"Are you Aubrey Ellis, by any chance?" Walter inquired curiously.

Aubrey's cheeks flushed. "Yes, that's me," she confirmed.

"It's truly a pleasure meeting you. You're making quite a name for yourself here. Congratulations on your well-deserved success." Walter's voice echoed through the air again. "Attention, everyone. We have the pleasure of having an extraordinary guest with us tonight. Let me introduce you to the esteemed author and beloved Connecticut native, Aubrey Ellis."

Garrett's heart swelled with pride as he joined the enthusiastic applause, his eyes never leaving Aubrey. Jasmine and Alexa's cheers rang out, their excitement evident as they wholeheartedly accepted her as the new woman in Garrett's life.

After the applause subsided, Walter graciously offered

drinks and refreshments to his guests. Aubrey and Garrett politely declined, while Jasmine and Alexa happily accepted glasses of flavored sparkling water.

Walter's voice resonated through the room again, drawing attention to the grand piano nestled in the corner. The guests had gathered eagerly, their excitement boiling over. Garrett exchanged a glance with his three girls, their loving smiles giving him the reassurance he needed.

Navigating through the crowd, Garrett settled onto the cushioned piano bench, feeling a sense of tranquility as his gaze encompassed his daughters within his line of sight. Their unwavering support and affection reminded him that their love transcended any performance.

"I've composed a song dedicated to these two amazing ladies standing before me. It's the first time they'll hear it. I present you with, 'Airplanes.'"

The room fell silent, awaiting when Garrett's fingers would meet the piano keys. Then, a tender melody emanated from the instrument, filling the space with a heartfelt tune. Aubrey observed Garrett from across the piano, captivated by the music that seemed to flow effortlessly from him. His black hair was neatly styled, and he wore a simple yet stylish ensemble— an athletic sweatshirt and faded jeans, emphasizing his rugged charm. It was as if he had been sculpted by destiny itself.

Garrett's voice resounded, weaving a spell that enveloped everyone in attendance. Jasmine and Alexa stood on either side of Aubrey, their hands seeking hers simultaneously. The song's lyrics unveiled a poignant narrative—a father's unwavering love for his distant daughters, symbolized by his relentless pursuit through traveling and airplanes.

The seamless blend of Garrett's voice and the melodic notes painted a breathtaking picture. Aubrey glanced at Walter, hoping to witness his immersion in the spellbinding moment that had entranced the room. With closed eyes, Walter seemed lost in the symphony, his face portraying an enigmatic expression. The music stirred emotions, evoking tears from various corners of the room, including the two girls standing beside her. Overwhelmed, tears cascaded down her cheeks, realizing that Garrett's daughters were experiencing the depth of love embedded in his composition. Sharing this intimate moment with them made her feel a profound connection.

Others in the room glanced toward the trio, sensing the rarity and beauty of the scene unfolding before their eyes. Garrett's eyes met his daughters', and he felt an explosion of emotions engulf him. Their tear-filled eyes and radiant smiles tugged at his heartstrings, enveloping him in a sea of love and pride. With a deep breath, he found comfort in the fact that he could continue his performance. Though a lump formed in his throat, he allowed the music to guide him, his fingers dancing in harmony with his voice. It felt like he had finally discovered his true purpose, his natural talent shining through. This song held immense significance, potentially shaping his future in music. With every ounce of passion, emotion, and conviction, he poured himself into the melody, leaving nothing behind. Knowing he had given it his all, he vowed to have no regrets. No looking back and staring at the past.

As the music gradually concluded, an unwelcome silence settled over the room. Garrett sat on the piano bench, his eyes fixed on the hands that had poured their heart and soul into the performance. Looking up, he met the radiant expressions on his daughters' faces, their smiles reflecting their pride and love. Soft claps emerged, increasing as the assembled guests acknowledged the song's end. Applause, whistles, and heartfelt congratulations echoed through the space, directed towards Garrett. Rising from the bench, he gracefully bowed toward the crowd, accepting their praise.

Aubrey couldn't contain her pride and admiration for Garrett's incredible talent. The song he had composed touched her soul, and she was in awe of the depth of his creativity. As she observed the faces of the strangers around her, their eyes shimmered with appreciation and recognition of the exceptional artist they had just witnessed.

Amid the crowd, Walter approached Garrett, his face adorned with a warm smile and contagious excitement. They exchanged a handshake, and Walter whispered something in Garrett's ear before excusing himself momentarily. Garrett walked around the piano, joining Aubrey and his daughters.

"So, what did you think?"

"Oh, Dad, it was amazing!" Jasmine exclaimed.

"The most beautiful song I have ever heard," admitted Alexa, a single teardrop still glistening on her cheek. They released their grip on Aubrey's hand and embraced their father passionately.

"Thank you, girls. Your love for it makes me incredibly happy."

Aubrey reached for her phone in that heartfelt moment, determined to capture the essence of their shared love. "Hey, guys, look at me and smile," she exclaimed, holding her phone and snapping several pictures.

"Thank you, Aubrey," Garrett responded, his eyes piercing her, leaving her breathless. The intensity of his stare stole the oxygen from her lungs, causing her cheeks to flush.

She stumbled over her words, trying to regain composure. "I'm fine, sorry. I need some water," she managed to utter, making her way to the kitchen. Grabbing sparkling water from the sleek granite countertop, she took a moment to collect herself, still feeling the lingering effect of Garrett's gaze.

As Garrett left to meet with Walter, he assured Aubrey that his daughters would keep her entertained in his absence.

She returned a playful smile, batting her long, dark eyelashes at him. "I would love to be entertained by them."

"I'll be right back."

"Good luck," all three girls chimed together, causing them to giggle collectively.

While Garrett departed, a couple approached Aubrey, expressing admiration for her books. They requested her autograph, which Aubrey happily provided. After bidding them farewell, Jasmine looked at Aubrey with a curious expression.

"I thought you looked familiar when I first met you. I finally realized where I'd seen you before. You were at Emilio's last Saturday night, right?" Jasmine's words made Aubrey's stomach churn, her heart threatening to escape her throat. She was filled with horror at the thought of being recognized. She remembered making eye contact with Jasmine at the restaurant but had hoped she wouldn't connect the dots.

A moment passed as Aubrey collected her thoughts, grappling with the rush of fear coursing through her body. Finally, she nodded in Jasmine's direction, prepared to confess fully.

"Yes, I was there with my friend Rachel. Like tonight, it was an incredible performance by your father," Aubrey admitted, her voice laced with vulnerability.

Jasmine smiled, evidently recalling that evening as well.

"How did you end up meeting my dad?" Alexa asked, her expression showing a hint of confusion. Aubrey explained how Rachel had inquired about their father with the restaurant staff. She recounted how she had luckily discovered him on Absolutely Single, the dating app. Both girls seemed enthralled by her story.

"How romantic!" Jasmine exclaimed, her eyes sparkling with delight.

"We're glad you two met!" Alexa added, her smile infectious. Despite Aubrey's underlying fear, she smiled back.

"Awe, thanks. Me too!" she responded, her heart heavier with the weight of her secret.

Walter and Garrett emerged from the office, making their way back toward Aubrey and the girls. Sensing the urgency, Aubrey knew she needed to speak with Garrett before his daughters could reveal the truth. As they approached, she quickly asked Garrett if she could chat with him. She could see the confusion forming in his expression.

"Sure, Aubrey. Walter, would you mind if Jasmine and Alexa

hung out for a minute while Aubrey and I talked?" Garrett requested, turning to Walter for approval.

"No problem at all, Garrett. Would you two like to see my Koi Pond out back?"

"Sure," they replied, following Walter towards the sliding glass doors that led to the back patio.

With his attention now solely on Aubrey, Garrett's anxiety started to build. He worried that the girls had mentioned something about his past, particularly his time in prison. Aubrey had a concerned look on her face, intensifying Garrett's nerves.

"Come with me," she said, holding his hand and leading him out of the front door. They sat down on one of the front steps, overlooking the surroundings. Aubrey looked into Garrett's light green eyes, her heart fluttering at the sight of a color she hadn't seen before.

"I have a confession to make, Garrett."

He could sense her apprehension, which only heightened his own. "What is it, Aubrey?" he asked, silently praying that it wasn't something that would drive a wedge between them. He listened attentively as Aubrey explained how she had first encountered him at Emilio's, recounting every detail. She shared the depth of her emotions upon hearing him play, the intensity of that evening for her, and Rachel's persistence in extracting information about him from the restaurant staff. Aubrey divulged how she had found him on Absolutely Single, admitting to creating an account specifically to meet him. She apologized for not being upfront about Emilio's, tears streaming down her cheeks as she waited for his response.

As each silent second passed, Aubrey felt she was already

losing him. Then, finally, after what seemed like an eternity, Garrett gently placed his hand under her chin, tilting her face upward to meet his. His eyes were forgiving, and his lips curved into a faint smile. "I forgive you," he whispered, catching Aubrey by surprise.

"You do?"

"Yes, of course I do. I'm so glad you found me, baby. Thank you for being brave and taking a chance. Otherwise, I wouldn't be sitting here with the most amazing woman."

Relief washed over Aubrey, her body relaxing. She had expected him to be upset, even furious. She had braced herself for the possibility that he might never want to speak to her again. Instead, he was understanding and even grateful. Overwhelmed with emotion, she ran her hand through his hair, pulling his moist lips onto hers. They shared a passionate kiss, fueled by a hunger they both felt but had yet to explore fully. When they finally broke apart, Aubrey stared into his eyes, appreciating that he had chosen to stay by her side.

"Thanks for forgiving my stalker-ish side," she joked, trying to lighten the mood.

Garrett laughed, his eyes filled with affection. "You're my stalker. And I wouldn't want it any other way."

He paused a moment before saying, "Walter wants to sign me to his label." As he kissed Aubrey again, he watched her expression transform.

Her eyes sparkled with joy as she couldn't contain her excitement. "Oh, Garrett! That's incredible news! I knew he would recognize your talent. You're one of the most amazing artists I've ever heard."

Garrett still couldn't fully process the news but needed to hear Aubrey's reassurance. "He wants me to fly out here again in three weeks to record my first single. Can you believe it, Aubrey?"

"Of course I can! You deserve this opportunity so much, Garrett. I hope you truly understand how much talent you possess."

"Thank you. We should get the girls so I can share the news with them. Thank you for being here. I'll miss you next week. I can't wait for our weekend together. I promise to show you a wonderful time in Idaho."

"Thank you for inviting me here. I'm going to miss you a lot too. I'll count down the days until I can return to your arms. And don't forget mister, you better plan on video chatting with me in the evenings."

"Absolutely," Garrett responded, a smile forming on his lips. They shared one last passionate kiss before heading back inside, ready to share the exciting news with his daughters.

The girls' faces lit up as Garrett shared the news. They couldn't contain their happiness and immediately suggested celebrating at a cozy local pizza parlor known for its delicious New York-style pizzas.

They settled into a booth, with Garrett sitting across from his two angels. As they savored each mouthwatering bite of the cheesy, saucy pizza, the atmosphere buzzed with hopes and dreams. Garrett listened attentively as his daughters spoke about his future as a star, their words filling his heart with joy. Garrett couldn't help but feel submerged with love for his daughters. He admired their unwavering support and belief in his talent. He reveled in this moment, knowing their faith in him fueled his desire to succeed.

Garrett's mind filled with a sense of calm. It felt as if everything was falling into place, and he felt hope in the possibility that Aubrey was a part of his life's journey, guided by something more significant. The thought of a future with Aubrey warmed Garrett's soul. He saw their path leading them toward a life filled with love and togetherness. Living together or marriage seemed like natural progressions, and the idea filled him with quiet contentment.

As the evening drew to a close, Garrett knew it was time to say his goodbyes. With heavy hearts, he helped his girls carry their luggage into their rooms, their excitement from the evening still palpable. Jasmine and Alexa shared the events that had unfolded at Walter's house, including the introduction of Aubrey into their lives. Garrett explained the recent turn of events to Julie and Ben, who were overjoyed for his success and newfound romance.

But now, the time had come to face the difficult part of his trips—saying farewell. Jasmine squeezed him tightly, expressing her appreciation for their wonderful week together. Garrett kissed her forehead, overwhelmed with pride for the woman she had become. He saw the glistening of tears in her eyes, and a lump formed in his throat as he held her one last time.

In an instant, Alexa rushed into his arms, her grown-up presence a reminder of how quickly time had passed. Memories flooded Garrett's mind: images of a young Alexa in a pink summer sundress and playful pigtails. He fought back his tears, not wanting to break down in front of them. He kissed Alexa on the top of her head, feeling the strength of her grip as she understood that he would soon have to leave.

"I am sorry I have to leave," Garrett whispered. "Thank you for making this week extra special."

As Alexa reluctantly let go, tears streamed down her cheeks. Garrett's heart broke into tiny pieces, feeling the weight of their separation. He knew he couldn't hold back his tears any longer. With a heavy heart, he mustered up the strength to utter the words they needed to hear. "I love you girls so much," he said, trembling. "You are both beautiful, wonderful, and the best daughters a father could ever hope to have. I will see you soon."

With those final words, Garrett left their home, tears flowing freely down his face. He sat in his car, his heart aching to see them just once more before his departure. Deep down, he knew that seeing them again wouldn't ease the pain of leaving. He wiped away his tears and summoned the strength to drive back toward the 1818 Estate.

Garrett settled into his seat on the plane the following morning. The familiar hum of the aircraft filled the cabin as he pulled out Aubrey's book, "Night and Day," from his briefcase. Running his fingers over the cover, he admired the image of a father and daughter, their hands intertwined. It struck a chord, reminding him of his bond with his girls.

Turning to the back of the book, he noted the substantial length of almost four hundred pages. Glancing at the blurb about the author, he found no new revelations about

Aubrey's life, but that didn't dampen his excitement to delve into her words.

With the plane poised for takeoff, Garrett opened the book and immersed himself in the story. Aubrey's words painted vivid pictures in his mind, evoking emotions he hadn't expected. As the plane ascended into the sky, he lost himself in her words, feeling a connection to Aubrey's storytelling that surpassed their budding romance.

The hours passed by, and Garrett found solace in the alluring narrative. Aubrey's words transported him to a world of love between a father and daughter that mirrored his loving relationship with his girls. He was engrossed in the book, oblivious to the passage of time as he turned page after page.

As the plane descended towards Boise, Garrett reluctantly closed the book, a mix of satisfaction and longing lingering in his heart. Aubrey's writing had touched him deeply, deepening his admiration for her. He carefully tucked the book back into his briefcase, ready to embark on the next chapter of his life as an artist and a man in love.

CHAPTER

SIXTEEN

Aubrey and Rachel sat at Dorothy's Diner, enjoying the familiar setting and the aroma of freshly brewed coffee. As Aubrey joined her best friend, she greeted her with a warm smile, feeling comforted in Rachel's presence.

"Hey, sis," Aubrey said, her voice filled with affection.

Rachel stood up, wrapping her arms around Aubrey. "It's good to see you, honey. I already ordered you a caramel mocha," Rachel greeted. She always had a knack for little gestures that brightened Aubrey's day.

The waiter approached, and they placed their orders, exchanging playful banter with the friendly young man. Rachel reveled in the attention, effortlessly exuding her natural charm. It was no surprise that men were drawn to both Rachel and Aubrey's magnetic presence. They were confident, successful, and undeniably beautiful.

As they waited for their food to arrive, Aubrey shared the details of her upcoming tour schedule, recounting the cities she would be visiting in the coming weeks. But Rachel's burning curiosity took center stage, prompting her to inquire about Aubrey's week with Garrett.

"So, spill the beans, sis! You've spent the whole week with Garrett, and I'm dying to know every juicy detail."

Aubrey chuckled, realizing she hadn't kept Rachel updated as much as she should have. She began to paint a vivid picture of their time together, describing the electric chemistry she felt and how her heart raced when he was near. She recounted Garrett's signing with Mansfield Productions, the unforgettable performances she had witnessed, and even the unexpected encounter with Jasmine.

After their plates were cleared, Rachel studied Aubrey intently, her eyes searching for answers. "You're falling in love with him, aren't you?" Rachel asked, a knowing smile playing on her lips.

Aubrey's immediate reaction was denial. "No way, Rachel! It's only been a week. How could I already be in love with him?"

Rachel chuckled, her laughter filled with wisdom. "I've known you for years, Bri. I've never seen you like this before. Who knows, maybe he's the one you've been searching for all along."

Aubrey pondered Rachel's words, allowing them to sink in. A part of her resonated with the idea despite her reservations. She couldn't shake the feeling that it was too good to be true, almost waiting for the other shoe to drop. "Honestly, I hope you're right. I really do."

Rachel reached across the table, taking Aubrey's hands in her own. Her eyes reflected both concern and love as she offered a gentle reminder. "Just remember, no one is perfect. You've always tended to run at the first signs of danger. Sometimes, it's worth staying and facing it. Try not to run away from this one, okay?"

Aubrey squeezed Rachel's hands, feeling the warmth and reassurance in her touch. She nodded, her voice filled with sincerity. "Okay."

Settling into his car, Garrett took a moment to savor the comfort of the familiar interior. The cloudy October skies matched his introspective mood. Before hitting the road, he reached for his phone and found several messages waiting for him. With a smile, he replied to Jasmine and Alexa, assuring them of his safe arrival and expressing his love and longing to see them again soon.

Next, Garrett turned his attention to Aubrey's message. He wanted to let her know how deeply her book had moved him. With heartfelt words, he expressed his admiration for her writing skills and the emotional impact her story had on him. He admitted that he missed her and was counting down the days until they were reunited.

As he connected his phone to his car's Bluetooth, Garrett decided to call Dave rather than send a text. He dialed the familiar number and navigated the on-ramp onto I-84, heading toward his parent's house in Nampa.

"Hey Garrett, did you make it home safely?"

"I sure did. Thank you for asking. How did your day go yesterday?" Dave had been concerned about a family function that may have had alcohol involved. Garrett had told him not to attend if he was uncomfortable with it. He explained how losing his sobriety and possible freedom was never worth it for these risks. After much discussion, they agreed he would attend a meeting before the function. They talked through escape strategies if it became too much for him. Alcoholics, especially those within their first thirty days of sobriety, had to be highly cautious and hypersensitive to risky situations.

"It went well. Some of my family drank, but it didn't bother me as much as I thought it would. The meeting yesterday left me with confidence, almost like a protective barrier that seemed to carry me through the night. Also, our escape planning helped me feel comforted, knowing I had different options other than drinking."

With those words, Garrett felt the finger of God touching his soul. What a wonderful feeling to be able to help another alcoholic find solutions to escaping their alcoholic prison. Garrett knew the alcoholic prison was much worse than the actual physical buildings. It was a place he never wished for himself or anyone else. The feelings of loneliness, fear, depression, and despair were so powerful that some less fortunate souls chose to end their lives rather than live another day in that horrible reality. This is what makes the work in the program so profound. By helping others, you were genuinely saving their lives and your own.

"I am happy it went well, Dave. How was the meeting today?"

Garrett and Dave went on to chat about Sunday's meeting and his step-one progress. They discussed his plans for the remainder of the day and agreed to get in touch with each other the following evening. Garrett was left with a peaceful, warm, tingly sensation as he disconnected the call. He knew it was God's will for him to be helping Dave. He was starting to understand why other recovering alcoholics with more sobriety had explained that this process would be a life-long journey. He had been told that helping others was the primary focus of maintaining long-term sobriety. It all made perfect sense to him now. Service for others was the key to sobriety!

As Garrett entered his childhood home, he was greeted by the familiar scent of wood smoke from his father's old-fashioned stove. The memories of melting snowballs on its hot surface made him smile.

Inside, the sound of excited barking led him to Paco, his parents' black Chihuahua, who showered him with affection. Garrett knelt and petted Paco, feeling the small dog's love for him.

In the family room, Garrett found his parents engrossed in one of their regular TV series on Netflix. Lewis, a retired railroad conductor, sat on a dark brown recliner chair, half-watching the large television and half-playing a casino game on his tablet. His mother, Diane, was in her beige recliner chair, diligently crocheting a pink and white baby blanket.

"Hello," Garrett greeted as he sat on the plush brown leather couch near them. Still excited, Paco hopped on the sofa and snuggled beside Garrett's leg.

"Welcome home, Garrett," Diane said with her sweet, childlike voice. "How was the trip?"

"It was amazing," Garrett replied, feeling the day's tension fading. The comforting smell of his father's cooking filled the air, prompting Garrett's appetite to grow.

"Are you ready to eat?" Lewis asked, getting up from his chair and heading into the kitchen.

"I am. I've only had peanuts and coffee today. Thanks, Dad."

Lewis, known for his love of cooking, took over the chef's responsibilities after retiring. He had prepared a BLT sandwich with avocado, a treat Garrett always looked forward to.

As they sat around the dining room table, finishing their sandwiches, Garrett shared everything that had happened over the past week. His parents asked questions, particularly about his record deal, which they found hard to believe at first.

"Will your songs be on the radio? And they'll pay you for your music?" Diane asked, her curiosity shining through.

"I'll start with recording one song, and if it goes well, I'll have the opportunity to record more," Garrett explained, hoping to convey the magnitude of his unbelievable opportunity.

His mother nodded, processing the information. "Do you have any pictures of Aubrey?" she asked, wanting to know more about the woman who had suddenly stolen her son's heart.

Garrett retrieved the photo Aubrey had sent him and passed the phone to Diane, who held it before her face. "Awe, she's beautiful. Who's the younger girl with her?" Garrett chuckled and explained that Aubrey's mother, Jenny, was in the photo with her.

"She writes books for a living?" Diane probed further.

"Yes, she just finished her fourth book, which is coming out tomorrow," Garrett replied, proud of Aubrey's accomplishments.

His parents expressed their admiration for Aubrey's achievements and were happy that she seemed to match the ideal partner Garrett had envisioned. Diane, who initially thought her son would be a terminal bachelor, congratulated him for finding such a fantastic match.

Feeling the warmth and approval from his parents, Garrett enjoyed their company for another hour before exhaustion finally caught up with him. He bid his parents farewell, giving Paco a gentle pat on the head, and left their home, looking forward to a quiet and relaxing evening delving deeper into the pages of Aubrey's book.

Garrett settled back into his routine. Mornings began with a visit to the gym in the basement of his apartment building, where he dedicated time to exercise before showering and enjoying a healthy breakfast. Once ready, he immersed himself in his work, following the stock exchange and its imaginary opening bell.

Garrett attended his regular Daily Recovery meetings and stayed in touch with Jasmine and Alexa, relying on various social media platforms to keep up with their busy lives. Phone calls alone were insufficient to maintain a strong connection with his daughters. Embracing the world of social media allowed him to stay updated with their pictures and posts, bridging the gap to some extent. Additionally, he ensured they video chatted at least once a week, cherishing those moments of virtual togetherness.

What made Garrett's routine different now was the inclusion of Aubrey and Dave. He and Dave spoke every night before Dave went to sleep, providing each other with support and encouragement. Garrett found comfort in their conversations, knowing he had someone who understood the struggles and joy sobriety created.

With Aubrey, their daily communication and frequent video visits during the week brought them closer together. The distance challenged their patience and forced them to explore new avenues of connection beyond physical touch. They had to delve deeper into their emotions, thoughts, and dreams, strengthening their bond through words and shared experiences. As each day passed, Garrett felt their relationship blossoming, even from afar.

SEVENTEEN

Aubrey's plane descended and touched down in Boise, her anticipation reaching its crescendo. The mere thought of seeing Garrett again created a tickling sensation inside her chest. The past week was a whirlwind of busyness and exhaustion for her. She had toured multiple cities, making guest appearances at various bookstore locations. The number of copies she signed for her new novel left her hand feeling arthritic. The unexpected success of her book surpassed all predictions made by her publisher and critics. National reviews from renowned critics showered her with glowing accolades. The financial success and growing fame were more than she had ever imagined from a career that came so naturally to her.

Despite the external accomplishments, the week took a toll on Aubrey's emotional well-being. The stress had been overwhelming, but Garrett's messages, phone calls, and video chats had been her lifeline. His presence in her life alleviated her anxieties, providing comfort and support. She marveled

220 | *The First Thirty Days*

at their growing bond, feeling a stronger connection than when she had left Walter's house a week prior. The ease with which they conversed surprised her. Even over the phone, they could talk for hours about almost anything. Garrett had become her boyfriend and one of her closest friends. Aubrey admired this combination, recognizing its immense value for their potential future.

As the plane taxied to its destination, the cabin lights flickered on, signaling the start of her much-needed vacation. Butterflies fluttered in her stomach as she joined the other passengers in making their way toward the front of the plane. The excitement of reuniting with Garrett fueled her every step and she couldn't wait to see him again.

Garrett sat in the bustling waiting area, surrounded by others who shared his anxious expression. Aubrey's plane had landed, and he could barely contain his excitement for her arrival. The knowledge that she was in the same building as him felt like a shot of euphoria had been administered into his veins. His eyes remained fixed on the glass walls, impatiently awaiting her emergence.

Garrett's heart raced as the passengers started to make their way out. Some walked with rolling carry-on luggage, while others clutched laptop bags over their shoulders. He mused that airports were fascinating places for people-watching, with diverse races, body types, styles, and ages coming and going with each flight.

Amidst the crowd, the one person he craved to see came

into view. Aubrey wore a stylish black sweatshirt paired with matching joggers, having forewarned Garrett that she would be dressed for comfort. Her hair was pulled back tightly into a ponytail. Even in her relaxed attire, she looked stunning. As her eyes met his among the crowd, a gorgeous smile spread across her face, filling Garrett's heart with joy.

Aubrey's entire being stirred as she laid eyes on Garrett. He stood beyond the double glass doors, exuding a magnetic allure. Her body reacted instinctively, various sensations and feelings invading her at once. His faded jeans accentuated his hips, making her catch her breath. A black jacket over a crisp white T-shirt was zipped up, adding to his undeniable charm. He held a single red rose in his hands, symbolizing his affection. His jet-black hair was meticulously combed back and neatly tucked behind his ears.

Aubrey's heart pounded in her chest with each step she took toward him. Her senses heightened, anticipating the touch of his hand, the scent of his cologne, and the sweetness of his lips. Time froze still as Aubrey found herself wrapped in Garrett's arms.

Their intense connection electrified every fiber of his being. Her touch, the scent of her perfume and body wash, ignited a symphony of sensations. Oblivious to the passersby, they held each other tightly, reveling in the intensity of the moment. Finally, Garrett reluctantly released her, their gazes locked as he planted a tender, lingering kiss on her lips.

Aubrey's lips tingled with the imprint of their kiss as she greeted him, "Hello, Garrett."

"Hello, beautiful. I'm so glad you're here. Welcome to

Idaho." He leaned in for another kiss, their lips meeting in a more passionate exchange, leaving Aubrey yearning for more. Their kisses felt like pure magic, rendering them invisible to the world, protected within their delightful bubble. Public displays of affection had never been her style, but with Garrett, she didn't care. The outside world faded away every time their lips met, and their private universe consumed them.

"How about we get out of here?" Garrett suggested, a mischievous smirk playing on his lips.

"You lead the way," Aubrey replied, gripping his strong, masculine hand, ready to embark on the next chapter of their story.

After collecting her luggage, Aubrey and Garrett found his sleek black Audi A6, which perfectly matched hers. As they merged onto the interstate, Aubrey stared out the windshield and marveled at the panoramic view of downtown Boise. The city lay nuzzled against majestic mountains, a sight that summoned a sense of peace and wonder within her. She observed Boise was a city of the perfect size, much like Hartford, Connecticut, offering a balance of amenities without the drawbacks of overcrowding and heavy traffic.

Garrett's apartment, located in the heart of downtown amidst other medium-sized skyscrapers, held a unique charm. Having been recently renovated, it was transformed from the luxurious "Owyhee Plaza" hotel into a modern, inviting living space.

As they rode the elevator up to the ninth floor, Garrett unlocked unit nine-zero-six and courteously held the door open for Aubrey. Stepping inside, Aubrey's eyes widened at the breathtaking views beyond the floor-to-ceiling windows. The cityscape stretched out before her, a sight that felt almost surreal.

Walking toward the window, Aubrey traced her fingertips along the glass, marveling at the bustling sidewalks below. People strolled, creating a vibrant atmosphere as they went about their day.

Garrett approached Aubrey from behind, his arms encircling her waist as he leaned in to brush his lips against her neck. Aubrey's breath hitched, and he pointed out some of the historic buildings within their view, including the Capitol, with its grandeur begging for their attention.

"It's beautiful," Aubrey whispered, enamored by the city's charm.

Turning her around with a playful smile, Garrett suggested, "Would you like to see the rest of my place?"

Aubrey chuckled, playing along. "I suppose."

They explored Garrett's family room, adorned with comfortable furnishings and offering a welcoming retreat. The nearby kitchen boasted a stylish breakfast bar and elegant design featuring light brown granite countertops, cherry wood cabinets, and sleek stainless-steel appliances. The living area showcased an oversized sofa and recliner, with a large television mounted on the wall above a mahogany coffee table, emanating a touch of sophistication.

Inside the apartment, there were two bedrooms. One room, adorned with bunk beds and stuffed animals, spoke of Garrett's love for his daughters. The second bedroom, Garrett's own, provided a similar view and offered a tranquil ambiance.

A queen-sized slate bed, complemented by a matching chest of drawers and a nightstand with a modern white marble lamp, stood as a testament to Garrett's simple yet refined taste.

Noticing a thoughtful gesture on the nightstand, Aubrey's heart warmed. She found a copy of her books there, symbolizing Garrett's support.

Placing Aubrey's luggage in the corner, Garrett teased, "What do you think, baby? Your main bedroom could probably fit this entire apartment."

Aubrey grinned, looking around as she imagined the size difference. "You're probably right." She laughed. "But I love it, Garrett. It's a perfect space for you and your daughters, and the location is amazing. I can't wait to explore the downtown streets."

"Thank you. I got us some sushi for lunch. How about we enjoy our meal and then go for a stroll."

They sat down and savored the variety of sushi rolls Garrett had picked up from a nearby restaurant. After their light lunch, Aubrey changed into more appropriate attire. Garrett took her on a charming city tour, hand in hand, exploring the coffee shops, art galleries, and other local treasures that caught their interest. They climbed the steps of the capitol building, marveling at the panoramic view it offered.

As they stood there, enchanted by the city's beauty, Garrett suggested taking a selfie with the capitol building as the backdrop—a symbolic moment marking the beginning of their time together.

Boise's laid-back and friendly residents left a lasting impression on Aubrey. Kindness and courtesy accompanied them everywhere they walked, creating a feeling of safety and geniality. Aubrey realized why Boise was considered a safe haven—its people embodied a genuine sense of community.

As the day transitioned into the evening, Aubrey and Garrett prepared for their dinner at Chandler's Steakhouse, an esteemed restaurant in the area. The air buzzed with romance as they got ready in their respective spaces. Garrett donned his three-piece gray suit, carefully selecting a black tie to match his belt and shoes. Aubrey emerged from the main bathroom, stunning in a sparkling sleeveless black dress that accentuated her features.

Garrett's breath caught as he beheld her, unable to find words to express his admiration.

Aubrey's eyes met his, and she playfully teased him. "You aren't so bad yourself," she quipped, drawn to his magnetic presence.

With their hands entwined, Garrett led Aubrey out of the apartment.

Chandler's Steakhouse was conveniently located a block from Garrett's apartment, and as they walked, the sinking sun brought a cool chill to the air. Aubrey wore a long black trench coat that elegantly draped below her knees while her high heels emitted a soft click on the pavement.

Upon arrival at the restaurant, Garrett checked in with the friendly hostess at the front counter. They were then led to their table by a courteous waiter. Settling into a booth at the center of the room, Garrett sat across from Aubrey, and their jackets were discreetly taken by the hostess, who disappeared into the background. Curious about her thoughts, Garrett asked, "What do you think of the place?"

Aubrey glanced around, taking in the scenery of the restaurant. Soft piano music played in the background, setting a romantic tone. The dim lighting and candlelit tables created an intimate atmosphere. They caught glimpses of the city lights twinkling outside through the large windows. The air was filled with the mouthwatering aroma of grilled steak and other delicacies. The elegant setting and Garrett's company made her feel like they were in their own little world.

"It's lovely, just like you," Aubrey replied, her eyes sparkling affectionately.

"You're too kind, Aubrey. You mentioned that you enjoy steak, right?"

"I do appreciate a yummy steak."

"Well then, the filet it is," Garrett suggested, pointing to the menu. "And perhaps we could start with some appetizers?"

Moments later, their waiter returned to take their orders. They chose the filet mignon, cooked perfectly with roasted vegetables and creamy mashed potatoes. To start, they decided on a shared plate of brochette and a Caesar salad. As they awaited their food, they engaged in light-hearted conversation, their laughter blending with the soft music in the background.

When their salads arrived, Aubrey chuckled as Garrett requested extra croutons, his childlike nature shining through. Seeing how he appreciated the small details and took joy in simple pleasures was endearing. The restaurant's intimate climate seemed to amplify their chemistry, and time seemed to stand still as they treasured each moment together.

As their main course arrived, Garrett watched with delight as Aubrey took her first bite of the main course. A contented smile spread across her face, and she closed her eyes briefly, savoring the flavors dancing on her palate. "This is delicious. You have excellent taste, Garrett."

"I'm glad you like it," Garrett replied. He savored each bite of his steak, appreciating the exquisite flavors and the joy of sharing a special meal with someone who held a special place in his heart.

As Garrett and Aubrey finished their meals, the excitement for the remainder of the evening began to build. Politely declining the dessert offer, they gathered their coats and made their way to the front of the building. Garrett had kept the next segment of their date a surprise. A cab awaited them as they stepped out of the restaurant, and Garrett gallantly held the door open for Aubrey as she climbed into the back seat.

Aubrey couldn't contain her curiosity any longer. Noticing stadium lights in the distance she asked, "Are you taking me to the blue field, Mr. Anderson?"

"Bingo, Miss Ellis. But prepare yourself for a unique experience. I don't think you've ever attended a football game quite like this in your elegant dress and heels."

Aubrey giggled softly, secretly wishing she had known in advance so she could have dressed more comfortably. As they exited the cab, Garrett's arm wrapped around her waist, creating a sense of affection and security.

"Do you trust me?" he asked, his voice sending a delightful shiver down her spine.

"Yes, I do," she replied. Together, they maneuvered through the excited crowd dressed in orange and blue, making their way into the circular-shaped stadium.

Once inside, they headed towards a set of elevator doors. An older man stood there, checking tickets as guests arrived. Garrett handed him his smartphone, and Aubrey watched as the man scanned it, emitting a pleasant beep and a green glow.

"Do you know where you're going?" the man asked, inquiring about their destination as he pressed the up-arrow button on the wall.

"I do, thank you," Garrett replied, leading Aubrey into the small metal box.

When they reached their floor, Garrett guided Aubrey to a luxurious suite. Inside, a dozen elegantly dressed individuals mingled, surrounded by food platters on the tables. The far wall showcased a breathtaking view of the stadium's magnificent blue field above the fifty-yard line. Garrett led Aubrey to two chairs near the far-right corner of the room.

"Surprise!" Garrett exclaimed, sitting down beside her. "What do you think?"

Aubrey's eyes widened in awe as she soaked in the breathtaking sight. The field was a vivid blue, an enchanting scene, unlike anything she had ever witnessed in a football stadium. The energy and excitement of the crowd below distorted her vision, immersing her in a world where romance intertwined with the love of the game.

"This is incredible, Garrett. Thank you!" She reached for his hand, leaned closer, and tenderly kissed his warm lips.

Garrett unlocked and slid open the window in front of them, allowing the sounds of the enthusiastic fans to echo through the small suite. The cool night air embraced them as the crowd's deafening cheers filled their ears. Aubrey reveled in the moment, the temperature drop reminding her of the unpredictable weather of Idaho, a place she was beginning to adore.

Amidst the frenzied crowd, a chant began to form. The fans in the distance yelled, "Booooiiiiiissssssssseeeee," while those nearer to Aubrey and Garrett responded, "Staaaaaaaaaaaaaaaaaaate." The chant soon swelled, spreading throughout the entire stadium. The united voices echoed respect and devotion to their home team, the Boise State Broncos, as they prepared to face their rivals, the BYU Cougars.

Garrett and Aubrey joined the chorus, their voices blending seamlessly with the crowd. Aubrey's enthusiasm and passion for the game mirrored that of the dedicated fans despite her elegant dress and heels. Garrett smiled, fascinated by how naturally she immersed herself in the moment. He chuckled as he noticed her pumping her fist in the air with each resounding roar of "state."

As the team burst onto the field, led by a player carrying a hammer, the crowd erupted. Garrett and Aubrey rose, cheering on the home team with unwavering support. Aubrey admired the contagious energy of the crowd, grateful to witness Garrett's animated spirit. It reminded her of her father, who had instilled in her a love and respect for the game through his passionate devotion.

"Do you always sit in the skybox?" Aubrey asked minutes before the opening kickoff. They snuggled closely together, Garrett's arm wrapped around her shoulders.

"This is only my second time. Usually, I'm among the other crazy fans in the stands. But tonight, I wanted it to be special, especially since we came directly from the restaurant."

Aubrey beamed, feeling grateful for the extraordinary experience. She leaned in, her lips locking with his as the kickoff soared through the night sky. Despite the roar of the crowd, Garrett felt lost in a world that existed solely for the two of them. When they finally parted, their eyes sparkled with passion. They sat back, stealing glances at each other, oblivious to the world below and the game unfolding.

His eyes, a deep shade of green, held a longing she hadn't felt with anyone else. In his presence, Aubrey found an undeniable sense of peace and completeness. The intensity in his gaze conveyed how much he wanted and needed her in his life. The night promised to be unforgettable, and though they had yet to discuss sleeping arrangements, the unspoken understanding lingered between them. Blushing, Aubrey redirected her attention to the game, deciding to appreciate the present moment without over thinking the events that might transpire later.

By halftime, the Broncos clung to a narrow seventeen to ten lead. Garrett and Aubrey mingled with the other guests, indulging in delectable finger foods. Once again, Aubrey was surprised by the warmth and friendliness of the people around her. Strangers complimented them on being a gorgeous-looking couple, and Aubrey felt proud to have Garrett by her side. She would often catch women glancing in his direction, but Garrett seemed oblivious to their wandering eyes. He made her feel secure and confident, focusing his attention solely on her and the game below.

When the final seconds of the third quarter ticked away on the giant jumbotron screen, the Broncos had extended their lead to twenty-four to ten. Garrett glanced at his phone and noticed it was a little past ten. Aware that Aubrey was exhausted from her long day, he whispered in her ear, "How about we get out of here?"

Aubrey looked at him, a confused expression crossing her face. "But there's still another quarter to go. Don't you want to watch the rest of the game?"

Garrett smiled gently, "I can put the game on at home. We have a busy day tomorrow."

Aubrey understood that he was being polite, a true gentleman. Before she could convince him otherwise, he was already on the phone with the cab company, arranging their transportation. When he ended the call, he looked at her and said, "They will be out front in five minutes." He had made up his mind, leaving no room for argument.

The anticipation of being alone with Garrett quickly re-entered Aubrey's body as he stood up and offered her his hand. They bid farewells, descending the steel elevator and stepping out into the chilly Idaho air. The cab waited for them in front of the venue, its engine humming softly.

Garrett opened the door and watched Aubrey climb in, sliding over to the other side to make room for him. As they settled in the backseat, their hands naturally found each other, and silence enveloped them during the ride back to Garrett's apartment. Both were lost in their thoughts, silently contemplating the evening and the possibilities ahead.

When they pulled up in front of Garrett's building, his heart began to pound against his chest wall. He paid the driver, his mind open to whatever the rest of the evening had in store for them, ready to embrace the unfolding moments.

He unlocked the door to his apartment, holding it open as Aubrey passed through. He caught a whiff of her perfume, bringing warmth to his nostrils. He helped her out of her long black jacket, hanging it in the small closet. "Would you like anything to drink? There is a full bar downstairs?"

Aubrey appreciated his offer but preferred a glass of water instead. Garrett retrieved two glasses from the cupboard, filling them with water and ice cubes.

"Would you like to change first?" Garrett asked.

"I'd like to watch the end of the game with you. I can wait a little bit to change." She kicked off her heels and settled onto the plush cushions of the couch, feeling herself relax. Garrett turned on the large flat-screen television and found the game, with the Broncos leading 24-17 and only five minutes remaining in the fourth quarter.

Sitting next to Aubrey on the couch, Garrett held her hand. He commented on the team's performance and asked if she had enjoyed the day. Aubrey looked at him seductively, causing a spark to ignite within him. He caressed her cheek and tucked a few loose strands of hair behind her ear. "You are so beautiful, Aubrey. Thank you for coming to visit me."

The touch of his hand and the sound of his voice intensified Aubrey's desire for him. She ran her fingers through his hair and pulled his face closer to hers. Their lips met in a soft and passionate exchange, their tongues intertwining. Aubrey let out a small moan, adding to the intensity between them. Unable to resist the growing fire inside, she straddled him, their bodies moving together with a steady rhythm.

Garrett's hands explored Aubrey's legs, gradually moving upward, feeling the softness of her skin. Their desire deepened as he reached her waist, his touch eliciting more moans. Her breathing became heavier, and her eyes were filled with longing.

Aubrey began unbuttoning Garrett's shirt as the passion grew, savoring each moment. He removed his shirt, revealing his bare upper body. She traced her hands over his well-defined muscles, feeling their strength. The fire between them exploded as he caressed her hips, then lower, igniting a plethora of sensations running wild through her body.

Garrett lifted Aubrey in his arms and carried her to his bed. Their eyes locked, conveying emotions that words couldn't capture. He whispered, "I love you, Aubrey."

"I love you too, Garrett."

EIGHTEEN

Aubrey woke up the next morning to sunlight streaming through the partially opened wooden blinds in Garrett's bedroom. She stretched and realized Garrett was no longer beside her. The enticing smell of bacon and oil wafted through the air, giving her a clue about where he might be. As she got out of bed a shy blush crept onto her face, recalling the magical night they had shared. She quickly dressed in a white sweat suit, replaying the memories of their intense and passionate evening. It was a night she knew she would never want to forget.

Following the delicious aroma, Aubrey found Garrett in the kitchen, tending to the bacon on the stove. He was dressed casually in a white t-shirt and gray sweatpants, his tousled hair making him look even more attractive. She sat on a bar stool, observing him as he flipped the bacon. Unaware of her presence, he jumped back in surprise when he finally noticed her. "Oh, Aubrey, you scared me!" he exclaimed, laughing as his face turned pale.

Aubrey frowned playfully, asking if she looked terrible. Garrett's eyes filled with humor as he reassured her that she looked beautiful. He greeted her with a warm, "Good morning" and asked how she had slept.

Glancing at the oven clock, she realized she had enjoyed a restful eight hours of sleep, a welcome change from her recent travels.

Garrett offered her a cup of coffee, which she gladly accepted. He poured her a steaming mug of black coffee with a hint of French vanilla aroma. Adding some coffee creamer, he stirred the liquid to create a light brown color. Aubrey noticed the omelets, bacon he had prepared, and sliced cantaloupe on the side.

"I hope you are hungry."

"Starving!" she replied.

Garrett sat beside her, hugging her sideways and kissing her gently on her hair. They ate their breakfast in contented silence, savoring the flavors. Aubrey complimented Garrett on his cooking skills, and he revealed that the recipe was a family secret passed down from his grandfather.

As they finished eating, Aubrey helped Garrett wash the dishes. With curiosity bubbling inside her, she finally asked about their plans for the day.

Garrett smirked and kissed her, whispering, "Not yet. You'll find out soon enough." He advised her to dress warmly and comfortably, including shoes she didn't mind getting dirty.

Despite her confusion, she felt excited about the mystery that awaited them.

While Aubrey got ready, Garrett packed a cooler with everything they would need for lunch. He dressed in jeans, boots, and a plaid shirt, ensuring everything else for their day trip was already in the car. After quickly looking in the mirror and brushing his teeth, he grabbed a baseball cap to tame his unruly hair. Feeling giddy about their plans, he hoped Aubrey would enjoy the activity as much as he did.

When he found her standing by the window, the sunlight illuminated her figure, making her look radiant. He wrapped his arms around her waist, kissing her neck, causing her to giggle. Her laughter warmed his heart, and he asked, "Are you ready to go, sunshine?" This prompted another burst of laughter from Aubrey, and he couldn't help but laugh with her, feeling a happiness he had never experienced before.

"Yes, I'm ready."

As they continued their drive, Aubrey couldn't contain her excitement at the unfolding landscape. The unfamiliar highway led them to breathtaking views of mountains that gradually appeared on the horizon. Garrett held her hand, their fingers interlaced, as they listened to soft rock music playing on the car's satellite radio. The music complemented the scenic journey.

They weaved through the towering mountains, their car traversing the winding roads that revealed new vistas at every turn. Aubrey's eyes widened as she admired the majestic beauty surrounding them. The mountains embraced them, inviting them into their serene and awe-inspiring presence. The transition from cityscape to nature's grandeur was nothing short of amazing.

Driving through the small town of Horseshoe Bend, they glimpsed its humble offerings—a few restaurants, a park, and a bustling convenience store. Garrett bypassed the city, their destination lying beyond, deeper into the mountains. The scenery continued to evolve, and Aubrey marveled at the transformation. The once sagebrush-covered slopes now gave way to a dense forest of various-sized pine trees, their lush greenery a striking contrast against the clear blue sky.

To their left, a river flowed alongside the road—the Payette River. Garrett shared with Aubrey that his family often enjoyed floating down this river during the hot summer months. As they meandered along the scenic and windy roads that carved through the heart of the mountainous region, Garrett opened up about his family. He spoke fondly of his parents and siblings, sharing stories from his childhood.

As an only child, Aubrey was enamored by Garrett's tales of a close-knit family. Despite their busy lives, they remained connected and supportive of one another. His parents still lived together just outside Boise, while his siblings resided and worked in the Treasure Valley—an area encompassing Boise and its neighboring cities. The more Aubrey learned about Garrett's family, the more she looked forward to the day she would meet them. They sounded just as wonderful as Garrett himself.

Observing Aubrey's reaction to the awe-inspiring scenery,

Garrett felt a sense of satisfaction. He noticed her eyes sparkling with wonder as they gazed at the towering pines, the steep mountains, and the rushing rapids of the Payette River. The weather was pleasantly cool, around sixty-five degrees, with a gentle breeze that added a touch of freshness to the air.

Approaching their destination, Garrett spotted a pull-off area on the right side of the road. He breathed a sigh of relief upon seeing the small dirt parking lot empty, knowing that they would have this picturesque spot all to themselves. They had arrived at the North Fork of the Payette River, which now flowed peacefully to their right. Garrett parked the car, turned to Aubrey, and locked eyes with her vibrant blue hue.

"We are here, baby."

Lost in the beauty of the surroundings, Aubrey twirled in pure delight, savoring every moment of their secluded paradise. The scent of fresh pine filled the air, invigorating her senses. The sun beamed down on them, yet the air remained refreshingly cool and dry. She could sense the change in elevation and catch a hint of the pristine water flowing below them. Silence enveloped the area, except for the roaring sound of the fast-moving river, creating a symphony of nature's music.

As Garrett wrapped his arms around her waist, Aubrey relished their intimate closeness. He pointed out a bald eagle gracefully soaring through the canyon above, captivating their attention. Aubrey's breath caught in her throat as she marveled at the majestic bird's flight. It was a sight of pure beauty, etching a lasting impression on her heart.

Once the eagle disappeared from view, Garrett twirled Aubrey around, placing her in front of him. They swayed together, moving to the rhythm of their love and the melodies of nature. Softly, Garrett sang "The Rainbow Connection" into her ear, his voice a tender serenade. Euphoria coursed through Aubrey's veins as if something holy had touched her. She felt a profound sense of God's love, protection, and spirit surrounding them—a connection to something greater than herself.

As the song ended, Garrett gently wiped away Aubrey's tears, their lips kissing tenderly. The depth of his love for her was undeniable. They shared a bond that enhanced every experience, making it more profound and meaningful. Aubrey's emotions were written all over her face, and Garrett did not need to ask how she felt. It was a moment of pure bliss and understanding between two souls deeply in love.

Garrett released Aubrey, popping the trunk open with his car's remote. He retrieved the green camping chairs, blue cooler, brown vest, and fishing chest containing his fly rod, reel, and flies, setting them carefully on the ground. Turning to her with a playful grin, he asked, "Ever tried fly fishing?"

Aubrey's eyes lit up. "No, but it's always been something I wanted to do!"

"Well, today's your lucky day."

Carrying the equipment and supplies, they went down to a small sandy beach by the river's edge. Garrett emphasized the importance of respecting the water and warned Aubrey about its hidden dangers. As they approached the water, Aubrey felt its power, its rushing sound growing louder. She marveled at the clarity and purity of the river, with white-capped rapids adding a touch of wildness. In the face of nature's grandeur, she couldn't help but feel a deeper connection to the presence of something greater.

Sitting in the comfortable green chair, Aubrey carefully watched Garrett prepare the fishing rod and reel. She had never fished before. She secretly hoped he wouldn't insist on her handling the fish if they were lucky enough to catch one. She found him irresistibly attractive wearing his brown fishing vest. It was a perfect day, just the two of them surrounded by God's beautiful creations.

With patience and expertise, Garrett guided Aubrey on how to hold the rod, demonstrating the graceful twirling and flicking motions needed to position the weighted line precisely. He explained the art of fly fishing, the delicate balance required to make the fly appear like an insect landing on the water's surface. Aubrey quickly absorbed the fundamentals and easily landed her fly in challenging spots. Garrett pointed out a swirling deep pool of water across from them, challenging Aubrey to aim for that spot and brace herself if a fish took the bait.

After a few tries, Aubrey successfully landed her fly in the deep gray water as instructed. She marveled at the elegant dance of her line and the constant movement of the clear, cold water. The moment's tranquility enveloped her as if her mind, body, and soul had synchronized perfectly.

Just as she was becoming lost in the serenity, a large fish burst out of the water, seizing the end of her line. Her heart raced as she instinctively followed Garrett's teachings, pulling back on the rod to hook the fish. The struggle began, and she felt the raw power of the creature beneath the surface. With every tug, her heart skipped a beat. Garrett sat beside her, laughing as he coached her through the exhilarating process. Holding a net near the water's edge, he stood ready to scoop up the fish as soon as it came within reach.

After what felt like an eternity, Garrett exclaimed, "I see it! It's a massive one!" His voice filled with childlike enthusiasm. With a swift motion, he scooped up the fish from the water, holding it high for Aubrey to see. The fish displayed a beautiful array of greenish-brown hues with a delicate pinkish tint along its body.

"You caught your first rainbow trout, baby! It's a beauty!" Garrett shouted, his excitement contagious. Aubrey's heart still beat wildly as she admired the magnificent fish. Garrett carefully held it by the mouth, removing the hook from its upper lip. Aubrey hesitated, unsure if she wanted to touch the slimy creature before her.

"Do you want to hold it?" Garrett asked, closing the distance between them.

"No, thank you," Aubrey replied, her voice filled with sadness. She observed the fish's gills rhythmically moving, desperately seeking its life-sustaining liquid. Garrett gently ran his hand along the fish's back, granting it a taste of what it longed for. "What will you do with it?" Aubrey asked, her voice filled with genuine concern.

Garrett's gaze turned serious as he replied, "In my family, we have a tradition of catching and releasing trout. There are only a few freshwater fish that I enjoy eating, and trout isn't one of them." He released the inpatient fish into the rapidly rushing water before them. Relief flooded over her, and she embraced Garrett, still catching a hint of the fishy scent lingering on his hands.

"That was amazing!" she exclaimed, her lips seeking his in a series of grateful kisses. "I can't believe it took me this long to discover how much fun this is."

Garrett looked at her, his eyes brimming with love. "You are already a pro, Ms. Ellis. I'm incredibly proud of you," he said, his voice filled with admiration.

Garrett leaned his rod against some large boulders by the bank, pulling the cooler closer to their chairs. Aubrey settled down beside him as he handed her plates and utensils. They shared a royal feast, indulging in bottled juices, a Tupperware full of mixed sliced fruits, thinly sliced turkey meat, brochette bread, and an assortment of packaged cheeses. They dined like a king and queen right on the edge of the bank, savoring every bite.

Aubrey excitedly recounted the play-by-play of catching her first fish as they enjoyed their meal. Garrett listened attentively as she relived the entire experience, from the fish leaping out of the water to the moment he let it swim away.

They arrived back at Garrett's place a little after four, carrying the cooler and fishing equipment to his floor. With their plans to grab dinner before Aubrey's eight o'clock flight, they had limited time left together. While Garrett unloaded the cooler, Aubrey slipped into the shower, washing away the lingering fishy smell that clung to her hands. As the water cascaded over her, she felt a well of sadness, knowing that their time together was drawing to a close. However, they had already made plans for Garrett to visit her in a few weeks when he would be recording his first single at Mansfield Productions. It offered a glimmer of hope, but the thought of the two-week wait weighed on her heart.

After Aubrey finished her showering and dressed, Garrett took a quick rinse, wanting to make the most of their remaining precious moments. He dressed swiftly, eager to seize every second they had left together. At five-thirty, they left his apartment, their destination set on a popular restaurant called "Cafe Rio." Renowned for their fast and delectable Mexican-style burritos, Garrett thought it would be the perfect choice to satisfy their hunger within the limited timeframe they had before Aubrey's departure.

Sitting across from each other at a small table, Aubrey struggled to contain her emotions. The food before her was delicious, but her appetite waned in the face of the dull ache in her heart. Long-distance relationships proved more challenging than expected, and the pain was unbearable. Setting her half-eaten food into the red plastic basket, she directed her gaze towards Garrett, the gorgeous man across from her. Seeking understanding, she mustered the courage to voice her feelings. "Do you feel it, Garrett?"

Garrett placed his oversized burrito on the plate, his light green eyes reflecting care and empathy.

"I do, Aubrey. I knew it wouldn't be easy, but this is much harder than I ever imagined," he confessed. Aubrey turned her focus away from him, momentarily distracted by a noisy family entering the restaurant.

"Does this make you doubt us? Is it worth it to you?" Aubrey struggled to hold back tears that threatened to spill down her cheeks. It pained her to hear that Garrett was finding it difficult, too. Suddenly, the fear of losing him due to the vast distance between them consumed her.

Reaching across the table, Garrett gently took her hands, his thumbs caressing her delicate knuckles. Offering her a comforting smile, he spoke earnestly, redirecting her attention from their intertwined hands to his intense, passionate gaze. "I need you to understand exactly how I feel right now," he began. "These past few weeks with you have been some of the best in my life. Getting to know you, I've never felt more connected to someone. Our compatibility surpasses any expectation I ever had for a relationship. Being with you has shown me love's true depth and beauty, like those love stories I've read and movies I've watched. Aubrey, you've helped me fully appreciate what love can be."

Aubrey's heart warmed, her fear melting away with each word he spoke. After a brief pause, he continued, his voice filled with emotion. "I care for you so deeply that it will only become more challenging. You ask if it's worth it. Aubrey, with all my heart, it is worth it to me. I don't want to let you go now that I've found you. Ever!" As he finished speaking, he leaned across the table, pressing his lips against hers. Aubrey felt the strength and power of the connection he had described stirring within her.

Pulling away, Garrett settled back into his seat, searching Aubrey's eyes with a hint of nervousness. "Now you know it's worth it to me. Now I want to know, is it worth it to you?"

She watched him intently, inhaling and exhaling deeply before making eye contact again. The intensity in her gaze almost took Garrett's breath away. "Yes, Garrett. It is worth it to me. I feel much the same way you do," she affirmed, her eyes drifting downward momentarily as she sought the right words to convey her deepest emotions. "You mentioned books and movies depicting love, romance, and the understanding and appreciation of finding the right person. I can relate to that analogy. I've been searching for a love like ours since I was a little girl. I've written books describing the love we're beginning to share. I thought I would never find that rare kind of love until you unexpectedly came into my life. Now that I've found this missing piece to the puzzle of my heart, I will fight to keep it whole and intact."

Aubrey smiled at him, her gaze unwavering.

"I love you, Aubrey," he declared.

"I love you too, Garrett," she responded. They shared one more kiss before tidying up their table, knowing it was time to head to the airport.

Garrett pulled up to the designated area where Aubrey's airline sign hung from the curbside awning. He assisted her with her luggage, making sure everything was in order. They embraced tightly, cherishing every second they had left together before the security guard gently reminded them of the impending departure. With a final passionate kiss, Garrett left no doubt in Aubrey's mind about the depth of his love for her. Reluctantly, he walked away, stealing one last glance before disappearing into his car.

Aubrey stood there, watching his taillights fade into the night, while her heart sank deeper. The absence of his presence caused tears to stream down her face, the pain of his departure more than she could bear. After a few minutes of uncontrollable sobbing, she took a deep breath and wiped her tears with the back of her hands, summoning the strength to carry on. With a heavy heart, she entered the airport, knowing that the road ahead would be challenging. But deep down, she held onto the belief that every moment spent with Garrett was worth it, and she was determined to keep their love alive despite the distance.

Aubrey and Garrett had a whirlwind week, each deeply engaged in their separate endeavors. Aubrey kicked off her West Coast tour, starting in Seattle, then Portland, and ending in Los Angeles, where her latest book's success skyrocketed her fame. Due to overwhelming demand, her tour was paused briefly to replenish book supplies. Meanwhile, Garrett maintained his routine and prepared for his upcoming trip to NYC to record his first single and visit with his favorite women. During a parole officer meeting, he nervously requested permission, eventually receiving approval after committing to share his full story with Aubrey.

Aubrey faced her own challenges, appearing on a morning show and sharing personal insights about her latest book, inspired by her loss. She also hinted at her budding relationship with Garrett, stirring curiosity among fans.

Despite uncertainties, both remained determined to embrace the future, facing challenges head-on and cherishing the connections that anchored them.

NINETEEN

G arrett settled into his seat at the breakfast counter, feeling pleasant muscle exhaustion from his earlier workout session. As he waited for his laptop to start, his phones ringing broke the morning stillness. He hurriedly reached the nightstand, picked up the phone, and answered on the third ring.

"Hey there, gorgeous."

"Good morning, baby; thank you for the lovely balloon and flowers! You know how to make a girl feel loved and special." Aubrey's voice flowed through the line, instantly bringing a smile to Garrett's face.

"You are welcome!" Garrett replied, his heart warming at the sound of her voice.

"It's easy to do when you have someone as amazing as you. You deserve every bit of joy they bring." They continued with their playful banter, exchanging sweet words and affectionate teasing.

Aubrey then filled Garrett in on the conference call she had just participated in, sharing the exciting news of her upcoming engagements and commitments. Garrett listened attentively, his admiration for Aubrey's accomplishments growing with each word.

"I'm incredibly proud of you, Aubrey. You've worked so hard, and your success is well-deserved. I feel lucky to be here, supporting you and cheering you on. Timing has a funny way of bringing people together, and I'm grateful for the moment our paths crossed."

Garrett's heart swelled with affection as Aubrey mentioned their relationship during public interviews. He had taken Aubrey's suggestion and watched her "Coffee with Kathy" clip on YouTube, touched by her genuine and heartfelt words.

"I watched the interview, and felt overwhelmed with love for you," Garrett confessed. "You have a way of touching my heart and bringing out the best in me."

As Aubrey chatted with Garrett, her mind wandered to her discussion with Rachel the night before, leaving her unsettled and anxious about the future. Wanting to understand their game plan, she decided now was the time to bring it up.

"I miss you so much, baby."

"I miss you too, honey. So very much."

Aubrey mustered her courage to express her desires. "I don't want you to leave again after you come to visit me. I want you to stay."

"At some point, hopefully, I won't have to leave," he said, echoing her sentiment. Aubrey's stomach fluttered with excitement, realizing that their desires aligned. She struggled to find the right words, but before she could, Garrett continued speaking.

"I've been thinking a lot about our future, Aubrey," Garrett began, his voice filled with earnestness. "I'd like to discuss it further in person while I'm there. There are things I want to share with you."

"That would be wonderful," Aubrey responded, her voice cracking. A wave of worst-case scenarios flooded her mind, causing her to seek reassurance. "Is everything all right between us?"

Garrett's soothing words washed away her concerns. "Everything is perfect," he assured her. "I just want to make sure we are on the same page. I'm falling more in love with you every day, and I feel it's important for us to have clear expectations regarding our next steps."

"I agree. I am falling madly in love with you, Garrett." She couldn't help but notice the lovesick tone in her voice, a testament to the depth of her feelings for him.

Anxiety plagued Garrett's chest as he thought about their upcoming conversation. He knew he had to share his past with her, as he had discussed with his Parole Officer. It was essential to be honest and transparent, even if it meant risking their relationship. He had decided to tell her everything early next week, allowing her the time and space to process it all.

"I love you, Aubrey. You have no idea how grateful I am to have you in my life. You are an incredible woman, and I thank my lucky stars daily for bringing us together."

Aubrey's response melted Garrett's heart. "I love you too, Garrett. I've always dreamed of finding someone like you. You've made me believe in the power of love and answered prayers."

Garrett experienced an influx of emotions as Aubrey expressed her feelings. He cherished their connection and hoped their conversation next week would only strengthen their bond. Saying their goodbyes, Garrett knew he would be devastated if their relationship didn't weather the storm. He held onto hope, praying that she would understand and accept his past. Only time will tell.

As the days passed and the twenty-third approached, Garrett felt the weight of his nerves and the pressure beginning to build. He knew that the recording session at Mansfield Productions would be a significant moment for him. The executives he had impressed surely recognized his talent, but the actual test would be how the public would receive his music.

Despite his doubts and insecurities, Garrett remained committed to his passion. He continued to practice, striving to deliver a performance that would captivate and touch the hearts of listeners. The journey of pursuing his musical dreams had been filled with ups and downs, but he remained hopeful that his dedication and talent would shine through.

With each chord he played and every lyric he sang, Garrett hoped that his music would resonate with others, just as it did with those who had witnessed his talent firsthand. He held onto the belief that his songs had the power to connect, inspire, and leave a lasting impression on anyone who would listen.

On the Friday before his departure, Garrett went to a familiar cemetery. The overcast sky cast a somber atmosphere over Boise, with the temperature resting at a brisk fifty-five degrees. Clutched in his hands was a vibrant bouquet of assorted flowers. He walked with purpose, heading towards the resting place of his best friend.

Since his release from prison, visiting Matt's grave has become a monthly tradition for him. It was a way for him to reconnect with his past and seek solace in the presence of his departed friend. As he approached the headstone, he took a moment to collect his thoughts and emotions.

Garrett placed the bouquet gently in front of the headstone. He sat down and began a conversation with Matt, recounting the happenings of his life. The upcoming week, with its bustling schedule and his blossoming relationship with Aubrey, took center stage in his narrative.

Garrett poured his heart out for hours, sharing his joys, fears, and dreams. Speaking to Matt felt cathartic as if his friend's spirit was listening attentively. In these moments, Garrett found comfort, a sense of peace in confiding in someone who had been with him through thick and thin.

The clouds hung low, their heaviness reflecting Garrett's somber mood. The cold air carried the scent of rain, adding to the gloomy atmosphere. As he sat near Matt's headstone, lost in his thoughts, he heard the sound of footsteps approaching on the narrow cement path. He looked up and instantly recognized the woman standing a few feet away—Matt's mother, Christine.

"Hello, Garrett," she greeted him, her voice barely above a whisper. Her large brown eyes met his, and he could see their pain and love intertwined.

"Hi, Mrs. Johnson," he responded, rising to his feet and embracing her in a warm hug. Garrett had prepared a quilt blanket on the grass, inviting her to join him. She kicked off her shoes and settled onto the plaid fabric.

"How are you?" she asked sincerely, her gaze burning into his soul. He could see glimpses of Matt in her features, and guilt consumed him—regret for the life he now had, knowing that Matt's life had been cut short.

"I'm doing well. Life has been kind to me lately," he replied, avoiding her eyes, and looking down at the colors in the fabric. "And how are you and Mr. Johnson doing?"

"We're getting by. Some days are easier than others. But that's life. We're embracing our retired life and traveling when we can afford it. And how are the girls? I'm sure they must be happy to have you out of that terrible place finally."

Garrett felt a painful twinge in his stomach at the mention of prison, a constant reminder of the accident that took Matt's life. "They're doing great. I visit them at least once every three months. They're growing up fast, becoming young women instead of little girls." He reached into his jacket pocket, pulling out his phone to show Christine a recent photo he had taken. Handing her the phone, he watched as her face lit up with joy.

"Oh my, they're stunning," she exclaimed, returning the phone to him with a smile. "Thank you for sharing this with me."

Garrett nodded appreciatively. "It's starting to feel a bit overwhelming, to be honest," he admitted, raising his eyebrows and wrinkling his face. Christine's smile reassured him before her attention returned to the grave before them.

In the silence that followed, Garrett could feel the weight of their shared loss. But then, Christine broke the silence, her voice filled with warmth and remembrance.

"You know, he was so proud of you. He admired you as an exceptional father, husband, and friend. You were the man he aspired to be." Christine gently took hold of Garrett's hand, her touch comforting. "It broke his heart when he discovered he couldn't have children. He couldn't understand why such joy and responsibility had been denied him. We spent many nights discussing this, and he often mentioned how much he admired you as a father. He would say, 'There's no other life I'd rather live through than Garrett's.'"

Christine's words pierced Garrett's heart, and tears welled up in his eyes. He looked at her through his tear-filled vision, his voice choked with emotion. "I'm so sorry. I wish I had just let him drive that night when he asked," he confessed, his sobs uncontrollable. Christine wrapped her arms around him, holding him tightly as he released years of guilt and grief.

As Garrett's sobs subsided and his breathing steadied, he heard Christine's voice again.

"It's not your fault, Garrett. We meant it when we said that at your sentencing. It was a tragic accident, and I genuinely believe your drinking had nothing to do with the outcome. I know my son, and he wouldn't have wanted anyone else in that passenger seat if he had known what would happen." Christine's voice was filled with conviction. "As much as I miss him, I believe it was God's will to take him and spare you. You have daughters who need you in their lives. Don't spend your days living in the past, burdened by guilt. Matt is watching over you, cheering you on as he did in life. You've been given a second chance at a happy, meaningful life. Embrace it fully, and never look back, Garrett."

With those final words, Christine released her embrace and stood to leave, slipping her shoes back on. Garrett held her for one last moment, grateful for her understanding and forgiveness. "Thank you for your kind words," he managed to say.

"You're welcome. Don't be a stranger, okay?"

"Okay."

As Christine walked away, he watched her go, knowing that he had received a precious gift in their encounter—a renewed sense of hope and the strength to embrace his life without the weight of guilt. He knew he couldn't change the past, but he could honor Matt's memory by living his life fully, embracing the love and joy he had been blessed with.

As the drizzle turned into heavier rain, Garrett stood there, his face turned upwards, allowing the raindrops to wash over his face. Each droplet felt like a connection to Matt, a reminder of their bond and love. He imagined Matt's presence in the clouds above, shedding tears of appreciation for the moment he had witnessed between two people he loved dearly.

With a sense of forgiveness enveloping him, Garrett spoke softly into the heavens, his words carried away by the rain-soaked breeze. "I love you, Matt. I miss you every day."

As the rain intensified, Garrett packed up his belongings, seeking shelter from the downpour. But within him, a new-found serenity and gratitude lingered. The rain had cleansed his soul, allowing him to let go of the burden of guilt and embrace the memories of his dear friend. With renewed purpose, he walked away, carrying Matt's spirit with him, ready to face the upcoming week.

Sitting in his car, sheltered from the rain, his phone began to vibrate in his pocket. He pulled it out and saw Jerry's name displayed on the screen. Garrett answered the call, feeling guilty for not reaching out earlier.

"Hey, Jerry. It's been a while. How have you been?"

"Long time no talk, my friend. I've been doing great. How about you?" Jerry's voice warmed Garrett's heart, and he realized how much he had missed their conversations.

"I'm doing well. Sorry for not keeping in touch. Life has been hectic lately. No excuses, in any case. I should have reached out."

"Don't worry about it. We all get caught up in life. It's not just your fault. We're talking now, and that's what matters. So, tell me, how are things with your girls, Aubrey, and your auditions? I'm curious to know what's been going on!"

Garrett felt enormous gratitude for Jerry's genuine concern and support. He proceeded to fill Jerry in on all the details he had missed. He talked about his work with Dave and how well the program was helping him. They discussed his upcoming trip to Connecticut and the importance of Dave's thirty-day token. Garrett shared the story of Aubrey's visit to Idaho, and finally, he mentioned the upcoming recording session at Mansfield Productions.

Knowing Jerry's musical expertise, Garrett sought his

opinion on choosing a song for the recording session. He mentioned the two options he had been practicing and asked for Jerry's thoughts.

"I think those songs are exceptional and showcase your talents beautifully. So, if this single sells, you'll have the chance to record more of your music, right?" Jerry asked, seeking clarification.

"Yes, that's correct."

"That's great. It sounds like an amazing opportunity. I understand why you're feeling the pressure to choose the right one. This could open up a whole new world for you."

As raindrops splattered on Garrett's car windshield, his mind filled with doubt and uncertainty. Sensing his unease, Jerry quickly added, "Hey, I don't mean to make you more nervous than you already are. I want you to know that I believe in you and your talent. You deserve this opportunity more than anyone else. It's just an interesting situation, is all."

"I appreciate your support, Jerry. Your words mean a lot to me. I'll always be grateful for your teachings and support in getting me to this point."

Jerry paused momentarily, and in the background, Garrett could hear the faint sound of ocean waves. Before Garrett could inquire about his location, Jerry spoke again. "Garrett, I have an idea. Before I propose anything, I want you to know how much I admire the songs you've written. I think they're beautiful. Could I offer a suggestion?

Intrigued and slightly puzzled, Garrett replied, "Of course. I would love to hear your thoughts and ideas."

"Do you remember the first song I taught you to play? The one I wrote for my daughter?"

A rush of memories flooded Garrett's mind, and he responded eagerly, "Yes, I remember. That song has always held a special place in my heart. I've only played it alone in my apartment. I have never shared that with anyone since I know how much that song means to you."

"Well, Garrett, I would be honored if you would consider playing that song for your recording session," Jerry offered sincerely.

Garrett's chest swelled with emotions, "Jerry, that's an incredible offer. Are you sure about that?" he asked, feeling the weight of Jerry's generosity.

"I'm sure. And please know that I don't expect anything in return. Hearing you sing over the years has brought me so much joy."

"Thank you so much. I will be forever grateful for this. If this single turns out to be a success, I'll make sure you receive the credit you deserve."

"There's something else I want you to know. You've made tremendous changes in your life. It's been an honor to be a part of your journey. I'm proud of the person you've become, and I look forward to seeing your continued success in life. Remember to keep making God your number one priority and your recovery your number two. With that, everything will fall into place, and your life will transform into a blissful paradise, akin to what the Buddhists call 'Enlightenment.'"

Garrett's heart filled with concern. Jerry's words felt like a farewell, leaving him puzzled. Negative thoughts began to consume his thinking, "Jerry, I appreciate your kind words and guidance. You've been instrumental in my journey. But I have to ask, is everything all right? Your words sound like a goodbye."

Jerry took a moment to respond, and when he spoke again, his voice exuded assurance and conviction. "Everything is more than all right. It's perfect, as it should be. I'm fine, so don't worry about me. I say these things because I believe you can achieve great things independently. You've learned how to stay sober and are now helping others. Your life is on its correct trajectory, its correct path. Don't let anything or anyone get in the way of your ultimate goals."

As those last words were spoken, his mind suddenly returned to that haunting flashback with Matt in the car. The present faded away, replaced by the vivid memories of that tragic evening.

Garrett found himself back in the wreckage, his head resting against the deployed airbag, bloodied and disoriented. Matt's face was turned towards him, both sharing a profound and sorrowful gaze. The weight of their unspoken emotions hung heavy in the air.

"I love you, brother," Matt's weak voice broke the silence. His voice was barely above a whisper. "This wasn't your fault, and you know it. You are a good man, Garrett. Find your path in life and never look back."

Tears welled up in Garrett's eyes, his heart aching with grief and desperation. "No, Matt! You can't leave me here. I need you in my life! Please, hang on. Someone will be here soon, and we'll both be all right. I promise, Matt."

But Matt's condition worsened, his coughs growing more violent. Thick, dark blood spilled from his mouth, staining his lips. Garrett strained to hear Matt's fading words as if time had slowed.

"I will always be with you, Garrett. I love you, brother."

The weight of those words pressed upon Garrett's soul as if etched there forever. He watched, heartbroken, as Matt closed his eyes, his body succumbing to the injuries he had sustained. Garrett's consciousness slipped away, merging with the present once more.

Returning to reality, Jerry's words resonated through his eardrums.

"Garrett, your girls need you out there, and this Aubrey woman sounds like a gift from above. It's time for you to stop relying on me so much and start believing in yourself. You give me too much credit for getting you to this point. The most influential and important person in your life is you, Garrett. You and our God deserve all the credit, no one else."

Garrett began to grasp the purpose behind Jerry's mood and message. He understood that Jerry wanted to gradually detach him from their reliance on each other as he prepared to embark on his new life in Avon. While the realization made sense, it also stirred a bittersweet ache within him, mingling with the unresolved emotions from the unexpected flashback.

Reflecting on the recent events and his progress, he recognized that he had accomplished much with minimal assistance from Jerry. Jerry was urging him to embrace independence and the possibilities that awaited him.

"I want to express my sincere gratitude, Jerry," Garrett responded, his voice filled with appreciation. "Thank you for your unwavering help, encouragement, and support. I understand your point, but I can't help but feel an overwhelming sense of gratitude for the pivotal role you've played in guiding me through the challenges I've faced. You've helped me replace fear with hope, pride with humility, and selfishness with compassion. I truly believe I'm better because of you and the example you've set. Jerry, I love you."

"I love you too, son. Good luck on Monday. Enjoy your upcoming visit and give the girls a warm hug from me. And please let Aubrey know how fortunate you are to have found each other. It seems like she's been searching for you her entire life, and you should cherish the bond you share."

Jerry ended the call with those words, leaving Garrett with a whirlwind of emotions.

Aubrey sat on the "The Today Show" set in NYC, enamored by the host's introduction and the cheering audience. She couldn't recall the host's name but found her familiar. The spotlight shifted to a piano in the corner, where Garrett sat handsomely in a gray suit, his smile reaching Aubrey's heart. The room grew silent as Garrett focused on the instrument before him, his fingers gracefully dancing across the keys. He played his creation, "Airplanes," enchanting the audience and casting a spell on Aubrey herself.

When the lights brightened again, the crowd erupted in applause. Garrett stood and approached Aubrey, their hands intertwined to symbolize their love. The host spoke up amidst the frenzied crowd, introducing Garrett's new hit single and praising their relationship. Aubrey felt self-conscious as she noticed the host's flirtatious look, but her attention remained on Garrett, who radiated love and pride.

The host shifted her focus back to Aubrey, proclaiming they had one more surprise guest. Aubrey's nerves tightened, wondering who else could appear. Then, her father's voice filled the air, causing her to tremble.

She whispered, "Daddy," in disbelief. The voice assured her it was indeed her father, even though logic told her otherwise.

Flooded with tears, Aubrey confessed how much she missed him. Garrett's touch on her hand offered comfort, and she met his teary gaze, finding comfort in their shared emotions. The studio was hushed, everyone enthralled by the heartfelt exchange between father and daughter.

Her father's voice continued, expressing his pride in Aubrey's growth and urging her to let go of the pain caused by his death. He emphasized the importance of accepting and moving on, assuring her that he would always be with her in spirit. Aubrey searched the studio's ceiling to glimpse her father's face, her heart aching for his presence. When she looked at Garrett, she noticed his recognition of the voice, as if they had shared a deep connection from another lifetime.

As silence enveloped her, urgency welled up inside. Aubrey pleaded for him to keep talking, fearing the loss of this precious moment. The audience erupted in applause, drowning out her father's voice. Aubrey stood, desperately trying to quiet them, but their noise grew louder, seemingly entertained by her distress. Overwhelmed, she fell to the ground, covering her ears to escape the cacophony.

When she opened her eyes, Aubrey found herself lying in bed, the dream fading. The echoes of her father's words remained etched into her heart, reminding her of the need to heal and embrace the love that surrounded her.

CHAPTER

TWENTY

Garrett's plane landed at JFK Airport late at night on October twenty-second. Mansfield Productions had kindly provided him with first-class tickets for the flight, making it a comfortable journey. During his last flight, Garrett struck up a conversation with a friendly older man who was traveling the world after retirement. They talked about various destinations, from exotic islands to beautiful mountains, and Garrett found it one of the most exciting conversations he had ever experienced. Upon landing, it was difficult for him to bid farewell to this newfound friend.

Making his way to the baggage claim area, he spotted a driver holding a sign with his name written in large black lettering. Tom had arranged for transportation, and Garrett introduced himself to the driver. The driver led him to a sleek black limo waiting outside the airport. Inside, he found luxurious beige leather seats, a small TV screen, and a bottle of chilled champagne. Soft background music played, creating a soothing ambiance. Garrett couldn't help but feel grateful for the special treatment he was receiving.

During the drive to his hotel in Midtown Manhattan, Garrett reflected on the remarkable changes in his life over the past year. It had been thirteen months since he left behind the life of a prisoner, bidding farewell to the fences and barbed wire that had confined him for five long years.

Upon arrival at the Westin Hotel, the driver assisted Garrett with his luggage. His fifteenth-floor room offered stunning views of the vibrant city below. As he stared out the window, captivated by the glittering lights and bustling streets, Garrett marveled at how far he had come. The hotel's elegance and comfort were far beyond what he could have afforded on his own, and he was grateful for the support he had received from Mansfield Productions. Settling into the plush king-sized bed, he soon drifted into a peaceful slumber.

At nine the following morning, Garrett anxiously awaited in the hotel lobby. Another man, dressed in a black suit just like the driver from the previous night, approached the front desk and inquired about Mr. Anderson. Garrett introduced himself, and together, they went outside, where another black limousine waited for him near the sidewalk. The drive to the studio was short yet exhilarating, with the skillful driver navigating the city's crowded streets. As they arrived at their destination, Garrett felt his nerves take hold. The pressure to perform at his best was starting to get to him.

While walking into the building, Garrett received a text message from Aubrey. Her words of love and support filled his warm heart and eased his anxious mind. He quickly typed a response before stepping into the elevator. "Thank you, my love! I'm on my way up now. I love you more than words can describe!"

After the elevator doors closed and reopened, Garrett was greeted by Dale, Tom, and Walter in the front foyer. Each of them expressed their excitement and welcomed him warmly. Leading him through the expansive offices, they guided Garrett to the back room where the recording studio was. Understanding the importance of preparation, they assured him he could take as much time as needed to practice and warm up in private.

Taking a seat on the bench in front of the grand piano, Garrett took a moment to gather his thoughts and find his happy place before starting his practice session. As he played Jerry's song, "Angel of Mine," the notes filled the room with an angelic and ethereal sound. Garrett couldn't help but feel immense gratitude for the priceless gift Jerry had given him. He was already contemplating ways to express appreciation and repay Jerry's kindness.

Feeling confident and ready, Garrett called Dale, Tom, and Walter back into the room, signaling that he was prepared to begin. By two o'clock. Garrett had successfully recorded his first single. Surprisingly, the process had been smoother and more straightforward than expected. Although he had to adapt to the constant criticism and feedback, he realized that it had ultimately improved his song through a collaborative "teamwork" approach.

Garrett expressed his gratitude and excitement to the team by explaining that his friend Jerry had been the talented songwriter behind the recorded song. They promptly provided him with a form to ensure Jerry received the proper credit he deserved. They also outlined the next steps in the process. The song would be released on iTunes and sent to music stations nationwide. Based on the sales and radio ratings, Garrett had the potential to secure a lucrative recording contract that would encompass his first full-length album, publicity tours, and promotional campaigns for his concerts.

Initially, Garrett would receive thirty-five percent of all iTunes sales, which would be transferred to his account on the first day of each month. It was surreal for him to contemplate that his music could generate income akin to his stock investments. He likened his single's success to the rise of a company's stock price, as his popularity expanded and resonated worldwide, he would be paid healthy dividends.

After completing the necessary paperwork, Garrett received multiple copies of his new single and was free to depart for Connecticut. Dale had arranged a rental car, waiting for him in the underground parking garage. Inside the vehicle, he discovered his luggage and a lavish gift basket filled with high-end delicacies, a thoughtful gesture from the team.

As Garrett drove away from the parking garage, he couldn't help but feel an overpowering sense of relief and joy. The weight of the day's events had finally sunk in, and he found himself laughing in disbelief at the incredible reality unfolding before him. The knowledge that his voice would soon be heard on radios nationwide and his song would be available worldwide on iTunes made him appreciate the blessings that had come his way.

A profound joy filled Garrett's heart as he recognized that he was on the right path, guided by a higher power. The happiness that eluded him for so long now permeated his being, bringing a newfound sense of fulfillment. He believed that God had orchestrated his journey, and this realization touched his heart and soul deeply.

Garrett believed this was a remarkable way to start his vacation, a true testament to the wonders that awaited him. He eagerly headed toward the three most influential women in his life, ready to share the incredible news with them and bask in their love and support.

Aubrey arrived at the IHOP a few minutes before seven, feeling slightly nervous. As she entered the restaurant, she spotted Garrett approaching her. Her heart fluttered as he enveloped her in a warm embrace. They shared a tender moment, their connection sparking a lovely sensation that danced across her skin.

Garrett looked handsome in his casual attire, wearing well-fitted jeans and a simple sweater. His jet-black hair was neatly styled, and a subtle cologne lingered. Aubrey's senses came alive with his presence, seduced by his touch and the gaze of his dark green eyes that matched the color of his sweatshirt. Jasmine's voice brought her back to this world.

"I've been following your interviews on YouTube," Jasmine exclaimed enthusiastically. Aubrey blushed, feeling slightly vulnerable under the spotlight of media attention. Sensing her shyness, Jasmine quickly added, "You've done an excellent job! I loved your outfit on 'Coffee with Kathy,' I could tell she was a little intimidated by you."

Aubrey smiled, genuinely appreciating the compliment. "Thank you, Jasmine. I was nervous during that interview, so your words mean a lot."

While waiting for her turn to join the conversation, Alexa said, "I agree with Jasmine. You're prettier than Kathy. I especially enjoyed hearing about Dad."

Blushing again, Aubrey replied, "I'm glad you enjoyed that part, Alexa. I wanted to clarify to the world that I'm taken."

The girls responded with an adorable chorus of "Awe!"

Garrett, his affectionate gaze fixed on Aubrey, held her hand beneath the table, providing a comforting reassurance.

As they settled into a booth, Aubrey asked, "So, who here is a big breakfast fan?" Jasmine and Alexa's right hand shot up towards the ceiling.

"Breakfast has always been a favorite for us," Garrett explained with a smile.

Aubrey recalled the delicious omelet Garrett had prepared for her during her visit to Idaho, causing a pleasurable flinch within her lower body. "Me too," she confessed, her mind still filled with fond memories of their time together.

Garrett's smile widened. "Good! You fit right in with this breakfast-loving bunch."

The attentive waitress took their orders. Jasmine and Alexa chose French toast with bacon and chocolate milkshakes, while Garrett ordered a classic breakfast with eggs, hash browns, bacon, toast, and milk. Aubrey was enticed by the picture of a cheesy southern omelet and decided to savor it along with a glass of milk. She appreciated the opportunity to enjoy breakfast for dinner, a delightful perk of being in the company of children. The thought brought a genuine smile to her face.

Garrett playfully inquired about her amusement, and Aubrey responded, "Just very happy to be here, Mr. Anderson."

Throughout the meal, the conversations flowed effortlessly between Aubrey and the girls. They exchanged stories, sharing details about their lives, interests, and aspirations.

While the waitress cleared their plates, laughter filled the air, and Aubrey couldn't help but feel a deep gratitude. In Garrett, she had found love and a loving family that welcomed her wholeheartedly.

As Jasmine and Alexa entered Garrett's rental car, Aubrey and Garrett approached her SUV. However, they paused in front of her vehicle, and Garrett stepped in front of her, taking hold of her hands.

"Thank you for coming tonight. You have two admirers, in case you hadn't noticed," Garrett said, his voice filled with affection. Aubrey's heart fluttered, overwhelmed by her love for him and his daughters.

"Oh, Garrett. They are amazing, and I admire them just as much. I'm so excited to spend more time with them this week."

He embraced her tightly, pressing her against his muscular chest. "You make me so happy. I'm deeply in love with you, in case you hadn't noticed that either," he whispered into her ear.

A playful smile graced Aubrey's lips. "I hadn't noticed," she teased. "Thank you for clarifying that for me. By the way, I'm crazy in love with you too. I don't want you ever to leave me again."

Garrett pulled back slightly, placing his hand on her cheek. He leaned in, kissing her with passion and desire. Time stood still. Their longing and hunger for one another permeated the air. When they finally broke the kiss, it took Aubrey a moment to catch her breath and regain her composure. Garrett's kisses could transport her to a dreamlike state where anything was possible.

"I'm so glad your recording session went well. I know you're going to be a huge success," she said, her eyes filled with love and pride.

Garrett smiled, his eyes burning with affection. "I hope you're right. I'll bring you a copy of the single tomorrow." They shared one more scorching kiss before reluctantly parting ways for the night.

"I can't wait to hear it. I love you. Sleep well, handsome."

"You too, baby. I love you the most."

Aubrey sat in her car, still basking in the lingering sensation of Garrett's kiss on her lips. She basked in the moment, not wanting the intense feelings to fade away. She longed to spend every waking moment with this incredible man. Tomorrow couldn't come soon enough.

CHAPTER

TWENTY-ONE

After dropping the girls off at their respective schools, Garrett returned to the welcoming ambiance of the 1818 Estate. Having had a positive experience during his last visit, he decided to stay there again. He had some work to attend to before meeting Dave for a coffee and a light breakfast.

Settling in his room, Garrett powered up his laptop and immersed himself in researching various tech companies that had caught his attention. Despite occasional distractions caused by his busy mind, he produced over five thousand dollars in profits over the last week, a testament to his astute decision-making. With each passing month, his average monthly revenue increased to an impressive fifteen thousand dollars.

Garrett's heart raced as he made necessary purchases and skimmed through his emails. The thought of his music and voice reaching the airwaves that day made him feel vulnerable and exposed. He yearned to gauge the public's response to his song, wondering how it would be received. The executives at Mansfield Production had advised him that it would take about a month to understand the audience's reaction to his unique sound and style. They emphasized that iTunes sales would best indicate the song's popularity and reception.

Feeling excitement and trepidation, Garrett closed his laptop and retrieved a jacket from the coat closet. Though the skies mainly appeared clear, the temperature hovered around fifty degrees. Glancing at his phone's clock, he realized he had just enough time to make it to "The Flying Cup" for his ten-thirty meeting with Dave. Today was significant for Dave as he would receive his thirty-day token, a milestone they had both looked forward to. After their coffee date, they planned to attend the noon meeting in Avon.

Driving towards his destination, Garrett's mind was plagued with thoughts about the conversation he would soon have with Aubrey. They planned to meet for lunch around one-thirty, and he had decided it would be the best time to reveal his past to her. He hoped and prayed she would be understanding and accept his history. The thought of losing her companionship was a heavy burden on his heart as he had fallen deeply in love with her. In just thirty days, their connection had grown to an inexplicable level, a love that he knew was rare and came only once in a lifetime.

Garrett parked his rental car next to Dave's truck, and they exchanged warm greetings with a handshake and a friendly hug. They entered the busy coffee shop, finding a quiet table in the corner. After placing their orders, they delved into Dave's progress with his step work. Dave pulled out his workbook, and they went through his step two homework together.

As Garrett listened to Dave's responses, he noticed a new-found confidence in his friend. Dave seemed more at ease, and Garrett felt a sense of joy witnessing his transformation. Their friendship was slowly taking root, and even though they hadn't shared much about their personal lives, Garrett valued the connection they were building. After discussing step two in detail, their conversation shifted to the strength of Dave's sobriety.

Dave spoke passionately about the daily meetings he attended, with the one they were about to go to becoming his home group. He shared the support he found in reaching out to other recovering alcoholics and the positive impact this fellowship provided. Despite occasional cravings, Garrett assured him they would lessen over time, though never entirely disappear. He commended Dave for his commitment to healthily dealing with these cravings.

During their discussion, Dave opened up for the first time about his past, revealing that he had spent fifteen years in prison for Aggravated Vehicular Manslaughter. Garrett understood why Dave related to him so profoundly at their first meeting. The power of the recovery program was evident in the connections they formed through shared experiences, past mistakes, and understanding.

As Garrett continued to listen, something about his story became eerily familiar. Initially, he attributed it to the similarities with his crime, but a nagging feeling tugged at the corners of his mind. There was something more that resonated with recent information he had come across. Dave's words cut through the air as Garrett began connecting the dots.

"Well, it's time for us to head over to the church," Dave declared with an infectious smile. The significance of receiving his thirty-day coin filled the moment with a sense of achievement and hope. Garrett nodded, pulling himself out of his deep contemplation. They settled the bill with the hostess and stepped out through the glass doors, the outside world beckoning them forward.

Much to Garrett's surprise, Aubrey's SUV pulled up in front of them, and her eyes met him with a warm smile. His heart skipped a beat, and anxiety coiled in his stomach as he anticipated the upcoming conversation. "Hey Dave, this is my girlfriend Aubrey, who just pulled up. I would like you to meet her."

Aubrey felt a faint shyness as she retrieved her purse and laptop bag, unaware that Garrett would be at "The Flying Cup" for his meeting. She didn't want to intrude on their time together, but she couldn't resist the chance to see him. Stepping out of her car, she was met with Garrett's embrace, a hug, and a kiss that brought much-needed comfort.

"Hello, beautiful! What a pleasant surprise to see you here."

"Agreed, Garrett. I had no idea you would be here. I planned to enjoy a mocha and finish some work while waiting for our lunch date."

"I'm glad you found me! I want you to meet my friend," Garrett said, leading Aubrey toward the stranger. Aubrey studied him as they approached, and a sense of familiarity lingered in her mind. He wore a simple outfit, yet his presence resonated with her. When their eyes finally met, Aubrey immediately reacted, retracting her hand as if in pain. Dave's face flushed with embarrassment, caught off guard by Aubrey's sudden coldness.

"Aubrey, this is my friend Dave Mills. Dave, meet my girlfriend, Aubrey Ellis," Garrett introduced, trying to make sense of the tension between them. Aubrey's eyes remained fixed on Dave, an intense, heated glare radiating animosity. Confused and exasperated, Garrett finally asked the question that hung in the air, "Do you two know each other?"

Aubrey didn't spare a glance at Garrett, her focus solely on Dave, her eyes filled with seething hatred. Dave, visibly uncomfortable, averted his gaze, not daring to meet her hostile stare. "I thought you were in prison," Aubrey uttered, the words dripping with contempt.

Dave's voice barely a whisper, he responded, "I got out a few months ago," his face reddening with shame. "I'm so sorry, Aubrey. I understand if you hate me, but please know ..."

"STOP!" Aubrey's shout shattered the silence, causing Dave and Garrett to startle. With a scowl, she continued, "I don't care how sorry you are. You are the reason my father is no longer alive. I pleaded with the judge to never let you out. It's infuriating to see you free while my father rests in a wooden box six feet under the ground."

Garrett's world shattered around him as he realized the dreadful truth. Dave was responsible for the accident with Aubrey's parents fifteen years ago. It all fell into place, and the weight of the situation pressed heavily on Garrett's chest. He was ill-prepared to handle such a catastrophic turn of events. He was speechless and stunned but could only bear witness as Aubrey unleashed her anger and pain upon Dave.

With each word Aubrey spat at him, Dave recoiled, his face etched with embarrassment, pain, and remorse. He tried to apologize repeatedly, but his words fell flat against the torrent of emotions pouring from Aubrey. Slowly, he started to retreat, the weight of her accusations too heavy to bear.

"I am so sorry. I am so sorry," Dave's voice trembled, his words a mantra of remorse. Aubrey fell silent as she watched him recede, her fists clenched tightly before her. She watched him enter his truck and drive away, leaving behind a shattered spirit. Garrett's heart ached at the sight, torn between running after his friend to ensure his well-being and staying by Aubrey's side to offer solace and apologies for not knowing the truth about Dave's past involvement.

As Dave's car vanished into the distance, Aubrey turned her gaze towards Garrett, her blue eyes mirroring the pain, anger, and hurt that consumed her.

"I'm sorry, Aubrey. I honestly had no idea he had anything to do with your parents' accident," Garrett's voice was filled with genuine remorse as he spoke. His words reached Aubrey, penetrating the shield of anger that had enveloped her. The rage began to subside, giving way to a deep well of sadness that was all too familiar to her. Tears streamed down her cheeks as the adrenaline from the anger gave way to immense pain.

Garrett's arms enveloped her, drawing her close to his warm, comforting presence. She buried her face in his soft white jacket, the fabric absorbing her tears as her body shook uncontrollably. At that moment, the floodgates of emotions burst open, releasing the pain and anguish she had suppressed for so long. She couldn't fathom that Dave was out of prison, free to roam, and here with the man she loved—the one person she had entrusted to shield her from the pain inflicted by Dave.

The sadness that engulfed her swiftly transformed into a powerful sense of betrayal. Aubrey felt a deep pang of hurt as she realized that Garrett had been spending time with Dave, even helping him, unbeknownst to her. The whole situation grew exponentially more devastating, intensifying her heartache and disillusionment. She squirmed out of his arms, wiping her tears away. She looked at him with a cold stare, anger pulsing through her veins again. "Why would you help someone like him, Garrett?" she asked through gritted teeth. "He's a murderer. He just spent time in prison. Why on earth would you want to try and save a low life like him?"

As he absorbed Aubrey's plea, Garrett's heart shattered into a million pieces. The pain and hopelessness overtook him, leaving him speechless and lost. He couldn't conjure up a response that would mend the damage caused. The weight of his guilt and the realization of his shortcomings overwhelmed him, driving him deeper into despair.

"Tell me you will not help him anymore. Tell me you will cut him out of your life!" Aubrey's voice pleaded, her face etched with tension and a straight line forming on her lips.

Garrett suddenly felt utterly calm, like he was experiencing a moment of clarity he had often heard about in his recovery meetings but never truly experienced until now. He understood that this was his chance to explain his past and disclose the truth he had kept hidden. He knew that if he didn't share his circumstances now, it would only create more pain and confusion for both of them in the future. Aubrey deserved to know the entire truth.

"Can we please sit in your car for a moment? I need to tell you something about myself," Garrett requested calmly. Aubrey looked puzzled, but after a brief pause, she nodded and entered her vehicle, with Garrett taking the passenger seat beside her.

As they settled into the car, Aubrey's discomfort was palpable. She locked her eyes onto Garrett's, awaiting the revelation she sensed was about to unfold. Garrett took a deep breath, steadying himself before he began to speak.

"Aubrey, I've been waiting for the right moment to tell you about my past." Garrett's voice trembled with vulnerability. "Jerry, my mentor, and I have discussed when would be an appropriate time, and today was the day we chose. But before I say anything else, I want you to know that I can refer Dave to another mentor. I have no problem doing that."

Aubrey's unease heightened, sensing that what Garrett was about to confess would not be easy to hear. She braced herself, eyes locked onto him, ready to face the truth.

"I help people like Dave because I am no better than him," Garrett's voice cracked, revealing the weight of his admission. "We both struggle with alcoholism, but that's not all we have in common. I, too, have spent time in prison. I was released over a year ago after serving a five-year sentence for an alcohol-related accident. I was convicted of a 'Vehicular Manslaughter' charge, similar to what Dave received."

Aubrey felt her breath catch in her throat. Anxiety gripped her chest, making it hard to breathe. It felt as if the air was being sucked out of the car. Darkness closed in on her vision, threatening to engulf her. But Garrett's voice pierced through the haze, calling her back.

"Take a deep breath, Aubrey. Breathe," he pleaded urgently, rolling down the windows, and inviting the cool air into her nostrils. Aubrey followed his command, gasping for air and filling her lungs with each inhalation. The darkness slowly receded, replaced by the life-giving oxygen. Minutes passed, and Aubrey gradually regained control, her panic subsiding. It had been years since she had experienced such a paralyzing attack, and she was grateful that Garrett had been there to guide her out of the darkness.

However, her relief was short-lived as the weight of Garrett's confession settled in her mind. "You killed someone?" she whispered, her voice barely audible.

"Yes," Garrett's voice trembled with remorse. "I was driving drunk with my best friend Matt when the accident happened. He was killed as a result of the collision with another vehicle. I was charged with a felony because of his death. I am responsible, just like Dave is for your father's death. Aubrey, I didn't know how to tell you, especially after hearing what happened to ..."

"Get out!" Aubrey's scream pierced the air, filled with rage and disgust. Garrett felt his heart shatter again, the pain intensified by her rejection. He looked into her eyes, seeing the contempt written across her face, and felt his self-worth crumble.

"Please, Aubrey, don't do this," he pleaded, his voice full of desperation. Aubrey's gaze softened slightly, indicating the internal struggle raging within.

"Please don't make any decisions while you're upset. Can you think about this before saying something you might regret?" Garrett implored, holding onto a glimmer of hope. He watched as Aubrey's expression relaxed slightly.

"You lied to me by omission, Garrett."

"I know. I should have told you from the beginning. I'm so sorry for not being honest with you sooner."

"Please, Garrett, just go. You should have told me about this way sooner than now. I don't know if it would have changed my feelings for you, but at least it would have been fair to me instead of waiting until after I fell in love with you," Aubrey's words stung, striking deep into Garrett's core. He felt a dagger thrust into his chest repeatedly, the pain unbearable.

Tears streamed down his cheeks as he realized the depth of his mistake. He knew this would be the last time he saw her. He reached for the door handle with a trembling hand, pulling it slightly open before mustering the strength to speak. "For what it's worth, Aubrey, Matt, and I were T-boned by an older man who had experienced a fatal stroke. He was unconscious when he hit us. I still take full responsibility because I might have reacted differently if I had been sober. I'm sorry for not telling you sooner. I know now that I've messed up. I also know that I will never find a love like ours again. This was a once-in-a-lifetime opportunity, and I can't believe it is slipping away from me. I love you, Aubrey." With one last tear-filled glance, he stepped out of her car, closing the door behind him.

As he walked away, the pain in his heart matched the weight of his footsteps. He knew he had lost her; the regret and self-loathing felt too much to bear. Garrett took a few moments to gather himself after Aubrey's departure. Tears continued to stream down his face. Amid his pain, he prayed, seeking comfort and guidance from a higher power.

He poured out his emotions, asking God for comfort and strength for himself, Dave, and Aubrey. He desired the courage to face the aftermath of their relationship, whatever it may be, and to continue moving forward in his life. Seeking understanding, he asked for clarity on God's will and the strength to fulfill it. And knowing that Dave was likely struggling, he sought inspiration to support him through his challenging time.

Once the prayer concluded, a determination flickered within him. The image of Dave's face lingered in his mind, and he felt an intense urge to find him. He knew that Dave must be grappling with devastating emotions—shame, guilt, and the temptation to turn to alcohol once again to numb the wound.

Garrett wiped away his tears and started his car. He couldn't let his sorrow and guilt overshadow his commitment to helping others. He vowed to find Dave and offer him support, drawing from his own experiences and the lessons he had learned during his recovery.

Feeling increasingly anxious as he set down his phone, Garrett acknowledged that Dave must have turned it off, adding to his sense of urgency. Since Dave's house had yet to yield results, Garrett knew his last option was to check the local bars in the area. Aware there weren't many options, especially at that time of day, he hoped to find some clue about Dave's where about. Garrett's mind raced as he drove from one bar to another. He couldn't shake off the feeling of responsibility and the urgency to find his friend.

Garrett's frustration grew as he pulled up to the third location on his list. He scanned the parking lot, hoping to locate Dave's truck, but it was nowhere to be found. Doubts started to set in, wondering if he was on the wrong track or if Dave had managed to find another place to drown his sorrows.

To stay positive, Garrett reminded himself that Dave might have returned to work or sought comfort at home with his understanding parents. He clung to the hope that maybe his friend had found a safe space to process the nightmare encounter earlier in the day.

With growing determination, Garrett checked his list's fourth and final location. As he arrived at the hole-in-the-wall bar at the edge of town, he noticed Dave's older pickup truck among the few vehicles parked outside.

Taking a deep breath, Garrett entered the dimly lit establishment. The atmosphere was filled with the scent of alcohol and the sound of cheerful and melancholic conversations. He navigated through the crowd, his eyes scanning the bar and the scattered tables and chairs, searching for Dave's familiar face.

Unable to spot him inside, Garrett's focus shifted toward a back door that led to an outside patio area. Following his instinct, he stepped outside and found Dave sitting and conversing with an unknown man.

Garrett's heart sank at the sight. He mustered up his courage and approached their table. "Hey, Dave," Dave's eyes opened wide with surprise hearing the familiar voice.

"What are you doing here, Garrett?"

"Can I sit with you?" Garrett motioned toward an empty chair beside Dave and opposite the stranger occupying the second seat. They were sitting around a circular glass table, with a large umbrella providing shade. Dave nodded reluctantly, and Garrett took his seat. He glanced at the shot glasses on the table, one full and one empty, with the full one in front of Dave.

The man across from Garrett stared at him, seemingly evaluating his every move. He wore a Patriots jersey over a white sweatshirt, dirty blue jeans, and a Patriots hat that concealed his eyes. Garrett looked away, focusing on his friend.

"How are you doing?" Garrett asked. Dave shrugged, his guilt-ridden expression still showing signs of distress.

"Garrett, this is my friend Justin. We did time together."

Garrett nodded in Justin's direction, and Justin gave him a somewhat challenging grin. Before Garrett could say anything else, Justin spoke up.

"I was just telling Dave to take some shots with me before you rolled up. Maybe you could help me talk some sense into him," Justin said with a slur.

Garrett felt anger rising within him, but he tried to remain calm. He looked at Justin, the anger simmering beneath the surface. "I don't think that's a good idea, Justin. I'm here to help him, not encourage him to drink."

Justin burst into laughter, provoking Garrett even further. "What are you, his pastor or some goody two shoes trying to save him from the evils of this world?"

Garrett took a deep breath, trying to control his breathing. "No, I'm just a friend who wants to see Dave succeed rather than waste it away."

Justin's demeanor became tense and irritated at Garrett's comment. "Are you trying to say I'm wasting away my life, homie?"

"I'm not your homie," Garrett said, his anger approaching its tipping point.

Justin leaned in closer to Garrett, his eyes narrowing and his expression serious. "You better watch who you're talking to. I don't know if you heard Dave, but we met in the joint. You cross me, and we're going to ..."

Garrett didn't let him finish. In a moment of rage, he exploded out of his chair and was at Justin's side in seconds. He grabbed Justin's jersey, and his hand contacted Justin's face, a slap rather than a punch. Justin's nose started to bleed.

Breathing heavily, Garrett spoke through gritted teeth, his aggressive stance clear. "Tell me, what do you want me to break, your arm or your leg?!?"

Justin looked at Garrett in shock, fear overtaking his body as it began to shake. After a moment, Garrett asked again, this time louder and more intense. "Arm or Leg?!?"

Justin put his hands up in the air, his voice trembling. "I'm sorry, man. I don't want you to break any of them. Please, just let me go."

Garrett released his grip on Justin, watching as he scrambled out of his chair and rushed for the back door. As Justin left, he muttered, "You're crazy, man."

Garrett's hands trembled slightly as he realized the consequences of his actions. He looked at Dave, whose confusion mirrored his internal turmoil. The realization hit him hard—this was a relapse, a return to his past patterns of using anger as a defense mechanism. With an understanding of the destructive power it held over him, this was a step in the wrong direction.

The memories of his violent past, the fights, and the pain flooded back with clarity. During his time in prison, the cycle of violence had finally come to a halt.

Garrett and Jerry were in their cell, engaging in a discussion about their recovery. It had only been a few weeks since Garrett had opened up to Jerry for the first time, and he had been actively participating in the program of Daily Recovery, making it a priority in his life.

They were focusing on a step that addressed unhealthy behaviors associated with their past struggles. Garrett recognized that his anger was one of the issues that needed attention.

Jerry gently approached the topic, saying, "You understand that anger and violence can be used as coping mechanisms, just like alcohol, right?"

Garrett appeared puzzled, furrowing his brows and squinting his eyes. "I'm not so sure," he replied, seeking clarification.

Jerry took a moment to gather his thoughts before continuing, "Let me explain. You've always been drawn to fighting, right?"

"Yeah," Garrett admitted.

"And does hurting others give you a sense of power and an adrenaline rush?" Jerry asked further.

Garrett considered the question. "I suppose it does. It makes me feel in control."

"Did alcohol also provide you with those same feelings?"

Garrett paused, reflecting on the question. "Yes, it did," he admitted, realizing the similarities between his anger and his past reliance on alcohol. He understood that both provided an outlet for his emotions, albeit in different forms.

Jerry empathetically acknowledged Garrett's realization. "It seems like you're gaining more clarity now. In this prison, you've earned a reputation as a skilled fighter, feared by others. But you also carry much anger, more than any other inmate here. You can influence others, but is being feared what you truly want? Would you rather be known for your aggression or your compassion? For your violence or your humility?"

These questions struck a chord within Garrett, causing him to contemplate his actions and their consequences deeply. Jerry's words offered a new perspective on his behavior, revealing the harsh reality of his choices.

Garrett's expression softened as he replied sincerely, "No, Jerry. I don't want to be that person anymore."

"Good. We still have some work to address the underlying painful memories and emotions you've been suppressing. But before we proceed, it seems some unfinished business needs your attention."

Garrett understood Jerry's allusion and knew exactly what needed to be done. Although Garrett had formed a close bond with Ty, he was reluctantly drawn into the world of SHFL. Despite not being an official member, Garrett had become Ty's trusted ally, taking on dangerous missions with unique skills he had acquired over time. His ability to navigate through prison cells undetected and incapacitate his targets swiftly made him an enigmatic figure among his peers. Garrett's presence alone instilled fear in the hearts of those residing within the confines of his unit, as they were all aware of the consequences that would follow his unexpected intrusion into their lives.

Garrett got up quickly and exited his cell. He found Ty talking with a group of guys at the poker table where commissary cash was being betted on with each new game. Once close enough, Garrett asked Ty to walk around the unit with him.

"What's up, brother?" Ty asked, draping his right arm around Garrett's shoulders.

"You and I have become very close over the last few years, and I want you to know I respect and care about you a lot, bro. I understand the dynamics of this place and how it operates. I've played my part in keeping things in order, but I can't do it anymore. I need to make changes in my life."

Ty pulled his arm off Garrett's shoulders and stopped walking. He looked at Garrett with disappointment and concern. "Are you telling me you're turning your back on me? After all we've been through?"

Garrett shook his head. "No, Ty, it's not like that. I'll always be there for you as a friend. But I can't keep getting involved in what we've been doing. I need to focus on bettering myself, finding a different path."

Ty's expression softened and he put his arm back around Garrett's shoulders. "I understand, man. I want you to succeed. You're smart, and you have a chance to make something of your life outside these walls. I don't want to hold you back. Just promise me you won't forget about your homie Ty."

Garrett smiled gratefully. "I could never forget about you, Ty. You've been like family to me. But I need to make some changes for myself. I hope you understand."

Ty nodded, a glimmer of pride in his eyes. "I do, Garrett. And I believe in you. You've got what it takes to turn things around. Remember, no matter where life takes you, you'll always have a friend in me."

Garrett shook the memory from his mind, finding himself back at the table with Dave. The hurt he experienced earlier that day resurfaced with a vengeance, coursing through his veins like a potent drug.

"I'm sorry about that," he said to Dave, hoping he hadn't scared him.

Dave shook his head, his expression filled with understanding. "Don't worry about it. I didn't like him anyway."

"How are you feeling?"

Dave shifted uncomfortably in his chair, his focus drawn to the dark liquid before him. "Terrible," Dave replied with a heavy sigh.

"Can I ask you a question? What do you think getting drunk will do to help you feel better? Can you honestly think of one positive outcome from consuming that poison?"

Dave sat in silence; his eyes fixed on the full shot glass.

Garrett continued; his voice filled with conviction. "Dave, I can tell you from personal experience that it will only make you feel worse about yourself, not better. I spent half of my life hiding behind a bottle and engaging in other destructive behaviors. It only led me to more pain, misery, and heartbreak. Is that what you want? To feel even worse than you already do. To make your life even more unmanageable. Or worse yet, to get drunk and potentially harm another innocent person."

Dave winced at the weight of Garrett's words, his eyes welling up with tears. His shoulders began to shake, and he couldn't contain the sobs that escaped his throat. "I'm such a terrible person. I killed her father, Garrett. She hates me, and I don't blame her."

Garrett scooted closer to Dave, placing a comforting hand on his shoulder. "How can I forgive myself if she can't even forgive me?" Dave cried harder, his face buried in his hands. Garrett rubbed his back, allowing him to release the flood of emotions he was experiencing.

After a few minutes, Dave wiped the tears from his face. Garrett handed him a napkin from the dispenser on the table. Dave blew his nose, disposing of the used napkin in the full shot glass. A smile formed on Garrett's lips, giving Dave a faint smile.

"I like that. It's better used as a garbage can anyway," Dave remarked, watching the napkin dissolve in the lethal alcohol.

Once Dave's breathing had steadied, he looked at Garrett bewilderedly. "I can't believe you came looking for me. I thought you wouldn't want anything to do with me once you found out what I did."

Garrett shook his head. "Dave, that's the beauty of this fellowship. We're taught to never judge someone for their mistakes. Yours are no greater than mine. We've all made mistakes; we're not perfect. That's why we can relate to each other so well. We're all humans experiencing the same journey. You never have to worry about someone looking down on you. My love and support are unconditional."

He smiled at his friend, pulling him into a tight embrace. As they held each other, Dave whispered in Garrett's ear, "Thank you. I prayed for God's help and protection right before you arrived."

TWENTY-TWO

Aubrey sat on the back patio of her mother's home, pouring out the dramatic events that had unfolded, her mother's quiet presence beside her. Every detail, every word exchanged, spilled from Aubrey's lips, along with the emotions that swirled within her—less anger, more betrayal towards Dave and Garrett. She expected her mother to be as upset as she was, but her expression remained unreadable. When Aubrey finished her tirade, she anxiously awaited her mother's response.

Jenny held her hand tightly throughout the lengthy description, her eyes reflecting immense love and concern for her only child. Her voice was calm and gentle when she finally spoke, causing Aubrey to lean in closer to hear her words.

"I'm so sorry you're having such a rough day, honey. I should have told you about Dave being released from prison. The Connecticut Parole Commission notified me once he became eligible for community supervision. I never expected you to run into him like this in a million years. If I had known, I would have given you the heads-up you deserved."

Aubrey was confused by her mother's confession, wanting to ask questions, but her mother asked for a fair chance to finish before she could inquire further. Aubrey nodded, trusting her mother's instincts, and urged her to continue.

"In response to everything you told me, I want to share a little about your father's drinking history. You understand he was an alcoholic, as you witnessed his active participation in Daily Recovery. However, you were too young to remember him as a drinker, and we rarely discussed those dark times in front of you."

Aubrey couldn't comprehend how this connected to her situation, but she gave her mother her undivided attention.

"Your father used to be able to drink like a normal person. It wasn't until his early thirties that his alcoholic tendencies seemed to escalate. It began with him passing out early during social gatherings at our home. Over time, I found him asleep on other people's couches. It was embarrassing and concerning for me. He tried changing his drinking habits, switching to beer or wine, or limiting his intake depending on the occasion. It would work for a while, but eventually, he would relapse and return to hard liquor, his preferred choice. He struggled to admit that he had a drinking problem. It wasn't until one night when his drinking landed him in county jail."

Jenny continued, "A police officer pulled him over for crossing over the center yellow lines on a two-lane road. His blood alcohol levels exceeded the legal limit, resulting in an

Excessive DUI charge. One more DUI could have led to a felony conviction."

"When I bailed him out that night, he wasn't scared of the jail; he was terrified because he finally realized the extent of his alcoholism. He understood that if he continued to drink, he would risk his job, his freedom, and everything we had. He didn't know where to turn for help. Fortunately, the courts knew exactly what he needed. They ordered him to attend ninety meetings in ninety days of 'Daily Recovery.' That's where he found his strength, his shield against King Alcohol, and his serenity. That's the only version of your father you were lucky enough to know."

"When the Parole Commission contacted me, they informed me that I had the legal right to attend Dave's hearing. I would have the opportunity to state whether I thought he should be released. It evoked so many emotions, and I struggled with the decision. I prayed for God's guidance, and one day, I received my answer. At the hearing, I told the Parole Board that I had forgiven Dave for the tragic accident that happened all those years ago. I shared your father's story and how easily he could have been in Dave's shoes. After getting sober, I spoke of the incredible man he became and expressed my hope that Dave could do something similar with his life. There wasn't a dry eye in that room, Aubrey. It was one of the most significant moments of my life."

By now, tears streamed down both Aubrey and Jenny's faces. Aubrey felt a whirlwind of conflicting emotions swirling within her. She tried her best to process everything her mom had shared, even though it wasn't what she had expected to hear when she chose her mother to vent to.

"Aubrey, I can't tell you what to do. It's up to you to forgive Dave and Garrett for their actions. All I can tell you is what I've learned from my experiences. For me, forgiveness is the only option. I held onto so much bitterness, hatred, and resentment for far too many years, and it only led to more misery and heartache. It was an emotional hell I never want to relive. You're still young, with so much life ahead of you. I would hate to see what happened to your father limit your capacity to love and be loved. If it were me, sweetie, I would forgive them both. And I honestly believe if your father were alive today, he would tell you the same thing."

Aubrey wrapped her arms tightly around her mother's slender frame. She let her tears flow freely. She missed her father more than ever but also felt a glimmer of hope for the possibility of finding her path to forgiveness.

In Avon, Garrett sat in a semi-circle of a "Daily Recovery" meeting, listening as Dave shared his story. Since they had missed the noon meeting, they had decided, after leaving the bar, to attend the six o'clock one. As a tradition, when someone receives a sobriety token, they are asked to share a little bit about their past drinking habits, problems that arose from their drinking, and how they got to the point they are at today.

He described his introduction to alcohol at a young age when he and a neighbor stole a half-gallon bottle of vodka from the neighbor's mother. Dave shared, "When I was thirteen, me and my neighbor snuck out in the middle of the night and drank that bottle. Man, that first drink ... made me feel invincible. All my anxieties, insecurities, and fears vanished."

Garrett listened intently, nodding as Dave continued, "By sixteen, I was already hiding liquor in my room, using it to help me sleep. My parents committed me at seventeen after being arrested for public intoxication at a school assembly."

Dave didn't shy away from discussing his crime, providing the group with vivid details, "I spent fifteen years in prison. Staying clean and sober was a constant struggle, even behind bars. But here I am today."

"At first, I thought you were all crazy!" Dave exclaimed, joining in the laughter that filled the room. "Then I realized that is a good thing because so am I. I wasn't sure if I would come to another meeting after that first one. I had planned on drinking myself into oblivion that night."

He continued, his voice filled with gratitude, "But it wasn't until someone came up to me after that first meeting, offered me a firm handshake, and a friendly smile that I reconsidered my options. He made me feel welcome and important. I wasn't sure if I would call him after he offered me his number, but I must admit that calling him was the best decision I have ever made. Garrett, thank you for all your help and support. I wouldn't be getting this coin if it weren't for you!"

The room erupted into applause as everyone stood. Garrett's eyes welled up with tears, touched by the genuine connection and support he had found in this community. It had been an emotional day, and this celebration helped dull the pain of his aching heart.

Embracing each other, Garrett and Dave shared a heartfelt hug. The room continued to resonate with the claps and cheers, a testament to the power of support and fellowship in their journey toward sobriety.

After the meeting, Garrett and Dave remained in the parking lot, saying goodbye to the other members. Once they were alone, Garrett asked Dave about his plans for the rest of the evening, curious about the critical task Dave had mentioned earlier in the day.

Dave replied mischievously, "I have wanted to do something important since I got out of prison but haven't made the time to do it. I figured tonight would be the perfect time to get it done."

Garrett looked at him suspiciously, his curiosity piqued. "Is it anything I should be concerned with?"

Dave chuckled, enjoying Garrett's reaction, "No, nothing you need to worry about. It doesn't involve alcohol. It's something I need to do in private. I will discuss it with you at a later time."

"Fair enough," Garrett replied, trusting Dave's words. "I am proud of you, Dave. Give me a call tomorrow."

"Thanks, Garrett. Will do."

When Garrett picked up his girls, they were taken aback by Aubrey's absence, wondering why she wasn't joining them as initially planned. Sitting at the bowling alley, munching on an assortment of fried foods, Garrett mustered the strength to share the events of his day. His daughters' painful expressions mirrored his own, and they hugged him tightly, offering comfort in their embrace. The sadness that gripped his heart felt foreign, a sensation he had previously drowned in anger and alcohol. He was determined to face it head-on, welcoming healthier and more productive coping methods.

His girls provided a comforting presence, yet the sharp pain inside him couldn't be completely alleviated. Throughout the day, he yearned to hear from Aubrey, and with each message alert on his phone, a glimmer of hope faded when it wasn't her. The subsequent wave of disappointment and depression was almost unbearable, but he persevered.

Bowling and laser tag with his daughters was a temporary distraction, granting respite from the emotional turmoil. By nine-thirty that evening, exhaustion settled upon them, their bellies full from the evening's indulgence.

While returning to the 1818 Estate, Jasmine absentmindedly flipped through radio stations until a familiar tune caught Garrett's ear. In awe, he asked her to stop, and together, they listened as his voice filled the vehicle, carried by invisible airwaves. It was his new single, "Angel of Mine." Following the song's conclusion, the DJ excitedly announced its release and the growing number of requests it was receiving.

Pride swelled within Garrett as his girls erupted in excited chatter. Their conversation for the remainder of the night centered on the song, and they wasted no time sharing the news with their friends, urging them to tune in. One of Alexa's friends responded, expressing genuine admiration for her father's music. Alexa's astonishment was palpable as her friend described how much she loved the song. The surreal feeling of having his music exposed to the world filled Garrett's heart, and he acknowledged that he and his girls would need time to adjust to this newfound attention. Above all, he cherished that Jasmine and Alexa loved his song, valuing their opinions more than anyone else's.

As the day's excitement faded and his daughters became lost in slumber, Garrett lay in bed, consumed by his thoughts. The day's events played on a relentless loop in his mind, each repetition deepening the ache within his heart. The memory of Aubrey's reaction to his confession, the disdain in her eyes, shattered him further. Silent tears streamed down his face, dampening the expanse of the pillow and cradling his weary head.

In his despair, Garrett turned to prayer. With a trembling voice, he poured out his heart, imploring God for assistance in navigating the turbulent path ahead. He longed to understand God's will concerning his relationship with Aubrey, pleading for strength and courage to confront his emotions with positivity and resilience. As his supplications drew to a close, weariness overtook him, and he succumbed to the embrace of much-needed sleep.

Aubrey parked her car in the familiar cemetery lot where her father was laid to rest. As she walked toward his headstone, she noticed a vibrant bouquet of autumn flowers bathed in the noonday sun, placed delicately atop his grave. It wasn't uncommon to find fresh flowers here; her father was revered in the community, admired by his students, and a guiding light for those seeking sobriety through Daily Recovery. He had touched countless lives, including her own.

The damp grass chilled her feet, the late October air offering no respite even as the sun shone. A gentle breeze caressed her face, adding a sting to her cheeks. Standing before her father's headstone, she read the epitaph slowly, as if etching its words into her heart. This sacred place had become a solace for her, where she could openly converse with her father's spirit, feeling his presence in the stillness. And today, she had come with a purpose, taking a deep breath before speaking.

"Hey, Daddy, I miss you so much. I want to talk to you about a new man who has entered my life. His name is Garrett, and he has been amazing to me. But things took a turn when I found out he went to prison for a drinking-related accident." Tears welled up in her eyes, overflowing down her cheeks. "Who am I kidding, Dad? You already know all about it. The dreams I've been having, so vivid and real, I can't tell if they're your way of communicating with me or my mind's attempt to hear the things I wish you could tell me."

Aubrey wiped her tears on her jacket sleeve, using tissues from her pocket to dry her eyes and nose. "Mom told me about your struggles with alcohol and the law. She thinks I should give Garrett a second chance and forgive Dave for what he did to you. I'm so confused right now. Part of me feels like staying with Garrett and forgiving Dave would betray you. Oh, Daddy, please help me know what to do if you can hear me. Please send me a sign, visit me in my dreams, and guide me to make the right choice. I love you so much, and I wish you were here."

With her final words, Aubrey surrendered to her grief, sobbing softly amidst the ancient gravestones. The sun hid behind dark clouds as she gazed through tear-blurred eyes, noticing a glimmering object near her feet. As the clouds parted, the sun's rays illuminated a bronze coin instantly recognizable to her—a token inscribed with "30 Days" on the front and the Serenity Prayer on the back, much like the ones her father had cherished and kept in his dresser drawer.

Realizing that someone must have inadvertently dropped the coin while leaving the flowers, Aubrey wrestled with the thought of leaving it near the bouquet or placing it back for its owner to find. However, she understood the significance these coins held for those in recovery, and she didn't want a passing stranger to take it. Instead, she decided to drop it off at the local church where Daily Recovery meetings were held. Perhaps the person who lost it would receive a replacement, and she took comfort in the thought that someone else would benefit from it.

After returning to her car, she cranked up the heater to its maximum setting, seeking warmth on this chilly day. She noticed a truck pulling up nearby. A man stepped out, and within seconds, she recognized him—Dave. He walked along the path leading to her father's grave. Suddenly, everything clicked into place. Garrett had mentioned that Dave would receive his thirty-day coin at the meeting they were supposed to attend the day before. Dave had left the flowers and the lost coin.

Acting swiftly, Aubrey called out Dave's name before he moved too far away to hear her. Startled, he turned, and fear flashed across his face upon recognizing her voice. He stood frozen, awaiting whatever was to come, his eyes darting between her and the ground. Closing the distance between them, Aubrey extended her hand, holding out the coin.

"Are you looking for this?"

Dave cautiously reached out and accepted the coin. "Yes," he replied, his voice cautionary and uncertain.

"And were you the one who left the flowers?" Aubrey inquired, her voice steady despite the swirling emotions within her.

He nodded, still unable to meet her eyes.

"They're beautiful. Thank you," she acknowledged, surprising him with her gratitude. "My father loved flowers, and I'm sure he would have appreciated the ones you chose for him."

Dave struggled to find the right words. Before he could speak, Aubrey continued, her voice unwavering. "My mother told me what she did for you at your parole hearing. Until yesterday, I had no idea she had attended or that she had forgiven you. It helped me see things more clearly. I can't say I'm ready to forgive you as she has, but I will consider it."

Tears welled up in Dave's eyes, a single droplet escaping and glistening in the sunlight as it traced its path down his cheek. "That's more than I could ever ask for from you," he whispered, his voice cracking. "Thank you." With gratitude, he slipped the coin into his front pocket.

"You're welcome," Aubrey replied, offering a hint of a smile. "Congratulations on your thirty-day anniversary. My father was an active member and would have been proud of you. Garrett talked about you a lot before I knew who you were."

Dave wiped away his tears and met Aubrey's gaze with newfound confidence. "He hasn't told me what happened between you two after I left, but I could tell he was hurting last night. He's an amazing man, Aubrey. Men like him are rare."

He glanced at the ground, seeming somewhat bashful, before extending his hand. Aubrey reached out and shook it firmly. "Thanks for finding my coin and keeping it safe. It was dark last night, and I was distraught when I realized I had lost it."

Aubrey released his hand, offering a parting farewell. "You're welcome. Maybe I'll see you around." She smiled at Dave, and he returned the gesture, a shy smile blooming.

Watching as Dave got into his truck and drove away, Aubrey settled back into her still-warm car, relishing the blast of hot air from the vents. A feeling of warmth enveloped her, and she basked in the satisfaction of treating Dave with civility, feeling a sense of intrinsic reward for her actions. A question lingered in her mind: Was finding the coin and being present when Dave searched for it a mere coincidence or a form of divine intervention? Deep down, she wanted to believe it was the latter. With that final thought, she left her parking spot, heading home with renewed hope.

As Aubrey drove, her phone buzzed with incoming text messages from an unknown source. Recognizing the potential danger of texting while driving, she decided to wait until she arrived home before checking them. The car's temperature monitor displayed a chilly thirty-four degrees outside, causing a shiver to run down her arms. Aubrey recalled the bone-chilling cold she had felt earlier at the cemetery. She hadn't anticipated such a drastic swing in temperature. Familiar with the unpredictable weather patterns of Connecticut, she glanced up at the gathering clouds overhead, wondering if they foreshadowed an impending snowstorm.

After arriving home, Aubrey turned her attention to the multiple text messages she had received. Curious who had sent so many in such a short amount of time.

"Hi Aubrey, this is Jasmine Anderson, Garrett's daughter. Dad doesn't know I am reaching out to you, and I would like to keep it that way. After he told me what happened between you two, I decided to find your number to share my feelings about your situation. Alexa and I were both sad to hear of your breakup. We don't blame you for being upset, but we hope you see our dad for who he is. I am currently at school, in a study hall period. I have been reading your book, which has quickly become one of my favorites. You told Kathy, during your interview, that this book was inspired by the relationship you once shared with your father. I want you to know that I can relate to how you feel.

Even while my dad was in prison, he always expressed how much he loved me and Alexa. He has always made us feel special, like we are his top priority. I remember one time, while he was away, he sent Alexa and me a fun questionnaire to fill out. One of the questions was what we loved the most about something he specifically did for us. My answer came quickly and easily. It was how much he always made me feel loved. He reminds me of the father in your story, which must have also been similar to your father.

I am messaging you today because I want you to give my dad another chance. I agree he made a mistake by not telling you about his past, but I don't feel that is unforgivable. He is a wonderful man, Aubrey. I know you already realize this. Today, at school, all my friends are gushing over his new hit single. The entire school has fallen in love with it, boosting me to overnight celebrity status. It is a little overwhelming, but I am sure you can relate. He is finally being recognized for one of his many talents. Soon, he will be one of the area's most eligible bachelors. I know he would rather have you in his life than be single. If it doesn't work out, I will still be your biggest fan."

Despite the conflicting emotions inside her, she missed him profoundly and believed that a conversation could help her make the best decision regarding their future. As she contemplated potential meeting places, she noticed snow-flakes starting to fall from the sky, gradually increasing in size. Entranced by the beauty of the snow, memories of her father and their shared love for the winter weather floated around freely in her mind.

Recalling the joyful moments they spent together, watch-ing snowflakes gently descend, Aubrey couldn't help but feel a sense of connection and approval from her late father. It was as if he was sending his blessing through the fluffy white snowflakes blanketing the earth. Embracing this hopeful interpretation, she sought to stay indoors near the warmth of a crackling fire.

Grateful for the gas fireplace in her front room, Aubrey sent a text message to Garrett, expressing her desire to discuss the previous day's events and asking if he would be available to come to her house. The anticipation grew as she awaited his response. Moments later, her phone chimed, indicating a message from Garrett. With excitement and a rush of sensations, Aubrey read his response: "I thought you'd never ask. I am on my way."

Her heart fluttered, and goose bumps prickled across her arms and legs. Garrett was on his way.

TWENTY-THREE

Garrett arrived at Aubrey's home just after one o'clock, keeping in mind that he needed to leave around two to ensure he could pick up his daughters from school on time. The roads had already become slick with the accumulating snow, which had been falling for about half an hour. Despite the challenging visibility during his drive, he remained determined to see Aubrey and have a meaningful conversation with her.

Garrett's nerves grew unsettled as he knocked on the large wooden door. He didn't know what to expect from her. Would she be angry like yesterday, or would she be the loving woman he had come to know and adore? The door opened, and there she stood, looking stunning as ever. Aubrey wore black tights with a gray wool sweatshirt extending past her upper thighs. Her matching gray wool socks reached about six inches above her ankles, and her silky dark hair hung straight on both sides of her face. A faint smile appeared on her lips as she greeted him.

Garrett's heart longed to embrace her, but he restrained himself. Aubrey motioned for him to come in, and he politely removed his shoes by the front door before following her into the front room. A blazing gas fireplace welcomed them. The modern decor caught his eye with its large fireplace, leather couches, fashionable coffee table, and contemporary art pieces adorning the walls. He could see the spacious front yard through the large windows behind the sofas.

Aubrey sat, patting the empty spot next to her on the couch, and Garrett removed his coat and placed it on the adjacent seat. Silence lingered between them until Aubrey asked if he wanted something to drink. Garrett declined, complimenting her on the beauty of her house and expressing his fondness for her modern décor. Aubrey playfully acknowledged his taste in decor, teasing him about giving him a tour before he left.

Garrett felt a glimmer of hope as Aubrey suggested the tour. "That sounds wonderful," he responded, grateful for the chance to spend more time with her. However, before their tour, he felt compelled to apologize and express his regret. He acknowledged that not sharing his complete story with her was unfair and sincerely apologized for his omission. He emphasized that he would understand if she couldn't forgive him, although it was not what he wanted.

Reading his thoughts, Aubrey asked, "Is that what you want? For me to never forgive you?"

Garrett quickly responded, "Not at all. I have never wanted anything as much as I want your forgiveness."

Aubrey ran her fingers through her hair, stirring his desire to touch her. "Tell me everything, Garrett. I need to know what happened and where you have been. I haven't heard your entire story, and it's difficult to decide what to do next without that understanding."

Garrett settled back into the couch, trying to get comfortable. He agreed with Aubrey that sharing his story was the best way to start their discussion. He told her everything, starting with how his drinking problem spiraled out of control during the final years of his marriage. He described the fight he got into at Bob and Linda's party, leading to him picking up Matt from his home and the subsequent accident. He shared the moment he woke up in the hospital the following day, learning about the tragedy and the charges he was facing.

Tears welled up in Garrett's eyes as he recalled the initial moments at the hospital. Aubrey placed her hand on his leg, offering comfort and affection. Garrett reciprocated by placing his hand on hers, relishing the tingling sensation it created. He continued to talk, recounting the court proceedings and his eventual five-year prison sentence. He conveyed how Matt's parents had shown up at his sentencing, pleading with the judge to drop the charges, as they believed it was a tragic and unintended accident. He shared that he could have received a much longer sentence without their pleas.

Garrett spoke about his experience in prison, the difficulties of not seeing his daughters, the dissolution of his marriage, and the loss of his coping mechanism—alcohol. He revealed his anger over his losses and the violent outbursts during his early years in prison. Aubrey's sympathetic expression gradually shifted to concern as he described those years of turmoil.

He also shared how he met his mentor, Jerry, who became his cellmate. Garrett recounted Jerry's introduction to Daily Recovery and how he taught him to play the piano. He mentioned the makeshift cardboard keyboard they used for practice in their cell and how he only had limited opportunities to play in the prison chapel.

Aubrey's expression turned to shock. "So, you learned to play on a cardboard cutout in your cell? And then you honed your skills through the church services?"

Garrett nodded, a breathtaking smile on his face. "That's right. I hope to have the opportunity to introduce you to Jerry someday. I think you'll love him as much as I do."

"I think I already do, Garrett," Aubrey replied, her eyes filled with admiration and love. "He helped you tremendously. I'd love to thank him personally."

Garrett squeezed her hand, feeling the connection between them erupting with love and understanding. "He was the one who suggested I go to Emilio's that first night you heard me play. So, we have him to thank for that too."

"He deserves a steak dinner at Chandler's for that," Aubrey teased, eliciting a chuckle from Garrett.

As Garrett finished his story, he mentioned the challenges of being on parole and explained that he couldn't move to Connecticut unless he found a resident to sponsor him. He revealed the difficulty this presented since he only knew a few people, including his daughters, ex-wife, and her husband,

Ben. Aubrey raised her eyebrows at the mention of this and said, "No wonder you gave bonus points to women who lived in the Northeast!"

"Well, you caught me," he said, surrendering his hands. "But just so you know, Aubrey, if I had met you anywhere else, I would have fallen in love with you just the same."

Aubrey's blue eyes softened, radiating warmth and a glimmer of lost love. "I sure hope so," she teased.

"I brought you a copy of my new single," Garrett mentioned, reaching into his jacket and pulling out the case. He handed it to Aubrey, excited for her to hear it.

"I'm excited to listen to it," she replied, accepting the gift.

"I need to get going soon. I have to pick up the girls from school, and the roads will probably be a mess," Garrett mentioned, glancing at the falling snow outside the window, which continued to blanket the surroundings.

"Can I give you a quick tour of the house?" Aubrey asked, standing up.

"I would love that."

While Aubrey showed Garrett her master suite, her mind wandered as she realized it was the first time he had stepped foot in her bedroom. Although cautious about their next steps, she gradually entered the forgiveness process. Garrett's inspiring story touched her deeply, revealing his remarkable progress over the past few years. She could already envision the media celebrating his extraordinary talent and the incredible journey that led him here. Garrett's story was destined to surpass all others, as everyone loves an underdog. Aubrey admired him for his music and the loving father he was to his girls.

As they emerged from the master bathroom, Garrett's attention was drawn to a framed picture on Aubrey's nightstand. He picked it up gently and asked, "Do you mind?"

Aubrey replied, "Not at all. That's the last family picture we took together." She referred to a snapshot capturing her, her father, and her mother. Aubrey watched intently as Garrett studied the picture, his brows furrowing in confusion.

"This is your father?" he asked, his face losing color.

Puzzled by his reaction, Aubrey responded, "Yes, why? Is something wrong, Garrett?" Suddenly, Garrett dropped the picture and collapsed to his knees, struggling to maintain his balance. Alarmed, Aubrey knelt before him, fear coursing through her veins. It was as if he had nearly fainted. "Take deep breaths," she urged, joining him in the calming exercise.

Aubrey tenderly touched Garrett's cheek, gently rubbing it with her thumb. "Are you okay?" she asked, her voice filled with concern. Garrett slowly sat down, leaning against the wall, and Aubrey settled beside him.

He picked up the picture again, a bewildered expression on his face. "I don't understand, Aubrey. Your father passed away fifteen years ago?"

Aubrey's surprise matched her confusion. "Yes, Garrett. I've told you before he died in a car accident when I was a teenager. Why? Do you think you knew him?" She couldn't fathom his thoughts, and he seemed reluctant to share.

Instead of answering, Garrett reached into his jacket pocket and pulled out his phone with a sense of urgency that perplexed Aubrey. She watched as he scrolled through his contacts, growing increasingly frantic when he reached the

J's. Mumbling to himself, he muttered, "Where is it? Where is his name? How can it not be here?"

Switching to his call log, Garrett's confusion and frustration deepened. "I don't understand. I just talked to him last week. How can it not be here on my phone?" His question seemed directed more at himself than at Aubrey.

Desperate for answers, Aubrey held Garrett's hand firmly, her eyes locked with his frightened and exasperated gaze. "Talk to me, Garrett. Whom did you talk to?" she pleaded. Seeing how the disappearance of someone from his phone was distressing him, Aubrey's concern grew.

Garrett's gaze remained fixed as he whispered, his voice barely audible, "I don't know what's happening or how to begin explaining this to you. Please, give me some time to process everything." Rising suddenly, he left the bedroom, with Aubrey trailing behind, utterly bewildered. They descended the stairs and returned to the front room, where Garrett's coat draped over a couch. He retrieved it and put it on, his movements mechanical and detached.

As Aubrey watched him, she knew something significant was unraveling in Garrett's life—a mystery entwined with her past. They stood in the entryway, facing each other, the weight of unanswered questions hanging heavily in the air. Garrett's eyes were filled with anguish, and Aubrey's heart ached for him.

"Thank you for inviting me over," Garrett said, his voice filled with gratitude. "I'm sorry I've been acting so strange. I promise to call you later and do my best to explain what has happened. Right now, I need some time to gather my thoughts. It feels like I'm losing my mind."

Aubrey gently pulled back, still holding his hands in hers. Concern washed over her, overpowering her feelings. "Please call me, Garrett. I'm glad you came over today. And I hope we can find a chance to get together again soon." Leaning in, she kissed him softly, their lips meeting tenderly. As the kiss deepened, passion ignited between them, and his touch's warmth and perfection swept her away. When they finally separated, she realized he had taken her breath away. She steadied her racing heart and weak knees, striving to regain her composure. "Is there anything I can do to help you?"

Garrett locked eyes with her, a slight smile forming on his lips. It was as if her question had sparked a thought or an epiphany among his distressed thinking. He stood there momentarily, soaking in their connection's intensity. "Yes, there is one thing," he replied, opening the front door to leave. "Listen to my song." With one final peck on her lips, he disappeared into the swirling whiteness beyond.

Aubrey stood by the door, feeling emotionally spent. She closed the door, leaning against it as she contemplated what had happened. Her heart was filled with curiosity, longing, and apprehension. She knew that Garrett's request held significance, and she couldn't help but wonder how his song might unveil the mysteries that had gripped his soul.Shrugging her shoulders, she picked up the CD from its place on the coffee table. She carried it delicately to the back family room, where her state-of-the-art electronics created a theater-like experience.

The flat-screen television and surround sound system filled the room with quiet anticipation.

Noticing that the CD was a simple burned copy, Aubrey understood why. Garrett had recorded it just days before giving it to her. As she inserted the disc into the DVD player, she couldn't help but imagine how the professionally packaged version would look. A pang of guilt washed over her as she realized she hadn't asked Garrett about the song he had chosen or expressed her genuine interest in this significant part of his life.

As the CD spun inside the player, Aubrey's excitement grew. The sound of a piano filled the room, and at first, she thought it might be a song Garrett had played for her before. But then, a realization struck her, causing her knees to feel weak and her heart to skip a beat. It was the song her father, Jerry, had written for her. "Angel of Mine."

Garrett's hands gripped the steering wheel tightly as he navigated the snowy roads to Jasmine's school. His mind was in a whirlwind, trying to process the events that had just unfolded. It all felt like a dream, something that couldn't possibly be happening.

The image of the picture he had seen at Aubrey's house replayed in his vision. It was a photograph of Jerry, his mentor, and best friend, the same image he had shown Garrett when they first connected in the prison cell. But that picture was also of Aubrey's father, who had tragically passed away in a car crash years ago. The realization hit him like a tidal wave, shaking the foundation of his understanding.

As he drove, Garrett searched through his phone, desperately looking for any trace of Jerry. But there was nothing—no contact information, no call logs. It was as if Jerry had vanished from existence. Confusion clouded Garrett's thoughts as he reflected on his memories of their time together. He realized that all his recollections were limited to the moments they spent alone in their prison cell during lockdown hours.

A sense of unease took hold of him. How was it possible that he couldn't recall any interactions with Jerry outside of their cell? He strained his mind, attempting to summon memories of other inmates talking to both of them, but nothing came. It was as if their friendship had existed within a bubble, isolated from the rest of the prison world. The realization struck him profoundly, leaving him grappling to understand the truth.

His heart pounded in his chest, the sound reverberating in his ears. Garrett focused on his breathing, trying to steady himself and maintain control. The road demanded his attention, and he couldn't afford to lose focus on this revelation. As he continued driving, his thoughts shifted from their time in prison to their interactions on the outside.

After his release, Garrett and Jerry remained close friends, speaking almost daily. But as he reflected on those early months, he realized their connection had always been through phone calls. Despite their plans to meet at Daily Recovery meetings, there were no physical visits. Jerry always seemed to have an emergency preventing him from attending. And then, Garrett's mind stumbled upon another strange realization.

He couldn't recall a single time he had initiated a call to Jerry. It was always Jerry who reached out, the phone ringing before Garrett could even search for his number. He had never thought much of it before, attributing it to mere coincidence. But now, it took on a deeper meaning. Jerry's presence had been more profound than he ever imagined. He was more than just a friend; he was a guiding force, a guardian angel watching over him.

A pang of sadness enveloped him as he acknowledged the truth. Jerry was no longer alive, yet his impact on Garrett's life was undeniable. The realization left him with a mix of emotions—gratitude for their connection, sorrow for the loss, and a profound sense of awe at the possibility of a higher power working through their bond.

As he continued his drive through the wintry landscape, Garrett carried the weight of this revelation in his heart. He knew that something extraordinary had touched his path that defied logical explanation. Jerry might no longer be physically present, but his spirit and influence would forever shape Garrett's life and future. And with that understanding, Garrett found peace in the belief that he was never truly alone, that a guiding hand would continue to lead him.

Engaged in a deep conversation with Gretchen later that evening, he found comfort in her understanding of ghosts and hauntings. He sought her insights on the woman who supposedly haunted their dwelling, wondering why she would linger instead of crossing over to the other side.

Gretchen offered her perspective, speaking of the enduring power of love, even in the afterlife. She believed the woman haunting their house clung to it because of her deep love for it—her attachment and fear that the current occupants would not care for it as she once had. The woman's appearance reflected her unrest and unwillingness to let go until she found peace.

Garrett absorbed Gretchen's words, finding resonance in the idea that love could be a powerful force keeping someone tied to this world. Just as the woman held on to the house out of love, Jerry clung to his earthly existence because of his unwavering love for his daughter, Aubrey. Their bond was so strong and unique that he couldn't leave until he was sure she would be okay.

Aubrey had faced immense difficulties moving forward after Jerry's death, but he remained by her side throughout the process. Jerry felt ready to let go as she found someone who loved her how she deserved. Garrett recognized the immense privilege and honor it was to be the one Aubrey chose to share her love with. He cherished his time with Jerry and felt blessed to have experienced their friendship and connection.

A smile formed on Garrett's face as he realized that Matt must have told Jerry about him. It all seemed so clear now. He felt deep gratitude and joy, knowing he was part of a greater plan guided by God's spirit. He marveled at the profound love that could only be truly understood through the parent-child relationship.

A peaceful calm enveloped him as he surrendered to the knowledge that everything would be as it was destined to be.

EPILOGUE

(1 year later)
9/23/2017

Dear Diary,

Today has turned out to be another memorable day. I finished my fifth book, "The First Thirty Days." How ironic that I finished it on the first anniversary of watching Garrett perform for the first time at Emilio's. Every day, I thank God and my father for helping Garrett choose that restaurant on that particular night to celebrate his freedom anniversary date with his daughters. I don't even want to imagine where my life would be had he not shown up that evening.

Writing a memoir versus a fictional story was different but strangely the same. Our lives are nothing but characters composed of descriptive words of what we see, smell, hear, taste, and touch.

The most significant difference between the characters of this book and the ones of my past is that they are real, and

I get to enjoy them every day. Living out the fantasies I have dreamt about and written about all these years is a blessing. What a joy it has been to write a book with my fiancé, Garrett. The fact that he made time for this, amongst his already busy music career, is incredible in and of itself. I am so very proud of him. His second record has become even more popular than his first. He is such an incredible person—someone I will always cherish and be grateful to have in my life. It is obvious why my father chose him out of the millions of other men in this country. At first, I believed it was all about me and my needs, but now I know the truth about Garrett and what makes him different.

I often wonder how the world will comprehend our story. Will they believe what we have written? Will they view Garrett as insane for claiming to have had a relationship with my deceased father? Or will they appreciate the beauty of what happened and the possibilities it could imply in their own lives? I truly hope my readers are inspired to feel and believe the latter. Some of my critics will have a field day with this story. At this point, I don't care. This is our story, and we are ready for the world to read it, applause or not. For those it touches, I hope it will offer them encouragement, strength, and hope through the most challenging times of their lives. People dealing with loss, grief, addiction, resentment, incarceration, or those needing to start anew should hopefully find a way to relate.

I pray that God will help those who need it most find this book in their lap. Garrett has set a great example to me of how to help others in need. He juggles so many responsibilities, being a mentor in Daily Recovery still being one of them. I will never forget what he told me a few weeks after I encountered him and Dave at the coffee shop. He told me how important it was to get out of himself and help others stay sober.

This, he had told me, was what motivated him in his program. And this motivation has helped him, including himself, save many people from incarceration or alcoholic death. He has explained to me how I can help many more people than he can with my God-given writing talents. I hope he is right. This is my way of giving back to the world, and I have never been happier writing a novel. Life has never been as wonderful as it is right now, but it's about to get better. Tomorrow, Garrett and I will be wed together in our love now and eternally. My dream will become a reality.

This is just the beginning of our story though. Now that we better understand Garrett's gift, we can only imagine what will come next...

THE END

ABOUT THE AUTHOR

Scott T. Young, a resident of Nampa, Idaho, is a seasoned professional with a rich history in telecommunications and entrepreneurship, who also attained an MBA in 2020. He is a devoted father and a romantic at heart, currently engaged and cherishing a connection that surpasses all expectations. Scott's debut novel, *The First Thirty Days*, draws from his personal experiences, exploring themes of love, spirituality, and mental health. His hobbies include golfing, skiing, fishing, rafting, music, and writing. Scott's resilience, especially post-pandemic, is a testament to his strength, which he now channels into his consulting firm, ST Consulting, LLC. His novel is a tribute to personal growth, redemption, and new beginnings.